BLOOD SECRETS

"The true story of the secret, bloody rituals of African mystical belief . . . It is disturbing and evisceral—literally and figuratively."

—New York Tribune

"Almost impossible to believe. But it's there in print before your eyes."

—Macon Beacon

"Oke provides a view of the jujuman's world and of modern Africa that only an insider could provide . . . Whether the reader brings assumptions about disease, modern Africa, or religion, Blood Secrets will challenge those assumptions."

—Gnosis magazine

"Here we have the true story of the demonology of the 'Invisible World' of the Africans as it was lived and believed by a boy who was trained in juju . . . full of the hell and fury of a major primitive religion that, according to Oke, has worldwide implications."

—The American Rationalist

PRAISE FOR
WICKED SECRETS

BLOOD SECRETS

THE TRUE STORY OF DEMON WORSHIP AND CEREMONIAL MURDER

BY FORMER JUJU HIGH PRIEST

ISAIAH OKE

AS TOLD TO JOE WRIGHT

BERKLEY BOOKS, NEW YORK

This Berkley book contains the complete text
of the original hardcover edition. It has been
completely reset in a typeface designed for easy
reading and was printed from new film.

BLOOD SECRETS: THE TRUE STORY OF
DEMON WORSHIP AND CEREMONIAL MURDER

A Berkley Book / published by arrangement with
Prometheus Books

PRINTING HISTORY
Prometheus Books edition published 1989
Berkley edition / August 1991

All rights reserved.
Copyright © 1989 by Indynaco, Inc.
This book may not be reproduced in whole or in part,
by mimeograph or any other means, without permission.
For information address: Prometheus Books,
700 East Amherst Street, Buffalo, New York 14215.

ISBN: 0-425-12852-0

A BERKLEY BOOK ® TM 757,375
Berkley Books are published by The Berkley Publishing Group,
200 Madison Avenue, New York, New York 10016.
The name "BERKLEY" and the "B" logo
are trademarks belonging to Berkley Publishing Corporation.

PRINTED IN THE UNITED STATES OF AMERICA

10 9 8 7 6 5 4 3 2 1

Contents

Blood
Secrets

THE
INITIATE

1

At about three o'clock, naked as I came into the world, they stretched me out face-up on the dirt floor of the hut. The *babalorisha* barked, "Don't move, boy," and then, from a soft wicker basket, he dropped a writhing serpent between my legs. The shock of it almost made me jump up in spite of his warning. But I was so tired from the journey that I just froze, gasping for breath, instead of trying an unlikely escape that would only have unmanned me in his eyes.

I was exhausted; we'd been walking since first light. I was required to do all the carrying, which was befitting, of course. Everything had been packed by the junior priests into one enormously heavy bundle. It contained all the ritual objects, the food and water for my guides, and the cages with the smaller sacrificial animals. This I was obliged to carry on my head, after the manner of a woman. The only things they didn't make me carry were the kid and the lamb which my guides condescended to pull along behind them on leashes. We could have completed the long trip before midday, livestock and all, in the old Model-A truck the village owned in common. But that wouldn't have been according to tradition and, of course, tradition was everything.

But whether it was exhaustion that made me freeze up or

3

panic, I felt paralyzed; I couldn't have moved even if I'd wanted to. Not so the frightened snake. As soon as he hit the ground, he slithered up onto my left thigh, seeking the security of warmth. As he did, my guides threw a raggedy net over the pair of us and quickly tapped some small pegs into the ground to hold it.

This made the snake sinuate wildly at first and that frightened me even more. But I kept hearing in my heart all that my grandfather had told me about the ritual: "Nothing your guides do can harm you if you are manly. But the *orishas* will reject you if they sense fear; they will judge you unworthy. So, fear nothing. And above all, remember who you are!"

My eyes were rolling uncontrollably and I was sweating profusely even though—as every Yoruba boy knows—the "poison" snakes in these rituals are always defanged. That's why a python, the true symbol of our religion, is never used; pythons kill by constriction rather than poison and there's no way to fake a python's deadly squeeze.

But the revulsion is the same whether the snake is truly dangerous or not. How would *you* feel if a snake was sliding itself like living sandpaper along your naked body? Even though you knew it couldn't bite?

See what I mean?

I stayed as stiff as one of Grandfather's ceremonial statues, recalling his assurances that nothing in the ritual could really hurt me, and the snake gradually calmed. Eventually it was still, just above my stomach. I think it slept.

I was badly frightened. And the knowledge that other boys of my clan had lived through all this was no comfort. For one thing, no one who completed his ritual had ever broken the taboo by telling any of us younger ones exactly what was in store. Instead, the young men all tried to outdo one another at the evening fire by making up the most frightening yarns, to the horror of us younger boys and the hilarity of our parents.

Furthermore, I knew that *my* initiation would involve far more of an ordeal than most because of my particular heritage, which demanded the most rigorous testing. In fact, both my guides were strangers whom I'd never seen before; it had been bandied about that Grandfather sent all the way to Gabon for them. The man's face supported that rumor. But the woman was so dark that I couldn't read her facial scarring. In any event, they were experts and could be expected to be very good at this.

As the Sun went down, the net and snake were removed and the man took them outside. I breathed freely for the first time since entering the ritual hut. I hadn't moved a muscle in six hours. Humbly, as befits a child in his thirteenth year, I asked for permission to sit up. The woman cuffed me almost absent-mindedly behind the head for my insolence and told me to fetch the two ritual water pots from outside. Normally, of course, carrying water would have been her job, and she seemed to take a special pleasure in making me perform such a degrading act. I scrambled out the doorhole, happy to be free, even if just for a moment.

The pots were gnarly and poorly fired, not even close to the quality of our local workmanship. They looked as if they'd been made by someone who had not the least experience of pottery. But I knew that only a very foolish man would judge juju-water pots by their looks; they were repositiories of enormous power, in the hands of a Man of Knowledge.

I wrestled the pots in through the tiny doorhole, then set them down where the woman pointed. As she commanded, I removed the stoppers. The pot with the skulls painted on it contained a foul-smelling brown liquid, viscous and sludgy. The red one with the serpents painted on it contained a clear but equally foul-smelling fluid. Neither liquid seemed to be any of the dozens of kinds of juju-water with which I was familiar.

The woman told me to make a fire in the center of the hut. And again, the corners of her mouth went up a little as I was forced to do women's work. She was much younger than I had thought she'd be, probably even without grandchildren yet. That made my embarrassment twice as deep. I was still burning with shame from the trick they'd played on me with the snake and I almost let my anger show. But the ritual would last for three days altogether and this was only the first night. Who knew what power she could unleash on me in that time? Young or not, insolent or not, she was still an *ayelorisha:* one of the very few women privileged to talk directly to the gods. I made myself hold my tongue.

It was cooling off rapidly. Western people—those from America or Europe—think of West Africa only as a hot, steamy place. But at night it can get bone-chillingly cold. By the time I had the fire going, I was shaking with cold, hunger, and fatigue. I cast a hidden look toward the white robe I'd had to wear for the last three days as a symbol of my approaching initiation. They'd told me to hang it on one of the roof poles as we came into the hut and there it hung still. I wanted to pull it back on but I saw the *ayelorisha* follow my glance. She turned back with her small unbearable smile again. "Are you cold, little boy?"

I chose to ignore her, like a man. I raised my chin in defiance and looked away from her. I thought how proud my grandfather would be if he could see me.

She dipped her drinking gourd into the serpent-pot, the one with the clear liquid in it. She stared at the dipper for a moment and chanted under her breath. She looked up at me and laughed, broadly and openly this time. Then she flung the dipper of water all over my shivering body.

I spluttered and coughed, as much at the indignity as at the cool water hitting my chilled skin. No woman, I thought, dares treat a man of the Oke clan in such a way, *ayelorisha* or not.

"But you are not yet 'a man,'" said the *babalorisha*. He was stooped over, squeezing in through the doorway. He was a big man, still strong and fearsome-looking in spite of his years.

"No," he repeated, "you are not yet a man. How is it, then, that it matters how a woman treats you?" It was as if he'd seen into my heart. "*If* you become a man of the Oke clan, then you will be treated accordingly. But only *if* you become a man."

I put my eyes down to the ground. There was silence for a time, broken only by the chattering of my teeth. My two guides went about their business, ignoring me as if I'd not been grievously insulted.

Then they squatted down to enjoy their evening meal of the yams and palm wine they'd made me carry. I'd not eaten all day. And I knew from the other boys that I would get no water nor solid food until my ordeal was over. The smell of the yams, the crunch as they were bit into, made the joints of my jaws ache with desire. I'd never wanted a fresh, delicious yam or a drink of cool water so much in my life. But I took pride in the way I was able to stand by—cold, wet, and silent, enduring all—while my elders ate.

When they finished, the *ayelorisha* removed the remnants and took herself outside. "The woman will sleep now. You will meet the *orisha*," the man said.

As he spoke, he removed his juju from the leather bag around his neck: a carved piece of wood that looked suspiciously like an old table leg; the neck broken off a green bottle; two items as big around as my fist that looked like dried apricots; a rusty knife; and several smaller bags of the type in which one carries ritual herbs.

"First, you will meet *Olu-Orogbo*." He leaned over and pulled one of the little cages toward himself. It was the one with a black rooster, the symbol of *Olu-Orogbo*. He took the bird out of the cage, raised it up, and looked at it face-to-face. Then he began an incantation that I'd heard my grandfather use many times: the one that asks *Olu-Orogbo* to act as special mediator between men and the other gods. Still holding the rooster before his face, he addressed it as "Brother Bird" and asked it to forgive him. Then, with one practiced twist, he wrung its neck.

He called on *Olu-Orogbo* again, this time in a louder voice. I'd never heard an incantation as mournful as this. The song was that of a hyena, morbid and without hope. I began to shiver again, just as I had when the woman splashed water on me.

Suddenly, with a keening cry, the *babalorisha* snapped the bird bloodily in two at the neck. According to custom, he kept the head and offered the carcass to me. We took the hot blood simultaneously from the two parts of the bird.

After I moistened my lips with the rooster's blood and swallowed a bit of it, I went to put the carcass down, since there was no one else for me to share it with ritually. But the *babalorisha* stayed my hand. "Drink deeply," he said.

His words surprised me. Rarely does one take more than a drop or two of sacrificial blood. Blood-drinking is, after all, a *ritual* in Africa; it is not a meal or a way to satisfy one's physical hunger. But I obeyed and put the neck to my mouth once more.

I had never had blood in such a quantity before. The salty, metallic taste of chicken's blood was nothing new to me, of course. But the new sensation of swallowing a whole mouthful of it— a heavy, stringy sensation—almost made me gag. I set the carcass down, the blood dripping off my chin onto my chest.

The *babalorisha* dipped his left hand into the skull pot. He rubbed his head, face, and chest with his wet hand, leaving little stripes of the pasty fluid. Then from the bag at his side, he reverently removed a singlet made of feathers. This he slipped carefully over his shoulders. While he did these things, he began to sing another incantation. This one was more rhythmic, less baleful, than the last. He chanted on and on, lulling us both with the repetitious drone.

Slowly, he began to crouch. His legs seemed to grow shorter and shorter. His arms went akimbo to his waist, palms out behind him. He took a hesitant step and his head bobbed sharply forward and back. He stepped mincingly around the dying fire a few times, letting out soft cackles. At last, having gained confidence in his identity, he stopped and let out a crow of pride in his roosterness. Then he stepped over to me and looked up, his head cocked to one side.

I didn't know at first what was expected of me. He scratched at the ground and crowed again. He was so complete a rooster that I almost saw the comb on his head and the wattles under his chin. After marveling at him for awhile, I asked, "Is it you, *Olu-Orogbo?*"

He toed the ground again and said in a scratchy kind of voice, "I am *Olu-Orogbo.*" He walked around in a tight circle, bobbing his neck which seemed somehow to have grown quite scrawny. He stopped and cocked his head again, looking unblinkingly at me with one beady eye, as if he had just thought of some great truth. "Without the chicken," he said, "the Yoruba could not live."

"That is so, *Olu-Orogbo,*" I said.

He walked around the embers again, scratching the dirt and snapping his beak thoughtfully. "Then," he said, "I shall tell you of our ways so that the Yoruba may live."

He walked around the fire again and again. Every time he completed a circuit, he told me a secret of the chickens. He told me how the egg got its shape and why chickens eat gravel. He told me how to make a baby chick follow around after a frog as if it were its mother. He told me why roosters crow at the dawn and what would happen to the world if they ever stopped.

All through the long night, he told me such secrets

—some big and some small. He told me how to read the
message of the future in the entrails of a freshly killed
chicken. He told me how to make a cure for skin diseases
from chicken droppings and how to use polished chicken
bones for luck when gambling. He told me why sacrifices of
chickens are so especially pleasant to the *orishas*. He even
explained how it can be that human beings and chickens are
one with all the rest of nature. He told me these and many
other mystical wonders. And the more he made me understand, the more I felt at one with the whole world of nature
around me.

Finally, as the sky began to lighten in the East, he
scratched out through the doorhole, like a rooster leaving
the coop. He crowed once, very loudly, and then came back
inside.

He dipped his left wing into the other pot—the one with
the serpents on it. He rubbed himself with the juju-water
and, as he did, he became once again a man.

Without speaking or looking at me, he went out of the
ritual hut for the last time. He left me alone with my
thoughts, which is the best way to leave someone who has
just had a transcendent religious awakening.

I lay there, happy and grateful that the gods were so good
and the world so filled with wonder, when the woman came
in. I wanted to tell her how childish I felt for having feared
the serpent earlier. I wanted to share with her my knowledge
that there was no reason to fear the *orisha*. But she was a
stranger to me and I couldn't find the words to explain any
of these things.

It wasn't until I heard a soft snarl that my attention went
to the burlap sack she was carrying. Without taking her eyes
off me, she pulled out a baby leopard, surely no more than
three days old, its legs bound.

The woman was wearing a spotted collar and her eyes
shone like those of a cat in a dark cave. When she smiled
her knowing smile at me again, I saw for the first time that

her upper teeth had been filed sharp where they poked into her lower lip.

Then she took a gleaming machete out of her bag. She gave me no time to adjust. Still smiling, she drew the machete smoothly across the leopard's throat. She handed the small, still-twitching animal to me and said, "Drink deeply."

All my dread returned at once, washing over me like the flood tide on the Niger. I'd been a fool to feel so secure about my initiation. Now the deepest fear of every African tribal man—the fear of the *orisha*—came into my stomach as strongly as an enemy's blow. It was all the worse for the false sense of security and well-being into which I'd been lulled through the night. It made me want to cry out, to ask for mercy.

But I dared not; the ritual had two more days to go.

2

I was being initiated into what Westerners know as "Traditional African Religion." Because the real name for our religion sounds humorous to their ears, anthropologists adopted this term so their study of it would be taken more seriously by their academic colleagues. But we Africans still call it what our ancestors did: *juju*. The word is flexible and takes its exact meaning from context. *Juju* can refer to our religion, to the paraphernalia used in its practice, or to the idea of mystical power, as in "so-and-so won the lottery; he has big juju." But however we use the word, it sounds ominous to us rather than humorous.

To us, juju is no laughing matter. We believe it to be a religion of total power and control. It is as formal and as structured as any other religion. And its high priests carry themselves with as much dignity and solemnity, in their own way, as the Archbishop of Canterbury does. Yet the average American or European thinks of juju as childish superstition. He or she calls it "devil worship"—which is not a bad name for it, actually—and thinks it is no longer practiced in the modern world.

On the contrary, juju continues to be practiced in one form or another by most Africans, even many of those who are nominally Christians or Muslims. It is also practiced by

those Africans who have been displaced into the New
World, whose weak and watery versions of juju are known
as *voodoo* or *hoodoo*. So, in terms of the total number of its
adherents, juju actually ranks among the world's dominant
religions. Yet little about it is known outside Africa.

Juju differs fundamentally from all the other major
religions. For instance, whereas Christianity is based on
love, juju is based on fear. Where Christianity seeks
salvation, juju seeks only power. So Christians worship a
god of love and seek to please him for his own sake. But
jujumen seek to appease the gods they fear, the gods of evil.

These gods are many because there are so many things
that can hurt us in Africa. Lion and rhinos probably come to
your mind. And I suppose they *are* a danger in some places.
But many Africans today live in cities that are much like
overcrowded cities anywhere: The roars you hear are more
likely to be from motorcycles rather than from lions. No,
the powers that we Africans fear and need to appease are
more subtle than lions. They are all the powers we lack the
science and technology to understand or to control. The
tsetse fly, for instance. And the mosquito. Drought. And
famine. Diseases like *kwashiorkor* and others, diseases so
horrible that you Westerners found them unimaginable—
until that one we call "slim disease" reached you. Western
medicine calls it AIDS.

Many of these powers, like the diseases that kill more
than half our children before maturity, are invisible. So we
find it easy to believe in an Invisible World all around us,
trying to do us ill. In fact, we would find it impossible to
deny that such an Invisible World really exists; all the spirits
who want to hurt us come from this Invisible World. So
there are many gods which we need to appease if we're to
live in any semblance of safety.

The names of our gods vary from country to country and
from tribe to tribe, but their characters remain the same. At
the very top of our pantheon is the supreme being. My

people, the Yoruba, know him as *Olodumare*. The Daho-
means to the west of Yorubaland call him *Nana Buluku* and
the Ibo to the east of us call him *Chineke*. His identity,
however, is the same everywhere: He is the one who made
the universe and everything in it. We don't worship him,
though; he is thought to be so far above us human beings
that all we can do is acknowledge his existence.

Olodumare has delegated the daily running of the world
to his subsidiary gods. Among these are the principal deities
known in Yoruba as the *orishas*. These are very important
and powerful spirits. They aren't fond of human beings, either,
so we find it necessary to appease them quite often.

Below the *orishas* are many, many minor gods of nature,
each with his own department to watch after: the god of this
particular river, the god of that particular tree, and so forth.
There is no end to these minor gods because we create more
of them continuously, as we feel the need to. Suppose, for
instance, that a man trips one day over a rock in the path and
injures himself. He may give the god of that rock a name
and invent a ritual to appease it in order that it might not trip
him up again in the future.

Along with all those nature gods are the spirits of our
ancestors who, knowing so much about us because they are
our forefathers, can be extremely dangerous to us human
beings. They need appeasement, too; in a juju household, it
is not unusual to set an extra place at table in case any
ancestor chooses to drop in for a meal. That place is always
set with the choicest food of the household. Our belief is so
strong that this practice continues even in times of great
famine.

And an ancestor who wants to stay longer than just for
dinner can incarnate into the body of a newborn baby. So
prudent parents always take a baby to the local juju priest,
the *babalawo*, to find out which ancestor lives in their child.

There are two levels of juju: one for all believers, and a
special one which is only for those who have had advanced

training. One of the characteristics that all the varieties of juju have in common is the secrecy that characterizes juju at that higher level of practice. I was undergoing the initiation to the higher level. Before an initiate undergoes any of the rituals, he is made to understand that death will surely follow if he should ever tell any of the secrets he learns. And, as you'll see, my fellow jujumen would do their best to see to it that the prediction came true in my case.

The secrecy is so complete that one might almost say there is another religion, unknown to the outside world, *inside* the religion of juju. For example, there are two kinds of sacrificial places. The *Temple* is relatively accessible and open. In our cities, there are some big juju temples that resemble Christian churches. Sacrifice is of grain or of paper money or—on some special occasions—of a chicken or a pigeon. Temples are unguarded and unhidden; some even permit tourists to enter—for a price—and observe the juju activities that take place there and which we refer to as *ceremonies*.

But there is another sacrificial place, usually well out in the forest, far from prying eyes and ears, that we call the *Shrine*. It is usually no more than a hut in a hidden clearing in what we call the *igbo-awo* ("the secret forest"). What is performed here is not the innocuous *ceremony*, but rather the gruesome and bloody *ritual*.

Our rituals are designed to appease the most horrid of our gods. And—because those gods are so fearsome—so must be the rituals: We believe that nothing better appeases the fierce spirits of juju than *blood*. We refer to this letting of blood as *ichu-aja*, a word which has been translated as "sacrifice." But, because "sacrifice" has overtones of charity and self-denial to Westerners, you might prefer to think of it as *ritual killing*, which would more accurately describe it.

Blood flows more freely than water in some shrines, but the modern Western world wants to remain oblivious to the fact. It does not want to know that we still appease the spirits of our gods with the blood of animals.

And even less does it want to know that the higher spirits demand the blood of a higher animal: the *human* animal.

Many in the West want to believe that all this juju, blood sacrifice, ritual killing, human sacrifice—is something from the distant past, a relic of darkest Africa from the days before it was "civilized" by the white man. That belief is far more comforting than the truth.

But juju in its bloodiest forms is still alive and well today. Not only in Africa, but among Africa's transplanted children in the New World, where it has now spread to whites as well. Hardly a week goes by that news of juju rituals is not reported somewhere in America by the press. But it's such a big country that the incidents seem isolated, the work of individual psychotics. Only when one becomes aware of how many such incidents there are altogether can one begin to see them as parts of a pattern. For example, the Cable News Network reported on September 1, 1988, that the remains of sixteen animals had been found in a public park in Newark, New Jersey. The remains were in plastic bags and included chickens, dogs, and a goat, the head of which was never found. But only a few days earlier, the Chicago television station WGN carried a film report about an apartment on the west side of the city which was used as a "holding pen" for sacrificial animals. Dozens of animals including chickens, pigs, goats, and dogs were kept in their own filth until sold to jujumen for sacrifice. Amazingly, the neighbors in this densely populated area claimed that they saw, heard, and smelled nothing.

Juju is in the midst of America now. It may be known by other names and some of its rituals may have been updated. But, basically, it remains the same as we in Africa have always known it to be: the religion that is believed to give power through blood. And that thirst for bloody sacrifice will explain much that has been happening in the West lately. As we will see, it may have an impact on even that most overwhelming social problem, AIDS.

Before I would come to recognize any of that, though, I would go through a mystical odyssey. My initiation was only the first step in that odyssey, but it was one that had been ordained for me from the day I was born.

3

The position of juju high priest—*babalorisha*—is not, strictly speaking, a hereditary one. In my case, there was no reason to believe that the honor would ever fall to me. Especially since my family had moved from Nigeria to another country altogether.

Our migration was a result of the Gold Rush that took place in West Africa in the 1930s. It was in the area called the Gold Coast which we know today as the country of Ghana. Visiting Americans often remark that it reminds them of Florida. On a map, it's a little closer to the West than my ancestral homeland of Nigeria.

In many ways, our Gold Rush must have been like the one that occurred in the American Wild West. Almost overnight, people from all over the world converged on one small spot on the West African coast. Few could understand the language of those working next to them. Fewer still could understand the other's culture or religion. Drunkenness and violence were common; it was not a good place to raise a family.

I was born in a mining camp there. Today the area is much more built up and modernized with a big port where the new cities of Sekondi and Takoradi squeeze the river. The people of Ghana call them the "Twin Cities," just like

Americans refer to Minneapolis/St. Paul. Sekondi/Takoradi is somewhat warmer, of course, especially in January.

My father brought my mother there from Nigeria some months before I was born. He supported my brothers, my mother, and me by laboring in the state mines. Whenever he felt he could spare the time and money, he would go off and search for a strike of his own.

The harsh, vagabond life we led surprises some of my American and European friends. After all, my grandfather was a *babalorisha* back in Nigeria—one of only a very few. That's an exalted position, roughly equal to a Bishop in the Anglican Church. My friends wonder why Grandfather didn't take my father into the "family business," so to speak, rather than let him scratch out a meager living in the mines of Ghana. But inheritance in Africa usually goes to the first-born son and that was not my father.

Sadly, Grandfather's first two sons both died in infancy. And in both cases, they died shortly after he officially named them as his successors. This seemed to discourage him from designating any other heir. He even ignored some of those who had strong cases to succeed him: Joshua, for instance, the seventh son of Grandfather's seventh son, should have been a strong candidate. But *nobody* was training to be the next *babalorisha*, so all the sons of my grandfather were required to earn a living any way they could, including my father.

To be designated as our next *babalorisha*, a man had to be chosen by the gods themselves. And that's why some sign was needed from Grandfather as to who the residents of the Invisible World had identified. But apparently, neither the gods nor the ancestors ever spoke to Grandfather on behalf of any of his sons, grandsons, or great-grandsons, even though he faithfully presented each of us to the *orishas* in elaborate juju rituals.

These rituals begin with circumcision—the boy's first experience with blood ritual. Also, facial cuts are often made which will heal into distinctive scars later. To accentuate the scarring, certain herbs are rubbed into our wounds. These inflame them so that a good, deep scar will eventually result. These scars can be used to identify a man's tribe, his clan, even his family. This practice has declined in favor of chalked facial markings; juju is, more than ever, a secret religion, so it's unwise for modern jujumen to wear permanent signals on their faces.

It is that willingness to adapt to changing circumstances that protects juju. A European friend recently asked me what my name was before I changed it. "What do you mean?" I asked him.

"How could your name have been given to you in a juju home? 'Isaiah' is a Christian name," he said.

"Ah, yes. But many Africans have Christian first names, even though they're jujumen."

I explained that Africans are resilient people. When any new concept comes to us, including a new religion, we take from it what we like and add it to what we've already got. The rest we throw away. The new idea doesn't replace the old one, but gets mixed into it like an ingredient in batter. It happens so consistently among us that the anthropologists have even invented a pretty name for it: *syncretism*.

So, many Africans who are nominally Christians or Moslems continue to practice juju in private. On the surface, they are all piety, and the minister or the mullah may count such people as members in good standing of his local congregation. But in reality, they are "closet jujumen."

Like most Central Africans at that time, my people were still thoroughly juju. But they were smart enough to prevent the outside world from knowing that. So when I was born, my parents took me to the local missionary and asked him to select a fitting Bible name. He chose Isaiah, a major Old Testament prophet.

Then my father turned right around and took me, Christian name and all, to the local *babalawo* for juju ritual.

A *babalawo* is a juju priest of the junior level who can lay curses, cast spells, and participate in public ceremonies. He cannot, however, officiate at secret rituals, not can he speak directly to the gods as a *babalorisha* can. *Babalawos* network among themselves just as members of every other profession do. They pass along information and establish each other's reputations for power: one might be very good at helping you curse an enemy, for example, while another might be renowned for lifting the curse that made your wife or your cow barren. Periodically, they even have international conferences and get-togethers, just as if they were hardware manufacturers or insurance salesmen.

The local man to whom my father took me turned out to be an old friend of my grandfather. He accepted the baby goat that would be sacrificed, but he firmly declined the few coins that would be his official fee; it was sort of a "professional courtesy," I suppose, toward my grandfather.

After what my father said was a very lengthy interview, during which he asked all about our family, the *babalawo* told my father to go away and to return two days later. In the meantime, he said, he had to consult with some of the local "specialists": the necromancer, the astrologer, and so forth. It was clear, he said, that a very important ancestor had become incarnate inside me and he needed to do some research and some tests and to consult with his colleagues in order to know who that ancestor was. In the meantime, he told my father, be very careful: You don't know who might be inside this child. This was all big news to my parents; they hadn't counted on anything except just another human baby.

The next couple of days must have been very difficult for them. Who was in me? A favorable, helpful spirit who would bring them good luck? Or . . .

Two days later, the *babalawo* dropped a bombshell. "In this child," he said, "is incarnated *Orisha-Oko*."

So! I wasn't just a spirit—I was a *god!*

Well, a godling, anyway. *Orisha-Oko* was the name of one we call a "household god." This was a special private god for the clan Oke only. Actually he was a demigod: half-god and half-ancestor. Legend has it that he was born with part of the amnion covering his head; the Europeans would say he was "born under a caul." This, of course, was very big juju, an omen of greatness. So he adopted the name *Oke*, which means "membrane," and became the founder of the clan Oke. The rough equivalent in the United States would be to say that the spirit of George Washington had been reborn in me.

My father was both proud and stunned. He was proud because a god had come into his child. Certainly the baby would grow to be very important and influential—perhaps a *babalorisha* or even an *oba* (king). Who wouldn't be proud?

But at the same time, he was scared and confused. How do you treat a baby who is the miraculous incarnation of somebody special? How was he to discipline me? How could my mother bear to feed me? Or change my diaper? None of this was the *babalawo*'s concern, of course. Juju priests, as a rule, feel themselves to be above the daily concerns of ordinary people; they do not show the care for their congregations that a Christian would call "pastoral."

So, without giving my father any counsel or advice about handling a child with a god inside him, the *babalawo* finished the ritual. With appropriate incantations, he killed the kid my father had brought two days earlier. It had to be a baby goat, rather than a calf or any other kind of young animal; in the secret symbolic language of juju, jujumen refer to themselves as "goats" and everyone else as "sheep." He smeared some of the animal's blood on all of us. Then, with the same knife, he circumcised me, thus making me a "brother in blood" of the goat.

Finally, he gave me my Name. The juju belief is that one's Name is heavy with juju, that it summarizes and symbolizes one's entire person, that it is the essence of one's soul. No one else—except my closest family members and my first son—was to know it. No woman—including my mother and my future wife—was *ever* to know it. Should it happen that my Name was ever learned by a tabooed person, the belief is that they would then have enormous power over me. I like to think of myself these days as educated—a traveled man, perhaps even a bit worldly. I no longer subscribe to juju beliefs or engage in juju practices. Nevertheless, even today, I would need a very good reason to reveal my Name.

This business of giving a baby a special Name, spiritual and hidden, seems at first harmless, trivial, even a bit silly. But it exemplifies the way juju thrives on secrecy. It shows how juju maintains its hold long after it had been consciously renounced. It demonstrates the *true* power of juju, the way juju can—and does—flourish unrecognized in the midst of any group of people. Even Western people—educated, sophisticated, rational people like your neighbors there in America.

But there was no reason to keep *Orisha-Oko*'s incarnation in me a secret. The only "secret" was how my grandfather would react.

4

They tell me that Grandfather killed a valuable ox when the good news reached back home about *Orisha-Oko* being inside me. He also sent a gift of two cows and a wife to his colleague in Ghana who had divined my true identity.

He immediately went into consultation with other important *babalawo* in the district. Many chickens and lizards were killed and their entrails studied. Every rain cloud was carefully examined by those who practiced that form of divination. And the graveyard was crowded with all the necromancers, seeking omens from the dead. In the end, these sorceries confirmed the news for Grandfather: His grandchild had been chosen as the earthly vessel for the great spirit *Orisha-Oko*.

It was inevitable, he declared, that I should succeed him as the next *babalorisha;* who was more worthy?

He sent detailed instructions to my parents about my care. Everything possible was done to assure my well-being. In effect, my parents and my brothers became my slaves. I always got the best and biggest portions of any food. And if I wanted some trifling trinket, I always got it. Even if that trinket already belonged to somebody else. It must have been easy for me to learn to walk because I don't think there was ever a time when anybody got in my way.

Even out in the streets of our village, people stepped aside for me. And anybody who had a sweet or a piece of fruit shoved it in my mouth, hoping for the smile that might indicate a blessing. So I quickly became very fat and very spoiled.

In my fifth year, my mother took me back home to Nigeria, to be with Grandfather and to learn the ways of juju. I never again saw my father after that. He hadn't ever been comfortable around me, always peeking at me out of the corner of his eye, afraid to raise his voice lest I curse him. It must be frightening to have a little god for a son. I understand he took another wife. He died some years ago.

As to my brothers, all of them still live in Ghana. We had no chance to be close, the way African brothers are supposed to be. Fortunately, there was a new family waiting for me at Grandfather's compound.

The name of our village in Nigeria was Inesi-Ile. It was a rural place in those days. It took a walk of about an hour through the savanna grass to get to the bus stop on the closest of our very few roads. And the district capital of Ilesha was more than two hours' additional journey away by bus. So those who had business in the city faced a lengthy commute.

There were a hundred or more homes in our village. They covered a very large area because a Yoruba home is more of a compound than a structure. It's a group of small buildings, sometimes only single-roomed, rather than one large building with many rooms, like in the West. The compound of my grandfather befitted his station as one of the principal *babalorishas* of Nigeria. It consisted of several buildings around a small yard and a little garden plot; the town's main square was just outside, in accordance with Grandfather's position as the principal man of the place. Juju ceremonies were conducted there as well as in our market.

Four of the buildings were quarters for Grandfather's wives. Each wife had her own room in one of the women's

buildings and he took his dinner at each woman's place in
strict rotation. There was also a granary, two livestock
barns, and several outbuildings of the type one finds on
farms anywhere.

In the garden we raised vegetables like cabbage and
carrots, and also some annual plants. The larger plants, like
bananas, and the produce that required several years to
yield, like our local apple, were grown on a somewhat more
spacious field that was a mile or so from the compound. In
that cleared area, which we called "the farm," we also grew
rice, beans, and several varieties of yam.

Toward the rear of the compound was the building that
housed Grandfather's private quarters. When the women
snickered among themselves, they referred to it as "The
Palace." In actuality, it looked no different from any of the
other residential buildings; it had but two rooms and an
enormous porch.

Just in front of the Palace was Grandfather's Temple: a
building that was used for consulting with other *babalawo*,
which Grandfather did frequently, and for certain ceremonies. It was also the place where I was to receive much of
my juju training over the next several years.

The whole of the compound was surrounded by a kind of
stockade fence with a single gate giving off onto the village
proper. These fences (or *odi*) are characteristic of Yoruba
architecture and have religious, rather than military, signif-
icance. They are designed to keep out not people, but *evil*.
To do this they naturally rely on juju.

The fence around a Yoruba city has seven gates, seven
being a sacred number. The *orisha* in charge of gates is
Legba. *Legba* is not a friend of man; no *orisha* ever is. But
he is the enemy of Fate. And it is Fate that sends bad fortune
to men. So we propitiate *Legba* in order that he will trick his
enemy Fate into leaving us alone.

Whenever an *odi* is built, therefore, *Legba* must be
appeased. This requires that three persons captured at

random be buried alive, still kicking and screaming, under each of the seven gates.

One of our legends about the power and the impartiality of juju involves just such a sacrifice. It seems that the firstborn son of a certain *oba* was weak, greedy, and despised by the people of the city. Yet it was he, the firstborn, who was designated to take over when it would be time for the old man to die.

The people of the city were at a loss at what to do. There was no democracy, of course, so the son couldn't be voted out. And a violent *coup* was out of the question because of the family's powerful juju; it would avenge anyone who lifted a hand against the sun.

But it happened that the fence was being replaced at that time and the *oba* had ordered victims to be captured so the appropriate sacrifices could be made.

One morning very early, the firstborn son stepped out of his house to respond to a call of nature. He was set upon by a group of the junior priests. They bound and gagged him and hid him in the forest. Then they went to the *oba*.

"Great *Oba*," the priests said, "we have secured victims for the sacrifice to *Legba*, just as you commanded."

"Well done," said the *oba*. "We will make ritual tomorrow morning. See to it."

But the men just stood here, looking from one to the other with worried looks on their faces.

"What's wrong?" said the *oba*.

"Great *Oba*, we captured the last man only this morning. It was still dark and we could not see him. He turns out to be an important man with great and powerful friends."

"Hmmmm." The *oba* thought for a moment. "But all men are the same to the *orisha*. If any man wanders into your grasp, surely it must mean that the *orisha* intended for him to be caught. It is his destiny. Do not think about it further."

But the men continued to look frightened. "Great *Oba*,

he is a jujuman, a Man of Power, a *babalawo*. His juju is great and powerful."

The *oba* half-rose out of his throne. "Wha-a-a-t? Do you think that *his* juju is more powerful than *my* juju?" He relaxed when the men quaked satisfactorily. "I order you to prepare for sacrifice tomorrow morning—"

"But the man we caught this morning—"

"Enough!" The *oba* boomed. "No man is greater than the rituals! Were it my very own son, I would carry out the ritual exactly as given to us by our ancestors."

Having said this, there was no turning back. His honor required him to bury his own firstborn son alive the next morning, which he did. History does not record what happened to the plotters.

During my years at Grandfather's compound, the fence never had to be replaced. A good thing for me. I had an enemy there who felt about me the way the plotters felt about the *oba's* son: he was Joshua, the son of my father's brother. That may seem a roundabout way of saying he was my cousin, but I have no other way to express the relationship: We have no word such as "cousin"; all are brothers.

My brother Joshua was twice my age when I came to Inesi-Ile and was already looking forward to his own initiation. His father was the seventh son of our grandfather and Joshua was the seventh son of his father. To be the seventh son of a seventh son is very big juju. I understand the same is true in Europe, where supernatural powers are often ascribed to the seventh son of a seventh son. No one in our village—especially Joshua—could understand why Joshua had not been made Grandfather's heir.

Of course, the day the news came that *Orisha-Oko* was inside me, Grandfather's peculiar behavior suddenly made sense to everybody; he'd obviously waited so that he could name me to succeed him. If anything, his reputation for wisdom was enhanced. So when my mother and I arrived in

Inesi-Ile, everyone chanted and bowed down to me. Except Grandfather, of course. And Joshua.

Even as a child, Joshua's hatred of me was profound. I remember how he used to try juju on me, to make me sick. At first, everybody thought he was cute, making his little hex signs at me and cooking up his little charms.

But in fact, shortly after my arrival, I did take quite ill. I developed a mysterious fever and nearly died. It was the end of the dry season before I recovered. People said it was young Joshua, strong with juju even at such a tender age.

For years, he was my constant torment. He would pinch me when we attended the adults so that I would cry out. Then, of course, I'd get cuffed on the head for disturbing my elders: God or no god, there were standards of behavior in the compound.

Even as we grew, so did out enmity for each other. It was a relief when his heart was finally captured several years later. Her name was Rebecca Abanogu. I remember once when I was about ten years old, he tried to trouble me in her presence and she rebuked him for it. She hugged me close and called me "little brother." It was the first time I'd ever been near the breast of a woman who was not my mother. Her breast was warm and firm and smooth. It yielded like a bag filled with duck feathers when she held my cheek to it and rubbed it comfortingly across my face. I became confused about my feelings toward her at that moment and finally decided that what I was feeling must have been gratitude for her kindness.

It infuriated Joshua, of course. But he never again taunted me when she could hear. And since he followed her around constantly, it neutralized him as a threat to me.

In any event, there was less time for me to come in contact with Joshua than there might have been. Most of my time when I was growing up was spent at Grandfather's side, watching him officiate at juju ceremonies. Because I had not yet been initiated, I was not allowed at this time to see or participate in any of the secret rituals out in the forest. That was good because it gave me time for school.

School was Grandfather's idea. Usually, our people didn't hold much with school, believing it to be "white man's magic." But Grandfather made an exception in my case. It was his long-range plan that I should record on paper the whole of juju knowledge. This had never been done before and he felt that it would make me the most powerful jujuman not only of Nigeria, but of all Africa.

Of course, that meant I had to learn to read and write. Rather than let me go to school to be "polluted" by outsiders, he found a tutor willing to stay on in the village: Mr. Olungwe.

Mr. Olungwe was a sad man, impoverished and wifeless. All his study had not helped him to get a job in the Civil Service, which is where most educated Africans wound up in those days. Nor was it his fault. During his last year in school, a kinsman of Mr. Olungwe's had led an abortive and well-publicized uprising in neighboring Cameroon in which hundreds were killed. The name "Olungwe" became a kind of curse and seeking work became futile for anyone of that name. His family's property had been seized, including the little money he'd sent them to save for him. Lacking a "bride price," his options were limited. But even families that had women who were difficult to marry off wouldn't allow them to go to an Olungwe.

So he taught me in return for his keep. I learned reading, writing, and arithmetic. He taught me in Hausa, English, and French. But the textbooks were left over from British colonial days, so I thought history consisted only of the Battle of Hastings, the Magna Carta, and Lord Nelson. Of African history, I was totally unaware.

Mr. Olungwe's difficult job of teaching me was made harder still by Grandfather's insistence that no "missionary juju" or "white man's juju" find its way into my young head. In other words, he was to teach me the mechanics of the "three Rs" and nothing else. As a graduate of the mission school and a European university, and as a consumer of Western books, he must have found it difficult to always avoid sensitive issues.

Whenever there was public juju ceremony (which seemed to be most of the time), school was out for me. For days at a time, my classroom would become my grandfather's side. The result of all these interruptions in my formal education was that it took me a long time to learn a little.

But gradually, the primer on juju that Grandfather wanted grew fat. In fact, I became somewhat of a fanatic about the white man's magic known as writing. The way the little black marks could make the paper talk seemed to me very big juju. Among our people, the mysterious sheets of marked-up paper were known as the "talking leaves." Through them, a man could speak to other men even after his death without a necromancer as a go-between, as our verbal system required.

I began to write down everything: the ceremonies that Grandfather told me to record, of course. But also chants. Curses. Charms. And, most of all, herbal recipes. Recipes for curing every kind of illness, for bringing luck, for male potency. I wrote with yellow #2 pencils sharpened with the edge of a machete. I wrote on big yellow tablets with green lines; those tablets had a wonderful pulpy smell about them that I remember to this day. I stored the pages in a big metal box which Grandfather hid for me at his Shrine way out in the forest. He carried the box back and forth himself, but he let me keep the key to it, which was a great honor and trust. I wore it around my neck, clanking against my cowries and all my other juju.

There seemed no end of information: Every jujuman adds something of his own to the standard procedures and recipes, and I tried to record it all. But, big as my manuscript was becoming, it still contained no information at all on the secret rituals that were for the initiates alone.

I'd only witnessed the harmless public ceremonies—the ones with which we amused ourselves by charging tourists and anthropologists to watch. In spite of my exalted position as the heir apparent to my grandfather, in spite of all I'd seen at his side, in spite of all I'd written during six years, I'd not even gotten close to *real* juju.

But that would be rectified as soon as I completed my initiation.

5

———

During all the rest of my initiation ritual, my guides spent time with me by turns so that I was never permitted to sleep. Nor was I allowed solid food or water in all that time. Instead, I was supposed to be sustained by the mystical wonders they served up for me. They took turns introducing me to the spirits that were important to my people.

The way of it was always the same. If the woman was finished with me, she would leave the ritual hut. Sometimes the sound of drums would then begin to come from outside but at other times, all remained silent; so, unlike me, my guides may have had opportunities to sleep. If the woman left, the man would come in. He would first conjure with various juju before sacrificing an animal of the type that was pleasing to the specific *orisha* he wanted me to meet. Then we would share the blood of the sacrifice.

After that, he would wash himself with the juju-water from the skull pot. Immediately, the animal whose blood we had just consumed would possess him. The animal would then proceed to tell me all that is good for a man to know about the secrets of its kind.

When it was finished, the animal would dip its paw or wing into the juju-water. Only this time, it would use the serpent pot. As the animal washed with the juju-water, the

man would repossess his own flesh. He would leave the hut,
drained and weakened. But the woman would shortly take
his place and the cycle would begin again.

In this way, I met many benign spirits: the wise tortoise,
the loyal and brave dog, and the fun-loving monkey. We
laughed together and they became like my brothers.

But I also met darker spirits: the slinking hyena, the
traitorous jackal, and the brooding vulture. Those spirits
called forth the horrifying *orisha* whom they represented.
Isa, the god of evil and illness, threatened me with every
kind of sickness. *Ifa*, the god of understanding, cursed me
and threatened to make me go mad. And *Ogun*, the god of
metals, threatened to cook me—"slowly and forever," he
said—in his forge.

I lost track of time and place. As I did, the world of the
ritual hut became more and more terrifying to me. At
one point, I felt my body was covered by masses of our
huge African termites. Later, I recognized snow falling
from the roof of the hut, even though I'd never seen snow
except in pictures. It buried me alive; I was colder than I
imagined anyone could ever be.

Toward the end, the woman appeared. She was wearing
a wrapper around her body—yellow with large black spots
surrounded with green rings. It was a very beautiful
pattern—familiar, though my mind seemed unable to make
sense of it. From her bag she brought forth a snake with
spots similar to her wrapper, but of different colors. I
wondered if it might be the same snake that had slept on my
stomach back when the initiation started.

She knelt by my side. "Now," she said, baring her
pointed teeth in a grin, "you prepare to meet *Orunmila.*"
She was panting slightly, as if she was short of breath, and
her skin glowed with perspiration, even though she'd not
yet started. It was as if she was excited, the way I'd heard
a woman was when she was with a man.

"*Orunmila?*" I repeated weakly. My mind seemed as if it

was full of smoke. I felt a perfect fool, aware that the name was that of one of our most important and powerful *orishas*, but still unable to place it.

"The god of all secrets," she breathed, stroking the snake. "Only he can tell you the ways of the most dangerous animals of all—other men." She rose gracefully, like an Ibo queen, still stroking the snake. In a few moments, it became limp. The woman slid her hand down to its tail and let the rest of its body dangle toward the dirt floor.

Suddenly, she snapped it—BANG!—over her head like a whip. Every bone in its body must have broken at once.

With a mighty jerk, she pulled the head off and dropped the rest on my chest, with the usual reminder to drink deeply of it. As I did, I saw her tilt the skull pot up on its side to scoop out the last of the juju-water. I remember how seeing her do this brought me joy; it meant the end was near. All I had to do was tough out this final exercise and manhood would be mine.

Drums started outside the hut. The woman began to writhe in time to them. As if by magic, the patterned wrapper she wore around her body seemed to stretch as I watched. It began to get longer, until it covered her feet. And it began to get higher until it covered first her neck and finally her face. At the same time, it began to get tighter and tighter, stretching until it fit her as tightly as the skin of a . . .

Python!

It opened its glassy eyes and wiggled its forked tongue in my direction, tasting the air to see if I would be as juicy as I looked. It was a very long snake—every bit as long as the woman had been tall. And it seemed very, very strong, heavy with juju.

There was nothing of the intangible about this giant snake, nothing that could have come from lack of sleep or food, nothing that could have resulted from the power of suggestion or from all the blood I'd ingested. The snake was

even more real than the other visions I'd had. It was as real
as I was, as real as my grandfather, as real as Africa itself.
In fact, I heard it tell me somewhere deep inside myself that
it was the very *soul* of Africa.

I had to face the most powerful symbol of a society
rooted in symbols and I couldn't do it. I screamed and ran
in a panic to the doorhole of the hut, willing even to give up
my manhood to escape. But the tiny hole undid me; before
I could wiggle out, the snake was on me.

I had already screamed all my air out. I could take no
more in because the python's coils bound me from knees to
neck and they were tightening. I cried out—but only in my
heart—to my ancestors, that they might receive me well in
the other world.

But suddenly, the pain of the python's coils was gone. I
took in air . . . no, I was as *light* as air! I opened my eyes
and saw the roof of the hut almost touching my face; it was
so close, I even blew away a fire ant from a piece of
thatching an inch in front of my nose.

I rolled over in space and saw my body below me, wrapped
in the coils of a huge yellow and green python. A hot feeling
came up to me from the green serpent, as if it hated me. Even
as I watched, the coils tightened until I heard popping noises
come from my body. But, somehow, I was not afraid.
Could this be the secret of Initiation? Did it explain the
warning my grandfather had always given me that, "Nothing can ever *really* hurt you"?

I heard a rushing sound, like the wind from the tropical
cyclone. I looked down again and saw the *babalorisha*
leaning over my body with a drinking gourd in his hand. He
was calling my name loudly enough for me to hear him over
the sound of the wind.

Suddenly, without having made any effort to get back to
my body, I was down on the floor again, looking up at him.
Next to him was the woman, the *ayelorisha*. She was

wearing a spotted wrapper, no different from the kind any
other Yoruba woman might wear.

I drank from the gourd. It was blood again. Not chicken
blood, which we tasted almost daily in my village. Not
snake, which I'd had earlier, either. Something I'd never
tasted before. A little like pig blood. But rather different,
actually. I looked around, but could not see what animal
they had killed to get the blood.

"Are you well?" the woman asked.

"Y-yes," I said. "but the serpent . . ."

"Serpent?" the man asked. "Look around you. Do you
see any 'serpent' here?"

"No, but . . ."

"Take this," he said. He ripped a long narrow strip from
the white robe I'd wore on my pilgrimage to the ritual hut.
The robe had been hanging from the roof pole ever since
we'd arrived, a silent witness to all that had happened here.
While I held one end of the long strip, he twisted it into a
tight, ropelike braid. "This," he said, "will become your
ibante."

I closed my eyes and nearly wept with relief: The *ibante*
is a jujuman's source of power. What he was telling me was
that I'd made it, that I was "in." From now on, I was going
to be a *babalawo*, a Man of Power, among my people. Even
more, I would become their *babalorisha* when my grandfather died. I would be privileged to talk to the gods and to
all of our ancestors directly. It meant that the way was now
cleared for me to become eventually the supreme juju leader
of all West Africa.

The *babalorisha* produced a needle from his bag. It was
threaded with some very strong, clear material. Then he and
the woman both emptied on the ground the last of their
bags, out of which fell many pieces of juju. He handed me
the needle and thread.

At his direction, I picked the juju from the dirt one after
the other and sewed them to the long skinny braid of white

cloth. Most of the juju were either cowries or small,
polished bones, although there were also a few metal and
wooden objects: buttons, they looked like. Sewing was
another of those tasks that were not appropriate for men in
my clan to perform, so I made slow and sloppy work of it.
But at last I was finished.

Then they helped me to drench the *ibante* in the last of the
unfamiliar blood that the *babalorisha* had given me from his
drinking gourd. I held one end of the braid just below my
navel while the two of them crawled around, winding it
between my legs, around, and back again. When they were
finished, it looked as if I were wearing crotchless, bloody
briefs, my manhood protruding from the stringy triangle so
formed.

It was intended that I should wear this power garment
under my outer clothes for the rest of my life. But the taboo
required that it be worn in the utmost secrecy. I could never
undress in front of anyone and, even when alone, I could
never undress in the light. I could never submit to an
examination by a medical doctor. And, when I married, I
would oblige my wife to wear a hood whenever we coupled,
lest she accidentally glimpse the source of my power.

The *babalorisha* threw me a pair of old khaki shorts and
told me to cover myself. Then the *ayelorisha* carried the last
of the drinking water to me, which was as things were
meant to be. She also brought me some fresh-dug yams, the
best I'd ever tasted. There were no congratulations to
accompany the meal, though—those would come later at
my celebration ceremony. Instead, I just fell asleep, half a
yam still in my mouth.

When I awoke, my two guides were gone. I have never
seen either of them again. Nor would I care to look for
them.

As custom demanded, I knocked down the ritual hut and
scattered the pieces. To the eye of an anthropologist or

tourist who ever stumbled on the spot, it would be as if nothing had happened in this place since the dawn of time.

When the Sun was barely above the horizon, I set off toward home. The three days of private ritual were finally over; the seven days of public ceremony were about to begin.

THE
JUJU
SCHOLAR

6

I made my way back to Inesi-Ile through a forest that had
become different to me in the past three days. It was
warmer, lighter, and less threatening than the ominous place
it had always been before.

Still, I knew it was me who had changed, not the forest.
The spirits that lurked behind every rock and inside every
tree were still there. And they were as vicious as ever; I still
wouldn't want to be caught out in the forest after dark or on
a day that had bad omens.

But I felt more secure because for the first time I had a
defense against the random evils that befall men. I now
knew that the ancestors and the nature spirits and even the
orisha could be appeased and thus (to some extent anyway)
they could be controlled. I was sure I would learn countless
ways to deal with them during my development as *babalorisha:* charms, hexes, and chants. But already I understood
the most potent appeaser of all: blood.

Nor was I unaware of the power my new knowledge
would give me over others—over many of the men and all
of the women. They would know I was different, reputed to
be a new and mighty man of knowledge. I was only just
beginning to flatter myself with the fantasies of all that such
a reputation could mean.

Because I no longer felt the need to move especially silently, a raggedy band of children heard me when I was yet some distance from the village. I barely saw them before they ran away from me in mock terror, a tangle of little brown arms and legs. In an instant, they were out of sight, racing toward Inesi-Ile. Every one of them wanted to be the first to have the honor to shout, breathless and wide-eyed, "A strange man approaches! A strange man approaches!"

The drums started almost immediately. So by the time I made my way to the ceremonial clearing by Grandfather's Temple, a large group of men had gathered. They closed in a big circle around me as I went to the center of the clearing. Spears in hand, they danced flat-footed and fierce-looking to the beat of the drums. They took turns stepping forward, shaking their spears menacingly in my direction and yelling dire threats. When the turn came round to him, Joshua glared at me as if he really did want to kill me.

For my part, of course, I simply stared indifferently off into space, as befits a Man of Knowledge. Out of the corner of my eye, though, I looked to see if Rebecca Abanogu was near Joshua. But, of course, it would have been taboo for a woman to be present in the warriors' circle.

Finally, after the last man had his chance to show his determination to defend our village against all comers, it was time for someone to step forward and "recognize" me. Custom dictated that it be my father. But in his absence, my grandfather himself honored me by stepping out of the circle of townsmen. He performed his part well, approaching me haltingly with much hesitation. When he was close enough to touch me, he stopped and squinted up into my face. He blinked a few times, as if trying to place me. Then, he let a big, toothless smile split his face. "People of Inesi-Ile," he shouted, "fear not! For this is my son, Isaiah—now a man!"

It was the signal. The men all threw down their spears and came forward, laughing, to embrace me. The women, who had all been inside, presumably quaking in terror, now came out singing and dancing in time to the music. Even the children dropped their act and joined in. All except for one little fellow who obviously hadn't been briefed; he picked up a dropped spear, charged me, and jabbed me painfully in the calf. I scooped him up and held him over my head. "This one is as brave as a man already," I shouted, and everyone laughed some more.

Everything from that point on is in progressively hazier detail because someone shoved a shell of palm wine into my hand and I downed it in salute. It was not the milky, mildly alcoholic drink that accompanies our food, but the strong stuff—"man's wine," we call it.

The first group of sacrificial animals was brought out immediately: the seven calves. There would also be seven he-goats, seven she-goats, seven cocks, seven hens, seven lambs and seven antelopes, all of which would be consumed with much palm wine in a seven-day feast of gigantic proportions.

One of the great things about a "new man" festival is that it's one of the few times we can celebrate in a purely "secular" manner. That is, the drumming, the fiddling, the dancing, and the drinking that accompany the ceremonies lack the religious overtones that color most of our activities. This festival is just for fun, an outcome of our exuberance for life.

And we certainly took advantage of the opportunity. The dancing and the music were as spirited as I've ever seen. Few of the celebrants even stopped their merrymaking to observe Grandfather's first ceremonial cut.

The calf was first anointed with the appropriate herbs by a group of women, one of whom was Rebecca Abanogu. Then they dragged it out and tethered it to a pole in the square. Two of the men, already giddy with palm wine, grabbed the calf's hindquarters and pulled backwards to make the animal stretch its neck.

Grandfather inspected his sacrificial knife with a practiced eye and bobbed his head in satisfaction. He pulled the calf's head back and swiftly drew the knife across its throat in the prescribed manner, from the left ear to the right. The left side being unlucky, this was a prayer that bad luck should turn to good.

But his knife missed the jugulars and he had to make another pass at the bleating creature. This was a major embarrassment for him because he was usually far more precise in his work. When he sprinkled the customary handful of blood on the crowd, his mouth was tight with shame. I noticed that, after that, he declined any more palm wine.

The women set on the carcass at once. Within minutes, it was skinned, gutted, split in two, and spitted over the fire. It smelled wonderful.

The men continued toasting me and each other; the palm wine flowed like water. There were strong, homemade cigars for all of us to share while we sang all the old songs to the accompaniment of the musicians.

People soon began to behave peculiarly. Men I knew to be quiet and serious became boisterous. Others who were always industrious and hard-working now lay around the fire, barely half-conscious. Well-behaved daughters and sisters were telling secret jokes to one another and laughing out loud quite unbecomingly. Of course, that was the whole idea of all the drinking and the other activities.

By the time the Sun was down and we were into the fifth calf, I noticed something that I'd never noticed before. Some of the women would roll their eyes, sort of, in the direction of the men. The men would grin and knock each other in the ribs until, after a while, one of them would get up from the circle and go speak to a woman. Then, full of palm wine and laughing, they would go into the bush together.

I had no doubt that this sort of thing went on at every big

celebration, but I'd never noticed it before. Of course, this
was the first time I'd ever had any cause to pay attention to
it; initiation in our culture is chosen to coincide with sexual
maturity. So, for the first time, I was a man in more ways
than one and that meant I found the women interesting,
especially Rebecca Abanogu.

She was one of the women standing around behind the
squatted circle of singing men, so naturally I just couldn't
help but notice her. Joshua had chosen his spot in the circle
to be directly in front of her, as always, and if I craned my
neck to see over him, I could just make out Rebecca's
breasts bouncing over his head. They were shiny with sweat
from the exertion of dancing and, as I watched them, I felt
myself becoming aroused.

As I explained, this was a new sensation for me and I was
embarrassed lest anyone should see my shame. For I was
wearing only a loose loin cloth over my *ibante* and it did
nothing to either hide or suppress my erection. So I sort of
hunched over uncomfortably and leaned in toward the fire,
trying to act casual and natural. I don't think I fooled
anyone because more of the rib-knocking immediately
started up and I could hear some of the women giggling
even above the sound of song. I was mortified, certain with
the self-consciousness of the newly pubescent that they
weré laughing at my lack of self-control. But I still found it
impossible not to stare at Rebecca Abanogu.

Then I looked up to her face and saw that *she* was looking
at *me*. To be specific, she was staring at my lap, in which
I'd placed my folded hands as a desperate attempt at
camouflage. Her wide-set dark eyes were big and she
appeared to be breathing through her moist mouth. Her
sweat was coming harder now, and the area around her full
lips was glistening with it. I was both panic-stricken and
aroused almost to the point of release but she didn't seem to
notice my discomfort.

When she finally raised her eyes to my face, she stunned

me by smiling pleasantly, as if she wasn't shocked by me in the least. In fact, she started rolling her eyes at me the way the other women had been doing to the men of their choice. I heard the newness of my loin cloth rustle in time to my throbbing. The thought that she was inviting me to go into the bush with her was almost more than I could bear.

I tore my eyes away from Rebecca and down to Joshua. He was rocking back and forth to the drums, his eyes glazed like those of a man with yellow fever. He held his wine gourd at an angle and the milky fluid was dripping onto the ground. Rebecca started dancing a private dance of her own behind Joshua. It was not a formal ceremonial dance, just the slow swaying of her hips from side to side, and then forward and back. Yet I knew instinctively that it was perhaps the oldest dance of all.

Grandfather leaned over to me, winking and laughing in rare good humor. "Joshua sleeps," he laughed, pointing, "even in the midst of much song. Clearly, he prefers wine to a woman tonight, eh?"

I could not speak.

He leaned even closer in the kind of conspiracy older men feel with the younger in such matters. His voice fell almost to a whisper. "You are a man now," he said quietly. "You may do as a man does."

I continued to be too embarrassed to answer; I just hung my head. When I didn't respond, his lecherous grin faded. "Unless you prefer otherwise, my son. We know, of course, that some men prefer for themselves the way of a woman, although I thought you . . ."

"No, Pa," I said. "It's not that. It's just that, well, how does one do it? I mean . . ."

He laughed again, his gummy mouth wide in mirth. "Is it for nothing that you have watched over our livestock all your life? That you were initiated as a Man of Knowledge? That the cock and the he-goat told you their secrets and gave to you of their blood?"

He was right, of course; it wasn't ignorance that was holding me back. The real explanation for my hesitancy was the same as it was for every other young man: fear of falling short of expectations. Fear of failure. Especially with this much older woman, the woman of my brother, Joshua.

But in the end, desire won out over prudence. Which, I understand, is the way it works in every culture. I rolled outwards from the circle, saving myself the embarrassment of standing up before the light of the fire. I walked uncertainly around the outside of the clearing until I was behind Rebecca. She turned to look at me, still swaying. I knew I was supposed to "talk her up" as the other men had done.

"Uh," I said, "uh."

Joshua was slumped forward now, but I didn't want to be too loud anyway. Rebecca didn't seem concerned about him at all, though. She laughed and said in a loud, mocking voice, "Is this some magical chant from the new Man of Knowledge? Some powerful new juju? Will it charm the birds from the trees, perhaps?"

I cleared my throat and started over again. "Uh," I said. "Uh."

Rebecca threw back her head and laughed heartily. "How can I resist the eloquence of this 'new man'?" She laughed again. "Very well, Spirit-Man," she said, "I am bewitched by your chant. Come." And with her leading me by the hand, we went off together into the bush so that I could learn the last secret of manhood, the one only a woman could teach.

7

The question of sex always comes up when I discuss juju rituals with my American friends. They expect to hear that not only is *sex* central to our rituals, but that *perverted* sex is. They seem to want me to tell them how juju high priests perform unspeakable sexual perversions in their dark and hidden shrines in the forest. And when I tell them that sexual perversion is not a primary factor in juju rituals, they seem disappointed.

However, it's true that for certain cults (mostly those dedicated to the *orisha* we know as *Esu*), violent and perverted forms of sex have an almost sacramental status. One such cult in Uganda, for example, practices *bestiality* (sex between humans and animals) as an essential ingredient of its rituals. After the private ritual, there is a public ceremony in which the animals so used are slaughtered and consumed raw by the population.

But such behavior is the exception rather than the rule in juju. The reason is that we Africans make less of a fuss about sex than do Americans. That may be because we live closer to nature than do many other peoples and our children are in a position to observe and understand sex from an early age. What juju perverts are those things that it regards

as *secret*. And, among us, sex is no secret. So it follows that
our rituals emphasize aspects of life other than sex.

But our juju ceremonies are something else again. Our
ceremonies are less "religious," more "secular," than our
rituals. And they are very sexy. But rather than being an
ingredient of these ceremonies, as most Westerners expect,
sex is a *consequence* of them.

Consider how some of the characteristics of our juju
ceremonies make sex among the celebrants almost inevitable. For one thing, our juju ceremonies often go on for
days, during which we continuously consume enormous
quantities of palm wine. While it's true that our wine is
weak compared to Western whiskey, it is quite intoxicating
when consumed in sufficient quantity. Even when consumed moderately, it weakens inhibitions (or so claims any
man caught in the bush with his neighbor's wife during a
ceremony).

Drums are another feature of ceremonies that contribute
to free availability of sex. They are played literally without
stop for days during a long ceremony, and their effect is
indeed hypnotic.

Then there's our local tobacco: very, very strong, and
rolled by the women into enormous cigars. And sometimes,
there's more than tobacco in them: Every village herbalist
knows more than a few recipes for hallucinogenic brews.
We use these concoctions to spike the palm wine and to
"sweeten," as we say, the cigar smoke.

Of course, the jujuman will never admit that his potions
are being used "recreationally," for the purpose of inebri-
ation; that would be too frivolous an application of juju
powers. Rather, he says that he is "awakening" the people,
"enlivening" them, so that they can participate more fully
in the ceremony. The ultimate goal is for the celebrants to
achieve an intoxicated and uninhibited state in which they
can do the things that our closely-regulated tribal way of life
ordinarily forbids.

All these activities—plus the general mood of fun and merrymaking—tend to stimulate sexual desire. Adding to that desire are our marriage customs. Marriage among us tends to occur quite late: when the woman is in her mid-twenties or so, and usually, the man is even older. So there is a long time, often ten years or more, between the onset of puberty and marriage—just when sexual curiosity and desire are at their peaks, in other words. During that time, we nonetheless expect both men and women to remain officially celibate. But note the word "officially." The reality is that sex is quite common.

Then, there's the issue of polygamy, though it's frowned on now in most modern African nations. But Islam tolerates it and juju positively encourages it—for the higher-ranking men in the society, anyway. You can imagine how the ordinary "man in the street" feels about it, how it adds to the tension in the community.

So juju people release their sexual tensions at festivals like our harvest ceremony, which occurs only after all millet and maize have been safely stored. It's a four-day ceremony that falls on a different date every year. One of the high priest's jobs is keeping the calendar and telling the people when it's time to perform such activities. The method by which the date for the harvest ceremony is determined gives insight into the surprising depth to which juju belief penetrates African life.

First, the high priest with his lesser priests in attendance tours the whole town and all the surrounding countryside to make sure all work is done. Then he calls for various predictions from all the area's diviners. He will consult with every prognosticator and fortuneteller from the *ifa* man (who employs a wooden instrument something like a *ouija* board) to the astrologer (astrology being a very important art in juju). Finally, he'll secrete himself in his Shrine in the forest for a few days where he'll make sacrifice, drink blood, and talk directly to the *orisha*. Only then will he be

able to direct the people to prepare for a feast. Several days
will be required for the community to get ready.

Part of getting ready involves the unmarried young
women. Through what is supposed to be a naive dance of
thanksgiving, each girl can show the community how
devout and innocent she is. But she really has a strong
sexual interest that our social rules do not let her satisfy.
The juju dance gives her a way to behave erotically while
outwardly appearing to be chaste.

The dance goes on all through the ceremony and is for
unmarried young women only; their ages are from about
thirteen or so, on up to the late twenties. Each girl has to
balance a grain pot on her head, so the dance is actually
more of a *walk*. Anyone watching her will understand that
to keep the pot balanced, the walk has to be slow, and very
rhythmic. Apparently, walking with the hips thrust sharply
forward while swinging the buttocks works well for most of
the girls. Of course, a young woman out in the Sun so much
during the festival time ought to oil her body frequently
with her best scented ointments. And it would be wasteful
to rub off all that luxurious, fragrant oil, so she parades
through the town naked. Well, not completely naked: All
the girls in the long, writhing-snake line wear jewelry made
of gold, cowries, and beads, and they also wear rouge on
their faces and their nipples.

The effect on our young men (and our old ones, too, for
that matter) is about what you'd expect it to be—the same
as it would be anywhere.

Of course, any man who desires to take one of these
young women into the bush has to do his part to foster the
deception, too. So he may paint his face or wear a cloth
mask. Then both the man and the woman can claim that her
seduction was by an unknown spirit who temporarily
possessed the man.

In this way, behavior that might have been condemned is
transformed into something that is socially acceptable.

What we actually wind up with is our young girls being ravaged repeatedly by men wearing grotesque masks, which you could probably sell tickets for in Times Square. But we soothe ourselves with the notion that it is an innocent ceremony of thanksgiving and no one is to blame if it gets out of hand. And, because this ordinarily contemptible behavior goes unpunished, it is repeated at every juju ceremony.

An obvious result of all this freely available sex is our unacceptably high rate of venereal disease in Africa. People intoxicated by the many raptures of a juju ceremony do not trouble themselves to practice safe sex. Nor is it likely we can ever convince them to do so; they are simply too carried away to think of such precautions. The ready availability of sex under juju may also explain some of the high rates of our other communicable diseases, although the link with diseases that are not sexually transmitted is less obvious.

But there is one tragedy that we may be *certain* results from juju sex practice: the distinctly African phenomenon of "throwaway babies." It is one of the saddest chapters of our history and a growing shame. What to do with all the unwanted children that result from our wild juju ceremonies? Abortions are almost unknown among us: They are too expensive and they seem contrary to our philosophy of life. So a woman who conceives during a juju festival will likely carry the baby to term.

But she can't keep it. A suitor might overlook her lack of virginity, especially if he can be persuaded that it resulted from a spiritual encounter. But what are the chances of convincing him that *he* has to raise the child? A child makes a young woman nearly worthless in terms of bride price. So she needs to get rid of her unwanted child *after* its birth rather than *before*, as is done in the West. Her parents may even have made it a condition of allowing her to stay in the family home during her pregnancy.

Juju has ritual uses for babies. And, given that the

problem is especially prevalent among jujuwomen, the answer would seem obvious: Present the child to the head priest. But *unwanted* babies are taboo to juju ritual; anything *unwanted*, anything *valueless*, doesn't comprise much of a sacrifice, does it? Juju can use only things of value for its blood rituals. So a *babalawo* must obtain a newborn baby before its mother has the chance to throw it away, which act would obviously alert the *orisha* that it's unwanted. If no cooperative mother can be found, jujumen will steal a baby for rituals that require one.

But the typical juju ritual does not require human sacrifice. So a woman who has an unwanted infant generally adopts the simple expedient of abandoning it, usually in the dead of night. For the woman who lives in the country, the nearby forest makes a convenient dumping ground. Clearly, a newborn infant can't be expected to last long there and the hyena and jackals ensure that there will be no carcass. City women have brought this abandonment practice with them, leaving their babies in the town garbage dump, where rats fill in for the hyenas.

Guilt is seldom a problem after these abandonments. Remember that a jujuwoman is quite accustomed to blood and violent death. Remember, also, that she considers the baby to be the spawn of an evil spirit who seduced her in the guise of a man. Her parents accept this too. And the real father may not realize the baby is his. Or he may even be unknown. So it's really not a matter of conscience for anybody involved.

The number of newborn infants abandoned in this fashion is incalculable. The dumping procedures automatically eliminate the evidence so people can plausibly deny that it happens. It makes it possible for tender-hearted Americans to doubt the truth of the whole ugly story. But there's an objective, scientifically verifiable fact that helps to convince them: If one calculates the ratio of pregnant women to live births, it is clear that there are far more pregnancies in Central Africa than there are infants.

So what happened to the "missing babies"?

The answer we often hear shows how the West misleads itself about Africa. Officials from such groups as the World Health Organization are certainly aware that there are fewer infants in Africa than the incidence of pregnancy would indicate. But these officials have been trained in Western modes of thinking; they can't imagine the world as it is under juju. The educated officials have to find some rational, acceptable explanation. So they assume that the missing babies were stillborn or that they died of natural causes shortly after birth. They ascribe the causes of these deaths to unspecified "poor health practices." Then they put out a report citing the poor health practices they just invented as the reason for Africa's "high infant mortality rate."

Happily, some people who have taken the trouble to understand Africa have now begun to address the problem. Pastor Danny Curle is one who comes to mind. With the support of sponsors like Diane Lewis in the United States, he cares for hundreds of these "throwaways" at "feeding stations" throughout Zimbabwe. And, in my own modest way, I am trying to follow his example in southern Nigeria. But we know we're just lighting one candle against the darkness of juju culture in Africa.

Sex and its aftermath represent one example of the way juju perverts normal human tendencies. Of course, I acknowledge that we Africans would still have our fair share of unwanted pregnancies and venereal disease even without juju. But the important words are "our fair share"; our problem would be more or less like anybody else's, rather than the crushing burden we now bear.

Juju lets people escape the social blame for the counterproductive behavior that would otherwise remain suppressed. And as long as it does, we Africans will be held back. This makes juju more than a religion—it makes juju the enemy of a modern Africa. It makes our people free to blame any ills not on themselves, but on a distinctively African phenomenon—spirit possession—which was the next thing I learned about.

8

The day after the ceremony began, I felt like a lion. I strutted about the town like one of the roosters that Grandfather was to sacrifice that day.

That afternoon when I saw Rebecca Abanogu at the feast, I almost committed the unpardonable blunder of acknowledging her. Fortunately, she was more experienced in these matters than I was and had better sense. When she saw me coming toward her, bright-eyed and eager, she turned and walked casually toward her girlfriends as if she didn't know me at all. Which, in a sense, was the case; from her standpoint, her lover had been a "Spirit-Man," not me.

I didn't see her for the next couple of days. She kept herself to her gaggle of girlfriends and ignored all the men of the village, Joshua and me included.

I mooned around a bit at first, barely aware of the celebration going on in my honor all around me. I cheered up only gradually as all the women of the town fed me morsels of the food their daughters had been preparing ever since they heard a festival was scheduled. I don't want to appear shallow about my feelings for Rebecca, but even the pain of unrequited love must give way when a teenage boy savors the delights of smoked goat, marinated cowrie meat, and fermented cabbage.

Besides, Grandfather took me to one side when he saw me so miserable. He explained how any woman of the village would find it a great honor to give herself to *Orisha-Oka*, the spirit that possessed me. I quickly tested his theory and found he was right. After that, I felt just fine.

By the time of the song circle on the third evening, I had recovered myself considerably. I sat in front of the fire, just listening rather than joining in, thinking about how we juju people really live two lives. One is our everyday life of work and family, and living by the rules of our society. The other is a life of wild and reckless abandon, quickly lived and easily forgotten—the life of the spirit-possessed.

Rebecca Abanogu had returned to the circle and I had half an eye on her when I saw Joshua rouse himself from his customary position near her. He was glassy-eyed, as though he'd had too much palm wine again. Without speaking, he left the circle on unsteady feet.

I leaned back and watched him leave us. I had good reason to watch him: Every time he'd looked at me the last few days, spears had come out of his eyes. I think he suspected what had happened between Rebecca and me. That would have been enough to get him angry at any man, let alone me whom he'd hated since I came to Nigeria.

He walked like a man in a dream to the garden area off to the side of the ceremonial clearing. He reached up to Grandfather's pecan tree and pulled on its lowest branch. He bounced it up and down several times and it finally broke with a loud snap. Sitting on the ground he quickly forged from it two long, skinny sticks, each with a V-shape on one end like a crutch. He stood, propped the crutches under his arms, and began to walk back toward the song circle.

And then a remarkable thing happened. With each step he took back toward us, he seemed to grow older. He began to bend over in the pain of advancing years. His back became hunched and he hobbled noticeably. Even his clothes seemed to go limp and hang from him like rags. A mangy old dog came out from somewhere and started hopping in excited circles, eyeing the sticks as if he expected a game of "fetch."

When Joshua got back to the group, he swung one of his crutches feebly and grunted, as old people do. The woman he struck turned to give him a piece of her mind, then stopped and gasped in amazement.

I saw her lips say, "Babalu-Aye," but I couldn't hear her. Then she said it again, louder this time so we all heard. She kept repeating the name over and over, rising in hysteria: "Babalu-Aye! *Babalu-Aye!*" As they figured out who was amongst them, the whole group in the clearing took up the chant: "*Babalu-Aye!* BABALU-AYE!"

For it was no longer Joshua among us; it was Babalu-Aye, the father of all *orisha*. He looked exactly as he did whenever we dared to depict him: a ragged old man supported on walking sticks and accompanied by a dog. In the flickering of the bonfire, even his skin looked old and lined, nothing like the young face of Joshua. It was the first public possession of the festival and the greatest.

Grandfather stumbled forward and greeted the *orisha*. "Great Babalu-Aye, how can we appease you? Is our ceremony not pleasant to you? Are the animals we sacrificed not. . . ."

Babalu-Aye waved his crutch and waited until there was complete silence. The dog seemed to lose interest as Babalu-Aye came to a standstill in the center of the circle. He scratched behind his ear a couple of times and then loped off into the darkness. When all was quiet and respectful, Babalu-Aye spoke softly in a hoarse voice, heavy with its coating of age. We all strained to hear.

". . . ceremony is acceptable," we heard him say. We all breathed a sigh of relief. "But I have a few things against some of these here," and we all held our breath again.

He started to turn slowly, sweeping his crutch slowly past

the people like a cameraman panning a camera. Every time the crutch lingered over someone, that person shrieked in fear and cringed. Finally, the crutch came to rest pointing at a man who lived over on the other side of town. I knew him slightly as one of our local blacksmiths but not a good one, apparently: Joshua had bought some *nganga* pots from him and complained about the poor workmanship.

"That one," said Babalu-Aye. The blacksmith's eyes got wide and he quivered with fear. "That one is a cheat."

The cowering man shrieked, "No, Babalu-Aye! Please! I—"

"Silence!" boomed Grandfather in his best ceremonial voice. The blacksmith fell to his knees.

"That one," Babalu-Aye repeated, "is a cheat. Now, a cheat is the same as a thief. So he will suffer the justice of the thief: His right arm will wither up and will no longer know its former cunning with metals."

It was a sentence worse than death for a blacksmith. The man groaned once and fell face forward in a dead faint. No one went to his aid.

The crutch moved on.

"That one," said Babalu-Aye, pointing at a woman, a cranky old crone who sat on her porch all day and yelled insults at anyone who passed her yard. "That one's tongue has condemned her. She will die. Tonight. Even before the Moon rises!" The old lady's lips flapped up and down a few times, but for once, she could find no words.

The crutch moved again. It stopped at Rebecca Abanogu.

"That one. That one is a harlot. She dishonors the people of Inesi-Ile." Everyone gasped and moved away from the hapless Rebecca. "She, too, will die. For her harlotry." Rebecca started to cry.

"But first, her beauty will decay. She will become a hive of open sores, so that no man can look upon her and hold his eyes open. Flies will breed in her body and fly out into the world through her sores."

People were staring at Babalu-Aye in amazement. Truly, this was big, big juju! Surely the father of all *orisha* would not have chosen just anybody for the delivery of such a powerful curse. Perhaps a mistake had been made in not choosing this Joshua to be the next *babalorisha* after all.

"And when the flies have consumed all of her that they wish," Babalu-Aye concluded, "then she will die." He cackled with laughter and started his crutch slowly moving again. In my direction.

When he got to me, he stopped. Then he lifted his other stick from the ground; he pointed *both* his crutches at me and my heart turned to wood within my thirteen-year-old chest.

"And *that* one," he shrieked in his creaky old voice. "*That* one . . ."

The mangy dog picked an ideal time to return. Running at full tilt, he playfully grabbed one of the sticks, spun the old *orisha* around, and sat him down irreverently in the fire.

I was the first one to run forward and help the leaping, hooting Joshua to put out the fire on his shirt. I knew the *orisha* had left him; it's common knowledge that spirits don't like fire.

We never heard what the *orisha* was about to say. But Grandfather fulfilled his duty as our *babalorisha* to interpret what Babalu-Aye *would* have said, had he been permitted to finish: That the *orisha* were most pleased with the progress Orisha-Oka was making in his spiritual development inside the body of Isaiah Oke and that he would become one day the greatest *babalorisha* in all Africa! Joshua made a face as if he wanted to challenge the authenticity of this interpretation. But nobody paid any attention to him; he was only Joshua again.

Rebecca Abanogu was helped off to her home by her friends, as was the devastated blacksmith. The gossipy old woman shook off all attempts to help her back to her home.

She stomped her feet and feistily demanded to stay for the rest of the evening's sing-sing.

The drums started up again but the heart seemed to have gone out of the festival after the apparition. Still we tried. And eventually, with more palm wine, we were able to resurrect at least a semblance of our former good humor. Until the old sharptongue suddenly let out a loud, shivering wail and fell over, stone dead.

Grandfather hurriedly conferred with his lesser priests. The remainder of the festival was canceled by unanimous agreement.

In silence, we all watched the Moon finish rising.

9

A few days later, Grandfather dealt with the curse on the blacksmith and healed him completely. The news spread rapidly around town that *babalorisha* Aworo Oke's power was equal even to a curse laid by the *orisha* themselves.

Grandfather later confided to me that the cure had actually been an easy one. He was able to completely skip the first step in the typical juju healing: finding out who bewitched the victim in the first place. This can often take a good deal of research—consulting with the various diviners, and so forth. But in this case, we had all seen the curse laid by Babalu-Aye himself.

The next job in a healing is to find a counter for the curse. Suppose, for example, that someone lays a curse of diarrhea on his victim. This is a very common scourge in Africa, especially in those areas where there are no rivers to flush away wastes. Americans sometimes make a joke of diarrhea, considering it to be, at worst, an embarrassing inconvenience that ends in a few days. But we lack the medicine and the technology to deal with it and, with us, it is serious indeed. In fact, it has been estimated that between two and three million children under the age of five in Africa die each year of the dehydration that results from diarrhea. The World Health Organization even lists "emergency rehydration therapy" as one of its top priorities for Africa in the 1990s. The West, of course, blames our high incidence of diarrhea on dysentery from stagnant water. But we Africans know that it comes from a curse laid by some enemy.

There are many counters for diarrhea cases; each herbalist has his own. Grandfather preferred this one (being unaware, as far as I know, that diarrhea which persists for more than about seven days will kill its victim):

Put a piece of raw pig tongue in a *nganga* pot. Add *kudu* urine to cover. Add several water hyacinth leaves. Boil until urine is gone. Remove tongue and discard. Add juju-water and honey to remaining leaves. Bring to boil again. (Make this up every month or so because it has a short shelf life.) Administer seven drops to victim for seven days and diarrhea will go away.

Grandfather's cure of the blacksmith was somewhat less unpleasant. According to my notes made over the years, I subsequently used the cure for other paralyzed limbs—legs as well as arms. I always found it at least as effective as the more elaborate cures of other *babalawos*:

Call on *Ogun* to observe the cure. Lay three copper coins on the affected arm. Light a white candle and wave it over the arm. Walk around victim nine times while shaking *ase* (a ceremonial gourd) and burning tobacco in a dish. Have the victim extinguish the candle flame by spitting on it. Then tell him, "As you have extinguished this flame, so I extinguish your pain." Then spit on his arm and pronounce him cured.

Having discovered the source of a curse and countered it, one task remains from the *babalawo*: turning the curse back on the originator. Obviously, this revenge can only be used when the originator is someone the victim dares to hit back at; turning a curse back on an *orisha* is not a good idea.

This "turning back" is responsible for the "juju wars" which break out between rival *babalawos* and which can continue for years. What happens is that the original curse-worker's reputation is damaged when his curse is turned back on his client. So he counters the counter with another curse, even stronger than the first. This needs a stronger counter measure which, if successful, becomes a further challenge, and so on. There are juju wars that have gone on for generations. The sad families of the victims troop back and forth from one *babalawo* to another for their entire lives. Whole villages can go to waste in the meantime (though whether from the "war" or from neglect is debatable).

So with relatively little effort, Grandfather further enhanced his already considerable reputation by curing the blacksmith. This brought many requests for his help. People whose families have fought a curse for generations will search all over Africa for help; they believe that the side which finds the most powerful *babalawo* or *babalorisha* of all will eventually win the feud. Grandfather had to begin turning away business from as far away as Togo; he had enough juju wars of his own right in Nigeria to worry about, and he didn't care to go looking for more.

His crowded schedule had an unplanned effect: He'd sent all his lesser priests out to other regions on his behalf, so he had to call on me to assist when Rebecca Abanogu's mother brought her for a cure.

Even though only a few weeks had passed, Babalu-Aye's curse of Rebecca was already being fulfilled in every particular. I cannot admit to any tender feelings for her; her condition was so gruesome that one noticed only the condition itself, not the person. She had lost a great deal of weight. She was dazed and listless and had to be carried into the compound on a litter by two of her kinsmen. There were

two enormous, festering sores on her face: one on her right
cheek and the other on her forehead. They did not give the
appearance of being on the skin, like ordinary sores. Rather,
they seemed to be deep, almost cup-shaped, as if the skin
were being eaten away by acid, down to the bone and
beyond.

Apparently, no one had had the courage to approach the
sores and Rebecca seemed unable to care for herself. So the
wounds had been allowed to become filthy, surrounded with
a ridged corona of dirt and pus. They gave off the smell of
rotting meat. Grandfather leaned over and studied them
closely, his professional curiosity overcoming the revulsion
that the rest of us in the Temple felt. "Hmmmm. This is not
an ordinary sore. Isaiah, see this!"

I swallowed hard and bent lower.

"This is the work of an exceptional spirit," he said,
poking his bony index finger into a prominent bulge in the
pus pile. The bulge seemed to slide easily around under the
mucus that covered it. He centered it between the thumb
and index finger of each hand. But it still slipped and
slithered under his pressure like a balloon filled with oil.

"Push here," he said to me, gesturing with his chin
toward the center of the lump.

I looked around in vain hope that he meant someone else.
"Me, Pa?" I squeaked.

He sighed. "Are you not a *babalawo*? Are you not he
who will follow me? Do as you are told!"

I swallowed some more. The fish I'd eaten last night felt
as if it had come back to life and was swimming about in my
stomach. I bent over and stuck my trembling finger into the
mess.

With my first touch, the bulge split open with a pop and
a little splattering of pus and mucus. The smell that came
forth was sudden and overwhelming. I jumped back but
Grandfather continued to lean over Rebecca, studying her
with intense professional interest.

After a few moments, he said again, "Isaiah, see this!"

"Aw, Pa!" I said.

"*Isaiah*!"

I bent immediately and at first wondered whether the old man just wanted to torment me, to "toughen me up," as he always liked to say. There was nothing about the vile sores that I hadn't already seen.

No, wait. . . . The bulge that I broke had released some grainy material from inside it. With their covering of pus, the grains looked like rice under a saffron sauce.

Then, as I watched, some of the grains moved.

I was too shocked even to faint, I think. I just continued to watch the wiggling grains, fascinated by the sight.

One of the grains separated itself from the mass of decay and shook itself, like a tiny wet dog. It was alive and, even as I watched, it flew unsteadily away. Others immediately did the same and in seconds, a swarm of flies flew in a black line out of Rebecca's cheek.

To my relief, I never did actually faint. Just almost. I remember the sight to this day: the flies zipping out of Rebecca's face in tight formation like a line of tiny, buzzing fighter planes. My Western friends always try to reassure me that a fly simply laid her eggs in the sore and, the sore never being cleaned, the eggs just happened to hatch as we poked at the egg case.

But being there was different from talking about it. What I saw was "flies coming forth into the world out of Rebecca's body," just as Babalu-Aye's curse had said.

"This is serious," Grandfather said in a masterpiece of understatement. "I suspect an evil spirit of extraordinary power and malignancy is inside her; she has been possessed." The assembled kinsmen gasped as one.

"Bring the truck," he told one of the men. "We must take her to the Shrine. We must make sacrifice."

10

We had seriously overloaded our old Model-A pickup truck, so I made sure to sprinkle a little "luck powder" over it before we set out. Rebecca Abanogu was stretched out on a makeshift cot in the back. Her mother and her two kinsmen rode back there with her. Also in the back were two big sacks, loaded with all the juju that Grandfather thought he might conceivably need. Grandfather himself rode up front with our usual driver, David, and David's brother, who came along to help us carry. The brother sat in the middle and held the goat between his legs. There was no room left for me except on the running board, where I held on for dear life.

Grandfather muttered juju chants under his breath the whole way; he never trusted anything with a motor. "White man's stink juju," he used to call engines. But we made much better time bumping along the forest path than we would have if we'd tried to walk. We reached the site of the shrine in about an hour, despite the fact that the last half-mile was almost virgin bush.

The Shrine was in a well-hidden clearing; one who did not know where it was would have to search for it very diligently. The site would have been disappointing to an outsider who expected it to be something grand. It was only large enough to hold maybe a dozen or so people standing close together. But there was no need for it to be large. What went on there was always secret; there would never be more people there at one time than had to be. There were only two small buildings: the Shrine itself and a shed used for storage. Attached to the shed was a small corral for penning the sacrificial animals.

Even someone visiting it for the first time would conclude that the site had been used a great deal. There were well-worn depressions in the ground at intervals around the clearing. These were the places where rituals required that fires be lit or that libations of water, oil, or blood be poured. Over the years, these spots had grown into little pits so that one had to be careful where one walked. And in the center of the clearing, there was a low flat stone where sacrifice was made. Where the original surface still showed through (in a few spots on its sides), it looked as if it had once been almost white. But now it was a streaky rust-brown from all the blood that had been shed on it.

Before starting his ritual, Grandfather needed to make sacrifice. He told Rebecca's kinsmen to set her cot down out of the way. He told me to get the he-goat from the truck and tether it to the sacrifice stone.

Meanwhile, he searched around in his big sacks, removing juju items that he then lined up neatly next to Rebecca; it was as if they would give her strength just by being close to her. Among the items were an old broken sword, a large round stone with symbols painted on it, several bottles with liquids of different colors, a little metal box that rattled when he handled it, and a human shin bone.

He also removed from one of the sacks several little pouches. He peeked furtively into each until he found one that contained a purplish powder. He poured some of this material onto a banana leaf and burned it. It produced the same kind of incense smell that sometimes used to come out of the Catholic church back in Sekondi/Takoradi. I won-

dered if it was some powerful juju that Grandfather had
stolen from the Catholics. I became convinced of it when he
dipped a stick in some juju-water and sprinkled it on
everything and everybody in the clearing, just the way I'd
seen their priests do.

He directed me to hold the goat for him while he killed it.
He was in such a hurry he used his everyday pocket knife,
not even bothering to find his sacrificial blade. He scooped
up some of the goat's blood in a gourd and mixed it with a
little green juju-water from one of the bottles. He poured
some of this mixture directly on Rebecca's sores. Then he
directed her mother to remove Rebecca's clothes and rub the
rest of the blood mixture over her body.

He rummaged in his sack again and discarded several of
the homemade cigars that he had in there until he found the
one he wanted. It must have been special in some way but
to me it looked exactly like the ones he had discarded. He
lit it and passed it around after taking a few puffs.

He dug in the sack some more and produced a box
containing a handful of little brown knots, like dried cat
turds. He handed three to me and told me to suck on them
until they were gone. I stared at them in my hand until he
took three for himself and, sighing at my lack of trust,
popped them in his mouth. Then I followed his example;
they were porous and had a vaguely peppery taste. Finally,
he opened Rebecca's mouth and dropped three of the pellets
under her tongue.

He slit open the goat he'd sacrificed and told me to
remove the entrails and place them in one of the depressions
in the floor of the clearing, all except the liver. This he
sliced up himself, putting one slice of it over each of
Rebecca's wounds and eyes.

He took his own clothes off and put on a considerable
amount of juju jewelry that he took from one of the sacks:
necklaces, arm bands, even a gaudy headdress of feathers

and cowries. As a humble assistant, I did not rate any
special costuming.

Having suitably prepared both his patient and himself, he
directed her kinsmen to move Rebecca into the Shrine. He
followed and called me in with him, but told everyone else
to wait outside. With Rebecca laid out flat on the floor,
there really wasn't room for anybody else in there anyway,
especially with the way Rebecca was thrashing around.

At first, I thought it was just her fever. But no. She was
moaning and writhing—not with pain, it seemed, but with
pleasure. Her legs were apart and as I watched, she slid her
hands slowly and voluptuously up to her waist, brazenly
spreading and displaying herself to us. What shocked me
even more than her wantonness was the sight of another of
the huge, weeping sores in her private region, its discharge
mingling with her own juices.

She was panting and her lips were drawn back to show
her white teeth clenched as if in ecstasy. Her hips, which
had been rolling in a slow, even circle now began to thrust
forward, harder and faster.

"Pa!" I said. "She looks like . . . uh, she looks like
she's, uh, ..."

He interrupted his private prayer and looked down at her.
"Yes," he said calmly. "This is not uncommon. She is with
her 'heaven husband' now."

" 'Heaven husband?' "

"Yes. What you see now is 'spirit rape'—what we call
'oko-orun.' "

I tried to look away, but I couldn't. She was twisting her
body as if in a fury, screaming and cursing—not at all as she
had done with me a few weeks earlier.

Suddenly, with a great cry, she was done. She was
covered with sweat by that time and the smell of her sex
mixed with the blood of the he-goat was overpowering. I
was embarrassed but Grandfather kept on with his work as
if nothing had happened. He squatted next to Rebecca,

shaking his *ase* gourd while he called softly, "Esu (*rattle*):
We seek you. Esu (*rattle*): We call you. Esu (*rattle*): . . . ."
And so on.

The use of Esu's name so surprised and frightened me
that I almost forgot about Rebecca altogether. I had not seen
Grandfather perform any acts of divination, yet somehow
he seemed to have learned that the spirit possessing Rebecca
was none other than Esu himself. Esu is the *orisha* that most
closely resembles Satan; all of our Christian churches in
Africa equate the two. Esu is called upon for help in all evil
purposes, such as laying down an *epe* (a curse) on one's
neighbor. He is the cause of all misfortune as well as of
death. He is vicious and ranks near the very top of our
pantheon. In fact, he is the most powerful—and so the most
feared—of all the *orisha*.

I may have been a *babalawo* but I knew I wasn't ready to
deal with the likes of Esu. I had to keep reminding myself
of what my initiation had been about: Nothing in the spirit
world can *really* hurt a Man of Knowledge. But it wasn't
easy to control my fear. The cases of possession by Esu are
among the worst on record. The behavior of the Esu-
possessed is always evil, even to the point of abomination.
A person possessed by Esu may go wild, hacking away on
a crowded bus with a machete. Or, as one possessed woman
recently did in Angola, kidnapping randomly-chosen school-
children and gouging out their eyes, only to set them free to
a life of total blindness.

Grandfather droned on, calling on Esu for what seemed
to me a very long time, during which I could only sit by. It
was a perfect chance for me to study every step of
Grandfather's procedure, trying to learn my future craft,
and I wanted to. But incredibly—despite everything that
had happened, even despite the fear that was creeping up on
me—I found myself passing into sleep as I listened to the
dreary, droning litany. "Esu (*rattle*). Esu (*rattle*)."

Then I heard a third voice in the shrine—a man's voice,

deep but nasal: "Leave us be, old man, me and my horse."
I started out of my doze and looked around. Grandfather
seemed to be in a trance state. The voice hadn't sounded
like his anyway. But there was no other man with us.

Grandfather continued his chanting in that steady, rhythmic way of his, never missing a beat. "Esu (*rattle*): Come
to us. Esu (*rattle*): We rule you."

About then I noticed a peculiar thing: Even though it was
still day outside, the shrine seemed cold—almost as cold as
night in the dry season. I looked down at Rebecca. The liver
slices were no longer covering her eyes, which were open
and shining as if with a light of their own. "Who dares
speak so to such a one as me?" she demanded in the deep
masculine voice.

Grandfather's eyes were still closed. He seemed to be
ignoring the spirit completely.

"You, old man," the voice boomed. "Why do you molest
me?" The voice suddenly took on a wheedling tone. "I am
merely a meek old ancestor, come for a nice visit. Can I not
ride this mare in peace?"

Grandfather continued to ignore the voice, shaking his
rattle and calling on Esu to come out and show himself.

The whine disappeared from the voice. "What do you
want of me?" it roared.

Grandfather finally roused himself. "Are you Esu?" he
said calmly.

"Yes, damn you. Yes, I am Esu!" As the voice said this,
a vapor came forth from Rebecca Abanogu's mouth, like
from a tea kettle. Only it was cold.

Then something like recognition passed over Rebecca's
face. "So you still live, old man?" the male voice said with
Rebecca's mouth. "You surprise me; I would have expected
you to be worm food long since. Ah, well—it will happen
soon enough, an old bag of bones like you."

Grandfather sat back on his skinny haunches, ignoring
the taunts. Except for a certain tightness around the mouth,

there was nothing to indicate he'd even heard. His eyes were still closed and his voice remained calm. "We command you to leave this person."

"*You* command? *You* command?" The voice roared with laughter. "How can *you* command? You are only a little old naked black man in a dirty, miserable hut in the middle of nowhere."

I felt compelled to take a slow look around. Then I blinked with shock: It was true—our Shrine really was just a wretched hut. Then I looked over at Grandfather's bony frame. For the first time, I saw what a frail and puny specimen of manhood he was; before, I'd always seen him as ten feet tall.

"You are good for nothing," the voice went on more quietly, "nothing but to grow old and die and molder in the ground. This is your only value, for you are just a foolish old man."

My heart was breaking for Pa. Surely his weary and worn old body could be no match for an evil spirit of this calibre. "Oh, Pa," I said, "let's stop this. You can't possibly—"

"Hush!" he hissed at me. "Never listen to Esu. I know this one from long ago; he is a deceiver and a liar. He will tell you any lies that suit his purpose. And he can make you believe them." Then, for the first time since he started the ritual, he opened his eyes. They looked sadly into mine. "Even worse, he may tell you the truth about yourself."

"Do you fear the truth, then, old man? Is it truth that makes you tremble so before me? Will I see you wet yourself before we are done?" asked the voice with a laugh.

It hurt me to hear Grandfather insulted so. Anger replaced my fear, giving me a false courage. "My Grandfather fears nothing! He is a great man, a Man of Knowledge; he is a *babalorisha!*" I said, addressing the spirit.

Grandfather reached out and slapped my face, hard. "No! Never talk with the spirit. If you do, you are undone!"

But it was too late. Rebecca turned toward me, her eyes

as shiny as obsidian. "What have we here?" The voice took
on a taunting tone. "Oh, I see who it is. He who can read!
And write! Now I am truly frightened. Indeed, the whole
Invisible World trembles at the name of Isaiah Oke." He
laughed heartily. " 'Isaiah Oke, Boy *Babalawo*,' we call
you."

"Remember," Grandfather said to me, "he cannot harm
you if you don't acknowledge him. Pride cannot tolerate
being ignored and Esu is the King of Pride. Ignoring him is
the only way to hurt him."

The voice laughed even harder. "I know you, boy!
You're the one who took my horsey here out for a ride at his
initiation ceremony. Do you want to know what she said
about you, little boy? Do you want to know how she
laughed at you? Eh, *little* boy?"

I felt rage rising, taking the place of my judgment.
Grandfather's hand was resting on my arm, as if to show he
was with me. But I shook him off violently.

The voice just kept laughing. "This is not much of a
grandson you have here, old man. He will never learn to
please a woman; he will be a *little* boy always." It was as
if the voice was physically *rubbing* its obscene, oily
laughter all over me. "No, he is not much of a grandson for
you. A bookworm. Or maybe just a *worm*, eh? He is very
fast for a worm, though. Do you want to know, Grandpa?
Do you want to know how *fast* your little bookworm is with
a woman?"

"Stop it!" I was losing control. "Stop it!"

Grandfather grabbed my arm with a grip stronger than I
would have believed and dragged me outside the Shrine.
Then he slapped me again and threw me to the ground.
"Learn from this!" he shouted.

I was weeping with rage and shame and barely heard
him. "You have let the Invisible World see your emotions,"
he said, "and you are vulnerable now forever." He shook
his head at me and then turned to look back toward the hut.

"I will have to finish with him by myself," he said, quietly. "It is now for you to wait and watch. Do not fail me further." He turned his back and straightened his scrawny shoulders. Resolutely he walked back into the hut to face the Devil alone.

Maybe he *was* ten feet tall, after all.

It took four days.

At times, the hut was silent for hours on end. At other times, we heard voices shouting and screaming; they were voices both of men and of animals. Once, there was a rumbling noise something like distant thunder on the northern mountains. It shook the ground on which we stood.

During the second day, I tiptoed to the hut and called out timidly, "Pa? Would you like something to eat?" But the only answer was a roar of such ferocity that it sent me scurrying backwards to the edge of the clearing. After that, I gave up any thoughts of trying to show courage and just huddled at the fringe of the forest with the others.

It was midmorning when it finally ended. There had been no indication that the battle was over; all had been quiet for hours. I was dozing in the truck when I heard Rebecca Abanogu's kinsmen cry out at the sight of her. She looked as if she were three times her twenty years; most of her shiny black hair had fallen out and her formerly firm and voluptuous breasts sagged halfway to her waist.

But of the sores with the flies issuing forth, there was no sign.

Grandfather was the most tired man I'd ever seen. He and Rebecca had to hold each other up, literally. Everybody in the clearing ran at the same time to help them but they both waved off questions. We headed immediately for the truck where Grandfather was unable even to boost himself up into the passenger's seat. I finally had to lift him; his body felt like an old sack of bones and weighed only as much.

He never talked about the incident later so I don't know what happened. As for Rebecca, she *couldn't* talk; she had been struck dumb at some point during the ritual and she never spoke again. She lived for about another ten years but seldom left the porch of her house.

Whenever anyone asked her, she indicated by gestures that it had been worth the price she paid—and that she would have been willing to pay even more—to be free of possession by Esu.

11

After that, changes came very quickly.

Grandfather changed. He started to age. He'd always been lean, but vigorously so. Now some of that vitality deserted him. He ate less and kept to himself more. He gave one the impression that he'd become somewhat frail. It was almost as if he was trying to make Esu's slanders about him come true.

My relationship with him also changed. Previously, I'd been at his side almost constantly, learning from him and recording his teachings. We had been almost like brothers, despite the enormous difference in our ages. But now we were both too aware of how badly I had let him down during the confrontation with Esu.

And I changed, too. I redoubled my efforts to absorb my formal education: Perhaps that was one way in which I could fulfill Grandfather's expectations for me. Certainly, it was a change for the better from the standpoint of my tutor, Mr. Olungwe. I suddenly became a very earnest pupil. Before, I'd always hurried through my lessons so I could go work juju at my grandfather's side. But now that he called for me less often, I retreated to the few books that Mr. Olungwe felt were "safe"—that is, devoid of any real ideas that might pollute my mind. Remember, it was Mr. Olungwe's job only to teach me reading, writing, and arithmetic, not thinking.

One day, Mr. Olungwe decided to change his job description and defy Grandfather by actually *teaching* me something. He had been making me read aloud from *The Theory and Practice of Colonial Administration in Africa* by Lord Emsworth. It was the wet season and, between my droning and the steady rain outside, I'm pretty sure I was close to putting us both to sleep.

"Stop," said Mr. Olungwe. "That would bore even an Englishman."

When I obediently closed the book, he stepped onto the porch and looked out into the heavy rain. He looked first one way, then the other, like a thief about to make off with someone's goods in the market. It wasn't really necessary to act so guilty; people stay indoors a great deal during the rainy season, so no one was about.

He came back in and carefully closed the door, despite the humidity. Then he pulled the shutters on the windows closed, as if we were going to start a secret juju ritual. He took something out of his rucksack and hesitated before finally handing it to me.

I studied it for a moment. "Honorable Olungwe, this item is like a book."

"It is a book," he said.

"But it is small. And it has no cover."

"It's what the Americans call a 'paperback.' It's about this man."

He pointed to the picture on the cover. The man had the familiar facial structure of the Ashanti but his name was quite foreign and unpleasant to my ear: George Washington Carver. "I do not recognize the name, Honorable Olungwe. What clan is he?"

He shook his head. "He is an American person. They do not have clans."

"No clans?" I was shocked; the clan is central to life in

Nigeria. I had never conceived of such a strange thing. "How can they survive, Honorable Olungwe?"

"That is why I want you to start reading some other books, my son—to find out that there are other ways to live than our way: other societies, other economies, other philosophies."

I guess I looked pretty dubious because he said, "Have you never wondered how other people live? What other places are like?"

I shrugged and munched a *kola* nut from the bowl between us. His question was meaningless: Why should I care about some other place when the only place I am is here?

I wistfully eyed the *ugbo-azigo* board over against the wall; Mr. Olungwe and I always had a rousing match at our national board game after one of our tedious reading sessions. He saw my attention wandering and cuffed me smartly on the side of the head. They have their own form of juju, these scholars, and can get away with treatment that would earn anybody else a good, solid curse from a *babalawo*. "Read," he said, pointing to the little book.

I made the bow of apology and started to read out loud. But it was even more boring than the book about colonial administration. And besides, the closed-up room was becoming stiflingly hot. All in all, I was very unhappy, but I kept reading. I was turning over in my mind whether to take the unprecedented step of rebelling against Mr. Olungwe when I got to the part about the peanuts.

Peanuts are a staple of life in West Africa. They are an ingredient in many of our foods and supply much of our protein. We also press them for the oil that we use for cooking. The husks that are left we grind into a kind of flour. The peanut is second only to the yam in importance in our food supply here. And not only for food. We make a die for cloth from the shells and certain medicines can be made from the little stem portions, if one knows how.

This Ashanti man with the funny American name knew all our secrets for living off the peanut. He told them to his American kinsmen, it seemed, and became renowned—very clever of him, I thought. The book related many of the secrets he had learned, some of which I hadn't heard before. It was a great deal like learning some new juju. Besides which, I enjoyed the story of the man's trials and tribulations for itself; we Africans love a good story.

So when Mr. Olungwe reached out and closed the book on me, I was startled to see that it was almost dark outside. "That's enough for today; more tomorrow," he said. "Perhaps."

"Oh, yes, Honorable Olungwe. Please," I added.

He returned the book to his rucksack. While he was looking in there, something else seemed to take his interest. He looked around the room, both ways again, as if someone might have snuck in while I was reading the forbidden book. Then he pulled out two more books.

One was thin with beautifully decorated pages. It was titled Koran and seemed to be associated with a man named Mohammed. He must have been from a very numerous clan because I'd met many men of that name on one of my trips up north with Grandfather. But I didn't think any of those fellows were capable of producing such a fine-looking book.

The other book was bigger with very small print. It was beautifully bound and was obviously of some great importance because the edges of its pages seemed to be covered in real gold, if one could believe such a thing.

The title was printed in gold on the cover: Holy Bible. I looked inside and saw what I assumed was the author's name. " 'Gideon,' " I said thoughtfully. "Sounds like he might be an Ibo."

Mr. Olungwe took the contraband books back from me and hid them back in his rucksack. "Perhaps when you are ready," he said. "Now, you won't tell anybody what you've

been reading, will you? Especially the Honorable Aworo
Oke?"

"Of course, Honorable Olungwe. If you wish it so.
Although I don't see why—"

I got another smart rap on the head and wisely shut up.

Two happy years passed in that way. Mr. Olungwe
frequently smuggled in books which turned me into an avid,
though not very selective, reader. They seemed to have
some magical power to shrink things, because my village
sometimes seemed a smaller place after I read one.

The books came from Ilesha where there was supposed to
be a thing called a "library," according to Mr. Olungwe. He
told me this was a building bigger than Grandfather's
complex and that it held nothing but books. I didn't believe
him, of course. I figured there was a point or a moral to his
story, just as there is to all the fables we tell in Africa, but
I confess that it eluded me. I had plenty of time to read all
the material he brought me, though, especially during the
rainy seasons. I never spent much time on my juju training
at that time of the year, anyway, because Grandfather made
few trips out to the Shrine. But ominously, on the few trips
he did make, he took Joshua as his helper.

It was all the more surprising, then, when Grandfather
called me to his meeting room late one night in my fifteenth
year to discuss my training. "Until now," he said, "you are
only *babalawo*. If you ever hope to become *babalorisha*,
you must progress further along the path of understanding
and knowledge."

"Yes, Pa," I said meekly, assuming that he was going to
correct me for spending too much time on my reading and
writing. But the written collection he commissioned me to
make of juju recipes, charms, and practices was becoming
truly enormous; I wondered if I could get away with using
that as a defense.

"So, I have arranged for you to go south," he said, "to
study in Lagos."

I was struck speechless. Lagos! To a village boy, it was more than a legendary place—it was almost mythical! The biggest, most dynamic city in Nigeria: crowded as Hong Kong, dirty as Calcutta, busy as New York. A crossroads for international business, bursting at the seams with millionaires and with poverty. An exciting but wicked place.

Inesi-Ile had begun to seem to me pretty isolated, so part of me was happy at the prospect of going to the Big City. An equally large part of me was frightened, of course.

Grandfather stared hard at me for a moment. I thought I saw a glimpse of something like pity in his expression. "You will be given the special opportunity," he told me, "to learn from Doctor Drago."

The frightened part of me suddenly flowed over the happy part and smothered it. Drago was a name pronounced throughout the whole of Africa.

But only in whispers.

They called him the "devil doctor of Lagos." He was said to be a *babalawo* of truly exceptional power. There were rumors to the effect that he refused to speak to the spirits, as the *babalorisha* do. Instead, he *commanded* them to do his bidding. He was supposed to be a deeply menacing figure. Some reports even said that he was the incarnation of Esu. I didn't want to believe those reports any more than I did Mr. Olungwe's wild tales about a whole building filled with nothing but books. But still. . . .

I tried to swallow whatever it was that had suddenly made my throat so dry. "Pa," I croaked, "this Drago—"

"*Doctor* Drago," he corrected.

"*Doctor* Drago . . . they say his power is unusual. They say he works evil. They say . . ."

" 'They say,' 'they say.' Do you listen now to the women while they wash clothes?"

"No, Pa. But if you could just tell me why. . . ."

"Why? To give you a second chance, that's why. To give

you the chance to redeem yourself, to show that you have what it takes to be *babalorisha* after me."

I looked down humbly. "Yes, Pa."

He nodded. "That's better. And you can thank your brother Joshua; it was his idea to arrange this chance for you to prove yourself. Now, make yourself ready; you leave for Lagos tomorrow morning."

"Tomorrow morning? But that's so soon. I've got some more pages for my juju record. I ought to go out to the Shrine to put them in the strongbox."

"You may leave them with me. I'll take care of them for you."

"But it needs a key. . . ."

"You may leave that with me as well." He held out his hand.

I trembled as I removed the key from around my neck. It had been there so long, clinking among all my other juju, that it seemed a part of me, like the *ibante* cord crossed between my legs. But I handed the key over humbly and obediently.

"Can I at least say farewell to my friends, to Mr. Olungwe and to. . . ."

"I will give your regards to everyone in Inesi-Ile."

There seemed nothing more to say. "As you will, Grandfather." I turned to go.

"Wait." He came forward and gripped my shoulders. He looked into my eyes and said, "I want you to succeed, son. I want to be proud of you. You know that, don't you?" I nodded.

Then he shocked me by falling forward and embracing me tightly. He held me that way for a long, long time, as if he didn't want me to go. He'd never done a thing like that in my memory.

At last, he stepped back. He instantly became his usual dignified self again—the *babalorisha* of Ile state. "You leave for Lagos at first light," he said briskly.

It was a dismissal.

12

In those days there was no direct route to Lagos from our part of the country, which is between the banks of the Shasha and Oni rivers. So I walked the hour's walk to the bus stop, getting there just after full light. Our buses out in the country operate on a timetable that answers only nominally to the movements of the Sun. So I had to sit by the side of the road for another hour or so, until the bus came along. It was a lovely morning, though, and I had a breakfast of some of the *fufu* that my mother had packed for me. She made the world's best *ofe*, too, which went so beautifully with the doughy *fufu* cakes. At home, we always refer to *ofe* as "palaver sauce" because every good home-maker always keeps some heated and ready to entertain any guest who wants to come over and "palaver" a while. But there was no convenient way to carry any with me, so I ate my *fufu* dry.

The "bus" I refer to was actually an old flatbed truck, which was far better suited to our modest dirt roads in the bush than a more comfortable vehicle would have been. It ran only between the various rural villages and the district capital of Ilesha. Its paint job was unique, exhibiting every color in the world, like an explosion in a paint factory. A big hand-lettered sign on the front shouted its name to waiting passengers: GLORY.

In Ilesha, I switched to a slightly more modern bus, bright yellow and fully enclosed. But the road to the south was still dirt in those days, and the machine broke down frequently with one malady or another. In the end, the complete trip of about two hundred kilometers took three days. Today, of course, there's a paved road between Ilesha and Lagos city. But it's always so choked with traffic that it can *still* take three days to drive. Or so it sometimes seems anyway.

The city of Lagos is on an island. But it has hills all around it that are crammed with the little homemade shanties of all the poor who leave the countryside to seek their fortunes in town. So we say that Lagos is the only island surrounded by people as well as by water.

My first sight of the city marked me as a country boy, I am afraid. But I couldn't help it; I'd never made such a journey all by myself before and I was excited. I leaned out so far to get a good look as we approached that I almost fell out my bus window. The driver stopped his machine in the middle of the road to pull me back in. He scolded me more than I thought appropriate. It reminded me of the way Grandfather always carried on and I found myself homesick even before we screeched to our final stop in Lagos Central Bus Terminal.

Lagos has been two and three million inhabitants, making it comparable to cities like Boston, Berlin, or Sydney, though, in reality, we fear that it may well be larger than any of those. There has never been an accurate census. One barrier to accuracy is the truly astounding number of squatters who have always lived on the hillsides around town. Another is our general reluctance to reveal too much about ourselves. Part of this reticence results from simple practicality: If the government doesn't know how many you are in your family, it's harder to tax you.

But there's another explanation, equally valid: We have carried our juju beliefs with us into the cities. Juju teaches that the more that's known about you and your family, the easier it will be for someone to lay an *epe* on you. That's why we always try to hold something back—from our neighbors, from the government, from everybody. So, no matter how bustling and modern the city of Lagos seems, no matter how much a Westerner is tempted to say, "Why, it looks just like Pittsburgh!" it's good to remember that appearances are surface only. Underneath, the old ways still rule us. In fact, we have a saying: "When a man moves to the city on his feet, juju moves in his heart."

So it really wasn't surprising that a renowned jujuman like Drago had chosen to hang out his shingle in this modern metropolis. What was surprising is how extremely *well* he did. I began to understand just how well when I stumbled out of the terminal, blinking in the light and heat and stench of Lagos city.

A very short man in purple livery waved and ran toward me, laughing out loud as if he were happy to see me. His uniform couldn't have fit any tighter if it had been painted on. His cap had a shiny black visor and a high peak with a bright gold medallion on it. His knee-high boots looked like they were made of flexible black mirrors. He had two gold teeth gleaming in front and I thought I had never before seen a man who looked so important.

I assumed he must be a general in the Nigerian Army, maybe even a field marshal. He started speaking to me very loudly and very rapidly in a language I didn't know. Why he would want to talk to me was a mystery, but I recognized my name in the flood of unknown words.

"Yes," I answered in Hausa, "I am called Isaiah Oke. Do you speak Hausa, please, sir?"

"Hausa, yes!" he yelled with a laugh. "Also Arabic, Swahili, Fula, French, English . . . what you wish, Boss?"

"Hausa, if you please, sir."

"Hokay, we speak Hausa! Very good, Boss! Welcome to Lagos!" He stepped back, clapped his boot heels together with a bang, and saluted me. I gave him back an embarrassed little gesture, a kind of weak and fluttery imitation of his salute. But it seemed to satisfy him and he laughed uproariously again.

Next, he leaped forward, grabbed my hand, and pumped it up and down vigorously in the manner of Americans. "Ojike, Boss—Nnaia Ojike, that's me!" He spoke loudly, and so rapidly that I could barely understand him. "But call me 'Speedy,' Boss. Everybody calls me 'Speedy'! That's right, Boss. Good old 'Speedy,' that's me!"

Before I had a chance to respond, he reached out and grabbed my arm tightly. He started to run across the street with me in tow. It occurred to me that maybe I was being arrested, though what crime I'd committed or why the officer kept calling me "Boss" was more than I could make out.

We ran over to an automobile that was the same shade of purple as Speedy's livery and as shiny as his boots. With a big grin, he ripped off his cap. Then he opened the car door with a flourish, and bowed low, his arm across his chest. It seemed that he wanted me to do something, but I didn't know what. So I just waited as respectfully as I could. We stood there in the hot afternoon Sun—him bent over and waiting, me confused and frightened—until he muttered a cue under his breath: "Get in, Boss! Get in!"

"Me? In there?"

"Yes, Boss! Of course!"

I still hesitated. The car was shiny-clean and enormously long, nothing like our village's truck at home or the buses that had brought me here. The rear was a comfortable, glassed-in compartment of purple leather and polished wood. Farther forward, there was an open area for someone to sit while operating the machine. And all the way up in the very front, in a place of great honor on top of the radiator, was this beautiful silver goddess with wings—*Shamanga,* I thought; or possibly even *Oya* herself. Obviously, she was there to watch the road and to protect one from the *epe* of flat tires, breakdowns, and accidents. It was like a shrine on wheels.

I paused in the doorway to wipe my feet off on the hem of the caftan that I was wearing for travel. I stepped into the car gingerly and instantly jumped out again, shocked.

"What's wrong, Boss?"

I backed away. "What juju is this? It's cold in there, cold like the rainy season. Has my family given you some offense, sir, that you should place such an *epe* of chills on me?"

Speedy laughed until he had to hold his sides; I'd never before seen a man of such easy and constant cheer. "That's just what we call 'air conditioning,' Boss. It's something new; a good thing—not juju." He took my arm and guided me gently back into the car. "Don't worry, Boss, you'll get used to it."

I sat down carefully, even though there was room enough for me to stand up back there. Speedy shut the door with a heavy thunk, instantly cutting off the sound of his laughter and all the other sounds of the busy city. I hadn't realized until that moment how noisy a place Lagos is.

Up front, Speedy leaped over the side of the car, landing in the operator's seat. He must have started the engine, though I couldn't hear it, because it began to get even colder in the back as we pulled out effortlessly into the jammed street. We were sharing the pavement with all sorts of lorries, carts, and bicycles. It was remarkable how they would all move out of our way after just one brief glimpse of the big purple car, though other cars on the street seemed not to intimidate them at all.

We rounded a corner onto a road that ran along the waterfront. For a few blocks, the traffic remained dense. Laughing all the way, Speedy worked the car through spots tighter than I would have believed, people miraculously making way for us. Then, traffic suddenly thinned out as we passed a line of warehouses marking the edge of the central city. In minutes, we were cruising easily along a blacktop road at about sixty kilometers per hour. Speedy pushed a button in front and the glass window between us went down into the back of his seat.

"So, Boss," he said over his shoulder, "What you think of Lagos? Crowded, huh? Noisy, huh?" I opened my mouth to answer him.

"Yeah, Boss," he said around another of his big laughs, "you're right about that. I know what you mean. Yes, indeed. Say, Boss, how you like this car?"

I cleared my throat and leaned forward, determined to try harder to catch his attention.

"Yeah, it's great, huh, Boss? A Rolls-Royce, the only one like it in Lagos: all custom. All of Doctor Drago's stuff is the very best. He insists on it; but you probably know that."

He paused and, for once, he didn't laugh. "How well you know Doctor Drago, Boss? You know him well?" I just shrugged, having concluded that conversation with Speedy was a road on which traffic could go only one way. But as I sat back to take in the sights for the rest of the ride, I saw his face in the rearview mirror: His whole attitude changed when he mentioned Drago. For the first time since we'd met, his face was drawn and tense.

"Yeah, Boss. I know what you mean; I sure do. But just do like he says, Boss. Yeah, do like he says and you'll be okay." He blew the horn at a farmer passing along in an ox cart. "Don't ever cross him, Boss. 'Cause he's a big man, the Doctor. That's right, Boss. A *big* man. *Big* juju. But you know that, right, Boss?" The farmer almost upset his cart, hurrying to get all the way off the road for the purple car.

"Don't ever cross him, Boss," he repeated. "You know

what happened to the last man crossed Doctor Drago?
That's right, Boss, that's right."

He went on cautioning me like that for the remainder of
our trip. On the whole, I liked the overly cheerful Speedy
better than the morose Speedy. But neither gave me a
chance to say a word on the whole trip. That was how I
learned the value of talking loud and fast in Lagos.

He was right about Drago's air conditioning, though; I
got used to it real fast. Being the "devil doctor of Lagos"
might cause people like Speedy to fear you. But it appeared
to have its compensations. I thought that the Doctor must
surely be an exceptional man. I couldn't wait to meet him.

13

Nothing had prepared me for the actual sight of Drago's compound—not the limousine, not the liveried chauffeur, nothing. Actually, we'd been on the grounds of the estate for ten minutes, Speedy told me, before we even came to the sprawling collection of buildings that made up the compound proper.

We pulled into a circular drive and stopped before what Speedy called the "Big House." It was the biggest building I'd ever seen up this close, bigger even than the Lagos Central Bus Terminal. It was as white as a chicken's egg and all of its many windows had glass in them. The roof of the front porch was balanced on four tall white pillars that looked like smooth tree trunks. The sprawl and height of the place made me think of our hills at home. But this was a hill squared off, hollowed out, and made into a dwelling for a race of giants. I suppose a European would have called it a palace but I'd never seen one and didn't know the word.

It seemed that Speedy didn't like to spend any more time than necessary around the "Big House"; I was barely out of the car before he roared off. I went up the stairs and stood before the two huge doors, carved wood and solid, not at all like the simple hides we hang across our doorways at home to keep out the drafts. I called out for permission to enter, as is our custom, and wondered how anyone inside the huge place could possibly hear me. But they did. Either that or else I was expected, because a tall, dark man opened one of the doors.

I stepped back a step, startled. His eyes were as black and shiny as Rebecca's had been when Esu was riding her. They seemed fixed toward the front, as if he'd have to move his whole body if he wanted to look at something that was not directly in front of him. He wore a black tunic and pants, filigreed with silver piping. My first thought was that he might be the master of the house, considering the cut of his clothes and the stiffness of his bearing. But my meeting with Speedy had showed me that all was not always as it appeared at first glance in Lagos. So I decided to wait before jumping to conclusions.

The man stepped to one side, still staring straight ahead and never blinking. "Come," was all he said. I stepped past him and found myself in a hall so vast that I had trouble thinking of it as a room. A room is just someplace to keep one warm and dry, so it's made in sizes that are right for a man. But this hall was more like a forest clearing than a room. It was as long as the main street in my village and the ceiling seemed as far away as the sky.

The tall, dark man closed the door, turned, and walked past me as if I weren't there. "Come," he said again as he passed me. There was a stairway off to one side that he began to ascend, slowly and methodically. He never looked back to see if I was following.

At the top of the stairs we turned down a much shorter hallway. He stopped before another of the solid wooden doors which seemed to be everywhere in the house. This one was carved with many juju symbols, only a few of which I could place. He opened it for me, stepped silently to one side and said, "Enter."

The room was as big as Grandfather's whole house back home. Yet it was clearly intended for a very small family.

Or maybe even for just one person, because there was only one of everything. There was only one bed, for example, rather than a mat. But it was big enough that four people could sleep in it comfortably. It was raised up off the floor in the European style and had its own little cloth roof overhead on four long poles.

There were other doors set into the walls of the room. The tall, dark man went to one of them and removed a suit of the type favored by Nigerians who live in the city: a long tunic, loose pants, and a visorless cap. He glanced at my feet, then produced a brand-new pair of sandals from the same place. He laid all this out on the bed in absolute silence.

He turned in my direction, still staring unblinkingly over my head. "Wash," he said. He made gestures, rubbing his face and body, as if to make sure I understood him. He pointed to the new clothing. "Wear," he said, pantomiming a man shrugging into a shirt. Then he turned without another word and headed toward the door to the hall.

"Please, sir," I said, "where is the stream?"

He stopped dead in his tracks. "Stream?" he asked in a hollow voice, still facing the door; it seemed he could only look straight ahead.

"How else am I to wash myself, sir, as you have directed me to do? Such a fine house as this must surely have a good stream nearby."

He turned around and bent slightly, as if to better bring his eyes to bear on me. For just an instant, I thought a look of amusement moved across his impassive face. Then he straightened and walked in his stiff way to another of the doors set in the wall. Behind this one was another room, much more the size a room should be. It was a lavatory, like the ones I'd used in cities and on trains. Only it was very clean. There was no one else in it and, like everything else he'd showed me, it seemed to be for use by me alone. He stoppered a big white tub and ran water into it for a few minutes from a metal pipe coming out of the wall. At last, he left without saying anything further.

I was afraid to dawdle in the tub. But I did, anyway: It was hot and clean—luxury like I'd never known before. Even my *ibante* came fairly clean and the rash that all jujumen get from it subsided a bit.

The sandals were slightly snug. But the rest of the fine embroidered outfit that had been laid out fit me perfectly. I dressed and then sat quietly in my room's one chair until the tall, dark man came for me. He knocked instead of calling out as we would have back home. I opened the door and he stood there, staring over my head at a spot on the wall behind me. "Come."

I followed him downstairs to another huge room. It faced out onto a sort of courtyard. The principle piece of furniture was a long table of dark wood, like the one Grandfather used for conferences, but even bigger and much better made. Two chandeliers sparkling with electric candles hung from the beamed ceiling above the table.

There were twelve high-backed chairs upholstered with red brocade around the table but only two of them were occupied. Seated on the long side was a man around my age, maybe eighteen or so. But there were tight little lines around his eyes that made him look somewhat older. He was lightly bearded and wore a *djellabah,* loose-fitting and hooded, after the style of the Moslems who live to the north. He rose and looked at me as the hawk looks at the pigeon.

Then I turned to the head of the table: There was a man there. A man with something not right about him. He didn't rise; he sat perfectly still, smiling like a statue. But his hands kept crawling slowly around the table in front of him as if they had minds of their own.

My eyes went to those hands and watched them, like a man helplessly watching a python. On each of his fingers, including his thumbs, he wore gold rings with massive colored stones. And the fingers themselves kept moving always, slowly and aimlessly, like the legs of a spider. Sometimes, the hands would stop and one or another of his fingers would raise up and rotate a little, like the tongue of a serpent tasting the air. I knew I was being rude, standing there dumbstruck, watching his hands. But I couldn't help myself.

He broke the spell when he spoke. His voice had the kind of rasp one hears when a carpenter saws wood: not exactly unpleasant, but high-pitched and impossible to ignore. "Ah, my new pupil," he said.

I started, then bowed deeply with greatest respect. For, surely, this was Doctor Drago. When I straightened, I was able to see the rest of him for the first time. His face looked as if it had been chiseled out of mahogany, the bones standing out in sharp relief against his shiny, stretched skin. His spectacles caught the light from the chandelier and made his eyes look like two solid white discs. He wore Western-style clothing: a three-piece suit with a white shirt and necktie. Across his stomach were several heavy gold chains, each of which ended in a pocket of his vest. Certainly, no one needed so many watches, so there must have been something else attached to them.

The tall, dark servant pulled out a chair opposite the younger man and I sat. Two more servants immediately came into the room, a man and a woman. They were dressed less well, but had the same look as the tall, dark man: stiff bodies with eyes made of glass. They held silver utensils for us while we served ourselves. The woman offered two kinds of cooked vegetables—fried cassava stuffed with *yabas* (our strong local onion) and a stew of mixed greens in chicken stock. The man brought around a tureen with a steaming *ragout* of well-spiced meat. It made me realize how hungry I'd become since eating the last of my mother's *fufu* for breakfast. My mouth started watering and I'm afraid I took rather too much on my plate. I tried to

eat with the fork that was laid out by the plate but I'd never
used one before and made a sloppy job of it.

Doctor Drago laughed with a sound like the cicada makes
in the forest. "It is good to see a boy with a healthy appetite.
I must always have some young man around to remind me
of how precious is youth." He nodded toward the young
man opposite me. "Mustafa here is leaving me today to go
back to his people. And today you come to take his place.
One goes, one comes; tell me, is it not wonderful how the
orisha provide?"

I nodded, my mouth too full to speak. The food was the
best I'd ever tasted. The vegetables were crisp and snappy;
we do not like our food cooked until it's gummy. As for the
meat stew, it was superb. Some of the spices were familiar
to me and the whole had a rather minty flavor. So I decided
it must be pork because we often prepare pork in a mint
base.

Then I noticed that Mustafa was eating it, too, with
almost as much relish as I was. This was strange because
even a Moslem who is a secret jujuman will not break his
cultural taboo against eating pig. I shrugged and helped
myself to another big helping. It was the best meat I'd ever
eaten.

"You will see much during your time here, Isaiah. Here
you will see juju that is a little . . . different from what is
practiced out in the country. Is that not so, Mustafa?"

Mustafa peeked furtively out of the corner of his eye
toward Doctor Drago. He'd done the same thing earlier,
before sitting down when I came in. And he'd done it also
before helping himself to any food. He acted as if he would
dare nothing without first trying to gauge Drago's reaction.
"Yes, Doctor, that is so," he finally murmured.

Drago ate far more fastidiously than either of us boys.
His elegant hands seemed to enjoy the fork more than the
food, stroking it and twirling it so it reflected the light. He
barely touched his food, preferring to talk and to watch us

while his hands amused themselves. I suppose it explained his cadaverous look.

"But for some days, Isaiah, I want you to simply get comfortable here. Later, perhaps, you can assist me in some small ways. I am very low on 'Gambling Soap,' for instance, and must make up a new batch soon; it is much in demand in Lagos. Perhaps you can help me with that."

Mustafa dropped his fork with a clatter onto his plate, spattering *ragout* everywhere. The two stiff-limbed servants stepped forward to wipe his *djellabah* clean.

"Hmmmm. Well, we shall see," said Drago, "we shall see. No real hurry, eh? Plenty of time. Meanwhile, if you should need to go into town, Speedy is at your disposal with the Rolls. Lucien, my *major domo,* will see to any of your other needs; you have but to ask."

Lucien moved stiffly into the room at that moment and said, "Speedy." Then he backed out with no more grace than he'd shown coming in.

"Ah, Mustafa. It is time to go for your train. I will miss you, my boy."

Mustafa rose from the table. "Thank you, Doctor. I . . . I will think of you often."

The Doctor came over to his side and embraced him briefly. It lacked the feeling that Grandfather had shown when I left the village. The Doctor's fingers twitched idly and impatiently on Mustafa's arms. "I know you will, my boy. I know you will. Now, go. And, until I see you again, take care of your soul for me." Which struck me as an odd way of saying farewell.

Mustafa turned. He hesitated a moment, as if he wanted to say something to me, then thought better of it. Without another word, he left us. We heard the front door close and the car drive away.

The Doctor took his seat again. "A strange boy. Juju on top of Islam. It's one of those combinations that never works out as well as one hopes: Something always gets held back." He turned his fixed smile toward me. "That's a problem your grandfather promises me I won't have with you. No confusion lurking in the back of your mind, is there, Isaiah?" I couldn't see his eyes through the milky reflections in his spectacles. "No Islam? Or worse—no Christianity? No 'higher education'? Nothing that might make a boy independent, might give him doubts?"

"Oh, no, sir," I was able to tell him honestly. Apparently, Mr. Olungwe had never decided I was "ready" and so had never allowed me to read his contraband religious books. Now I could be grateful for that omission in my education.

"Ah, good." He sat unmoving, his eyeglasses aimed at me and his fingers restless as seaweed in the current. He stared at me until I got nervous, feeling that there was someone *inside* me, turning me over and studying me as a boy might study a beetle.

Finally, he roused himself and said, "You must be tired after your long trip. Go to bed now. We'll talk more in a few days, after you've settled in."

I belched loudly to show my appreciation of the excellent meal and went up to the wonderful chamber that I had already begun to think of as "my room." I undressed and got into the four-poster, luxuriating in the comfort of a soft mattress and smooth, clean sheets. I fell asleep thinking how lucky I was and blessing good old Joshua for the great idea of sending me here to prove myself.

14

There came a day when a motorcade pulled up in front of the Big House. I'd been with Drago for about two months. Two very pleasant months, I should add, marked by frequent dinners of the delicious *ragout* that we'd had the first night. I ate so much of it that, for the first time in my life, I was beginning to put on weight.

My duties were rigorous and time-consuming, but on my infrequent free days, Speedy drove me into town where I enjoyed the wonders of the Lagos Central Library; there really was such a place! He would roar away in the car after dropping me off but he always rejoined me for lunch. I enjoyed his manic conversation and we were becoming friends. I still didn't understand why he looked as if someone had damaged his car every time I mentioned Drago.

On the day of the motorcade, I was in my room, making a few notes on a juju recipe the Doctor had taught me for arthritis. Because my room looked right down onto the driveway, I'd learned over the past couple of months not to be surprised by fancy cars coming to Drago's compound. Men would step out of the cars cautiously, glancing around as if they were afraid to be seen. Sometimes Drago would get in the car with his customer and they would go off

somewhere, occasionally for days at a time. But more
frequently, the caller would leave after a few minutes, his
hand buried deep in his tunic pocket. Most looked relieved
when they left. But they all looked around just as furtively
as they did when they'd arrived.

But this was different. There was a big, big limousine
preceded by a jeep full of soldiers and followed by another.
The soldiers were very tough looking. They wore helmets
and balanced carbines on their knees. Bringing up the rear
was a white ambulance with red crosses on its sides and
roof. Nor was the sedan itself the usual Mercedes, Peugeot,
or Rolls that always brought the most important men to the
Doctor. This was an American car, like nothing I'd ever
seen before. It was huge, with big fins sticking up in back
like the sharks that sometimes appear off Lagos Island. The
windows were greenish and seemed very thick, much
thicker than ordinary automobile glass. The rear windows
were fitted with gray drapes that had been pulled closed
from the inside. The shiny, black car was longer than some
of our public buses; there must have been room inside for a
dozen passengers.

But only one figure stepped out when the car stopped. He
was a mountain of a man, as big around as he was tall. His
uniform was that of a senior military officer, although not of
the Nigerian army. He wore his chest full of medals like
they were juju. He didn't look embarrassed or afraid, as did
most of Doctor Drago's customers. Instead, he laughed
loudly when Drago himself came down the front stairs to
meet him. His face was round and shiny, like a dark Moon.

For the first time during my stay, I saw Drago humbled.
He bowed and scraped before the big man. "Colonel, I was
not expecting you until sometime next week," he said in
English.

"In my business, my frien', one get away when he can
do," Colonel Moon-face answered in a deep, loud voice.
Then he laughed again, heartily, and embraced Doctor

Drago, much to the Doctor's distress. Even from my second floor window, I could see that the big man's features were not those of the Yoruba nor the Ibo, the Hausa, the Fulani, nor any of the other nearby peoples. Nor did he know any of the languages in common use around Nigeria. Otherwise, the Doctor wouldn't have chosen English, a language in which the Colonel was obviously not very skilled.

The Colonel released Drago, turned, and snapped his fingers. The soldiers immediately jumped down and removed small wooden boxes from their jeeps. Small or not, it took two men to carry each inside while a third man stood guard.

The Colonel stopped the men before they entered the Big House. He slammed the palm of his hand against one of the boxes with a slap hard enough to make the bearers groan. "Here," he said to Drago. "Here you fee, Doctor. Gold, jus' like we agree on. You like inspec' it?"

The Doctor's fingers fluttered greedily for a moment over the boxes, as if they wanted to fondle what was inside. But instead of telling the soldiers to open them, he said, "No need, Colonel. You are an honorable man."

The Colonel threw back his big head and laughed with a sound that shook the windows in their frames. "Ah, yes! 'Honorable man.' Ver' good, Doctor. I like you. You my frien'." He flung his right arm around Drago again and shook him. Even behind the white discs of his glasses, I could see the Doctor's distaste for this big, loud, uncouth man.

While this was going on, two men in white suits removed a litter from the ambulance. The body on it was strapped down and covered completely with a sheet, as if it were a corpse. But I could hear some muffled noises and could see movement under the sheet, as if the person was trying to get up from the litter. I concluded that it was a case of possession and that we were about to see a healing of a very important person.

The entourage went inside then, the Colonel and Drago bringing up the rear. The Colonel kept laughing and babbling all the while in his broken English, as if he and Drago were old friends.

I suppose the men had some private business because it was more than two hours before Lucien came to get me. I had grown accustomed by this time to the lethargy characteristic of all of Drago's servants, with the exception of our driver, Speedy. I'd even gotten bold enough to amuse myself at their expense sometimes. For example, I used to see how long I could keep Lucien in the doorway, saying, "Come," over and over again at one minute intervals. In the end, I became bored with the game before he did; otherwise, I think he might have been standing there passively to this day.

But obviously, I wasn't about to try any childish mischief when it was Drago who had sent Lucien for me. Especially when someone as imposing as the Colonel was with him. So this time, I obediently lined up behind Lucien who, much to my surprise, did not turn toward the Doctor's study. Instead, he led me out the back door and across the lawn to Drago's *ile-agbara*—literally, his "Power House."

The Power House is a mystical place. It is sort of a private Shrine, and each jujuman provides one for himself according to his means. A poor man might have only a corner of his home with a curtain that can be drawn across it for privacy. Those of greater affluence try to set aside a room where no one but the *babalawo* will ever enter, it may only be the size of a closet, but it is still a special place to the jujuman.

In Drago's case, his wealth was such that he had a separate small building behind the Big House to serve as his *ile-agbara*. It is only by comparison with the Big House that I can call it "small"; a few months previously I would have been awed by its size, thinking it fit to be the home of the *oba* of some entire nation of people.

Drago's Power House was several times the size of
Grandfather's Shrine. It was built of beautiful, cold, white
limestone blocks and was surrounded by its own well-
tended grounds. I'd been inside it many times, but only in
the central room, the one set aside for sacrifice. Drago
required me to do all the sacrificing while he and his lesser
priests negotiated prices with the customers in the smaller
rooms around the outside.

And it was long and hard work, I can tell you. I've lost
track of how many hours I had to labor over the killing
table. We used a special one made of stainless steel that the
Doctor imported from a place called Sheffield in England.
It had been designed for use in the embalming trade and had
little gutters cut into it so the blood and other bodily fluids
could drain away into an *abattoir* down at the foot of the
table. Sometimes the blood was saved in buckets for use in
further ritual. But often, I was liberating so much of it
during my day's work that Drago told me to just let it go
down the drain. There were times when I went to bed with
a sore arm from all the ritual killing work I was obliged to
do to earn my keep. I may not have been learning as much
new juju from the Doctor as I'd hoped, but there was
probably no equal in all of Africa for my skill with the
blade.

And it was to the large sacrifice room that Lucien brought
me once again. Only this time, I had company. The staff
had been pressed into service as musicians and were all
sitting glassy-eyed on the floor just inside, softly playing
ritual drums. Doctor Drago was standing at the head of the
table, his eyeglasses like silver coins under the fluorescent
lights. The Colonel was there, too, next to Drago; every few
seconds his big belly shook as if with silent mirth at a joke
no one else could hear. They were both dressed completely
in white, the juju ritual killing color. Two of the soldiers,
apparently picked at random to represent all six, had been
given white tunics to wear over their fatigues. They stood

along the wall, huddling into themselves as if badly frightened. I was a little amused by their nervousness; they probably weren't jujumen at all, just common soldiers. They probably had never even seen a blood ritual, let alone participated in one.

Well, boys, I thought, *there's a first time for everything.*

"Colonel," said Drago, "this is my new assistant, Isaiah."

"He look like good boy. You good boy, Isaiah? Is good to be good boy."

"The Colonel," Drago said, "has asked that you be present. The soldiers are here at his request, too."

The Colonel beamed. "I like many witness. Juju too secret, too quiet. But I like many people to know how I do things—to know how I get power, how I use power. So you be witness—tell other jujumen. These men be witness—tell other soldiers."

I bowed politely. "Yes sir, as you wish." I turned to Doctor Drago. "Do you wish me merely to observe, sir? Or would you like me to execute the sacrifice?"

"You will do the killing, Isaiah. But this is the first time you will be performing this particular ritual. I want you also to observe closely, to learn all you can. It is not often we are find ourselves commissioned by some great patron"—here he bowed in the direction of the grinning Colonel—"to perform a ritual as powerful and important as this."

"Really, sir?"

"Yes. Even I myself have had the opportunity to perform it no more than two or three times each year during my career."

I found myself becoming excited. This was the kind of training Grandfather had sent me here for! The only thing spoiling it for me was the two soldiers who looked so out of place. In fact, one fellow looked as if he might faint at any moment. I suppose just the thought of seeing a goat or a ram sacrificed was curdling his stomach because he kept staring at the table behind the Doctor, swallowing and swaying. I found it distracting; I would have asked him to leave, if the matter had been up to me.

"This ritual is called '*iko-awo*,' " the Doctor said. "Do you know it?"

I shook my head thoughtfully. It translated roughly as "spirit slave."Not only did I not know it; I'd never even *heard* of it. It was that way with much of this big-city juju, though. The Doctor sold juju remedies through distributors all over Africa. Trucks were always pulling up to be filled with items we'd never heard of in the countryside: *Gambling Soap. Better Luck Candles. Lover's Oil. Lord Mnube's Health Elixir.* I assumed they were the same kind of remedy our herbalists back home made up out of local ingredients. But Doctor Drago had a large wholesale volume, so I figured he just made them up in bulk and packaged them under his trademarks.

There was only one sure thing: Doctor Drago had made his reputation by guaranteeing that every remedy was *absolutely authentic*. It was a good answer to those who said that the Doctor didn't even really believe in juju, that he was just in it for the money. But his insistence that every remedy, every curse, every ritual be 100 percent authentic showed his true juju nature. And if Drago said a ritual was important, it was *important*. And if he said it was authentic, it was *authentic*.

"So this ritual is new to you?" he asked.

I nodded.

"Well," he said lightly, "there's a first time for everything, isn't there?" He stepped to the side, his active hands fluttering about as if they were congratulating each other.

And there, bound with leather straps to the table behind him, was this skinny white man.

15

The ritual we were about to perform was an example of a new style of juju—what we sometimes call "money juju." That's actually a slang term for the brand of juju in which making money seems to be the *babalawo's* only motivation.

That is, juju's traditional objectives—curing or preventing misfortune by appeasing the *orisha* and one's ancestors—seem to be not at all important in "money juju." The only goal seems to be the acquisition of obscene power for oneself (or for one's client) in the Invisible World. So the rituals of "money juju" are deliberately cruel and vicious because the customer is supposed to receive enormous power from the diabolic behavior.

"Money juju" is a product of city life; it could never exist in the country, at least not on any large scale. It depends on the anonymity and fragmented society found in big city life. In our cities, people of many tribes and cultures are thrown together into an amorphous heap, so that there are no community standards. In the countryside, everyone knows everyone else and we all have the same rules by which we have to live. In such stable communities, word spreads quickly about any jujuman who is insincere, because taking juju lightly might bring the fury of the *orisha* down on his whole village.

So, if a man is thought to be guilty of perverting juju, he will receive the tribal man's ultimate punishment: He will be shunned—ostracized, ignored, psychologically exiled. He will be cut off from all those with whom he has a common culture. No one will speak to him, his wives will ignore his needs, his children will withdraw their respect, and his neighbors will pass him by, paying him no more notice than they would a goat turd drawing flies in the road. He will be completely alone in the midst of many others.

Life without community is not worth living for one who has grown up in a tribal culture. Being shunned is even worse than being rejected by one's own family. In fact, for the tribal member, being shunned by one's fellows is the worst punishment possible, short of death.

But the city dwellers are already cut off almost completely from their traditional culture. They no longer have a community to ostracize them. So they no longer fear the shame of standing guilty before their peers. In the city, they can be punished only by the impersonal written law of the courts. And the law's only eyes are those of the policeman, while the village has eyes everywhere.

So there are few controls on the city dwellers, and they feel they can get away with anything. In the first place, there are not the thousand prying eyes of the village to find them out. And in the second, what can city people do to them even if they catch them? Put them in jail? The threat is hollow: For tribal members, being in the city and away from their people is *already* something like being in jail. Where village members are held back by their fear of what the community will think, city dwellers *have* no community to fear. They simply don't care what you or I think and are quite candid about letting us know that.

This indifference to the good opinion of one's fellows has let *cruelty* become the primary characteristic of the modern phenomenon of money juju. In fact, the crueler the ritual is in money juju the more power it is believed to have. The idea probably stems from one of the most ancient of our ceremonies: the annual ritual killing of the scapegoat.

Each spring, the *babalawo* sacrifices a goat in the town square. The ceremony is a solemn one. It is three days long and starts with a period of quiet, during which no citizen may work. Rather, each member of the community is expected to examine his or her conscience during this time. Each tries to remember anything done during the last year that might cause those who populate the Spirit World to be angry with the people. On the third day of the ceremony, the people assemble and symbolically pile all their moral transgressions on the goat. The belief is that, with the animal's death, all these sins will die as well, and the citizens of the Spirit World will have no cause to harm the community.

This custom is not unknown in other parts of the world. But whereas the ancient Israelites, for instance, used to send their goat out to wander to its death quietly and alone in the desert, we take a more direct approach. At sunup, the *babalawo* begins to make slow, shallow cuts all along the flanks of the sacrifice. Then he pulls off the long, thin strips of skin between the cuts and throws them to the watching crowd, who eat the flesh raw.

Our traditions say that an animal will survive two hundred such cuts, if they are made with an extremely sharp knife, which is why we call the ritual "The Two Hundred Cuts." But just because the ritual is thought to be survivable does not mean it is painless. In fact, it's intentionally hard on the poor animal, deliberately brutal and inhumane. The belief is that the "soul" of the goat must be "charged up" by pain and agony, and that makes the animal's suffering an integral part of the ritual. Indeed, the more the beast suffers, the better, from the standpoint of the believer who wants forgiveness of his or her sins.

To make it all as gruesome (and, therefore, as "powerful") as possible, the poor animal is never gagged; the more noise it makes during its ordeal, the more the *orisha* will come to see what all the fuss is. In between cuts there's a good deal of celebration, so the whole procedure takes about twelve hours, running from sunup until sundown.

Finally, the 201st cut is administered. It's the only one that's supposed to cause death, so it's always across the throat. It's the only one that's deep. Not until that 201st cut is the poor animal finally put out of its misery and sent to the Invisible World to intercede on behalf of its tormenters. Just to make sure it does so, its head is removed and placed in a specially prepared *nganga* jar. The head is held as ransom until the next year, when a new victim is chosen.

This ritual is unusual for its cruelty. For the most part, it is blood that plays the sacramental role in juju, not pain or suffering. Admittedly, we adorn our bodies with blood, we sprinkle it over each other—even *drink* it. But the animal from which we take that blood is almost always killed *fast*. To deliberately torture a sacrificial animal is not our way.

The difference was defined by a man with whom I appeared on an American television talk-show recently. He was a professor from the American city of New Orleans and billed himself as an expert on *voodoo*, the watered-down imitation of juju that slave owners grudgingly permitted their slaves to practice in the American south and in the West Indies. The talkshow host is widely known for his liberal views and had been assailing me for cruelty to animals. I was getting the worst of it, I'm afraid; my English was not adequate to debate someone so glib.

"The thing you fail to understand about voodoo ritual practice," the professor told him, "is that it's basically humane."

"*Humane?*" the liberal host yelled. "*Humane?* How can you say it's humane when they kill helpless animals?"

"And where do you think meat comes from for your table? 'Helpless animals' are killed to feed you and your family, aren't they?"

"That's not the same thing at all," the host said.

"You're right," the professor admitted. "The African jujuman kills his sacrifice with a single stroke. Death would appear to be almost instantaneous. As far as we know, the sacrifice is painless—"

"Aha! 'As far as you know'!"

"That's right. Did you know that the jujuman uses the same technique required by *Leviticus* for *kosher* slaughter? It's supposed to be the least unkind method. That's not how our American packing houses do it, though."

"What do *you* know about packing houses? You never worked in one. You're a *professor*." The host said the word as if it were a curse.

"No," the professor admitted, "but I read Upton Sinclair's novel, *The Jungle*. That's where I learned about how cows and pigs are really killed in our packing houses. Do you know how a cow is killed? They chase her into a chute that runs down to the slaughtering floor. The chute is so steep that she can't stop herself from falling and bouncing all the way to the bottom once she sets foot on it. When she finally hits the bottom, her legs may be broken and her skin is all ripped. The man at the bottom of the chute is supposed to put her out of her misery by slugging her between the eyes with a sledgehammer."

The audience started acting restless and the host said, "That's not what we're here to talk about."

But the professor continued. "This usually doesn't kill her right away, though. So the workers jam a metal hook with a chain on it through her neck. Then they drag her off with a tractor to this huge pile of other slowly dying cows. They all lay in their own blood and filth for hours, blind and bawling in terrible pain, until they die.

The host broke for a commercial at that point and some of the audience left. I think it was a less-than-successful show for the host. The professor had been right, though: Compared to other methods of slaughter, juju does tend to treat its sacrifices humanely—except in those special instances

where we want the animal to carry messages for us into the
Invisible World of the spirits. Then we use rituals like "The
Two Hundred Cuts" that are so deliberately abusive,
painful, inhumane, and cruel that they make Mr. Sinclair's
slaughterhouses look like amusement park rides.

Now here's a pretty obvious idea: If juju like "The Two
Hundred Cuts" works with a goat, it should work even
better with a man, right? The *babalawos* are not fools; they
figured that one out ages ago. So they have long believed
that the ritual torture and killing of a human being should
gain enormous power in the Invisible World. But because of
the social scrutiny that's a part of tribal life, that kind of
murder was really only an isolated problem with us.

Until, that is, we Africans found freedom from social
judgment in the anonymity of the big cities like Lagos,
where I was living. And also—as you'll see later—New
York and London and Los Angeles, where *you* might be
living.

16

There was a tennis ball stuffed in the skinny white man's mouth. A leather thong had been passed through two holes poked in its sides and tied behind his head. It made a very effective gag. His eyes were bulging, but that seemed to have been due to fear, because he didn't appear to have been injured in any way. Rather, he seemed quite fit. He was lean and wiry, like a runner, and there were no cuts or scratches or bruises on him anywhere.

In fact, he appeared to be unblemished.

The situation couldn't be what I was afraid it was. It just couldn't be. "Do you know the 'Two Hundred Cuts'?" Doctor Drago's voice asked. I don't think I was aware at first that it was me he was talking to. My complete attention was given over to the man on the table.

My surprise at finding a stranger restrained against his will was understandable, I think. But there was also the fact that I'd never before seen a white man this close up with no clothes on. It was fascinating, of course, to see a body so *pale*—almost the bleached color of a leper's scars. But what really drew my attention was that the fellow had a thin coating of *hair* all over his body, stiff and straight, just like a goat. I couldn't stop staring at him.

Doctor Drago whacked me over the head with his *ofo*, the

staff of office that many *babalawos* carry whenever they are at ritual. An *ofo* is usually only a couple of feet long and maybe an inch or so in diameter—more a switch than a staff, in fact. So it just sort of naturally lends itself to helping a student focus his attention. But Drago's *ofo* was made of almost indestructible *ahayan* wood and was as thick as a man's wrist. It was about seven feet long and shaped like a big, dark question mark. A leather sack of sacred alligator pepper was bound to the foot of the staff and rattled whenever he shook it. When Drago hit you with his *ofo*, it did more than get your attention; it hurt like the devil.

And it also made the Colonel laugh hysterically. He seemed to enjoy watching someone inflict pain.

"Isaiah!" the Doctor said. "I asked you a question, boy! Do you know the 'Two Hundred Cuts'?"

"Oh, yes, Doctor," I said fearfully, rubbing my head. "Sort of, that is; I've seen my uncle do it."

Drago was wearing a starched, white tunic buttoned up high around his neck, and white trousers over white shoes. He looked like a medical doctor from an American movie. "Hmmmm," he said, "but you've never performed the rite yourself, is that correct?"

I became aware that I was trembling. I desperately wanted to believe that I misunderstood what he had in mind. I reminded myself of the strange tourists that would offer Grandfather exorbitant sums to watch one of our sacrifice rituals. One of them—an Englishman, I recalled—had himself tied up by a companion while he watched us sacrifice a ram. His behavior made no sense to any of us, but surely something like that had to be the explanation for the skinny white man.

"The 'Two Hundred Cuts'? Oh, no, sir," I said. "I never did. Not me. You see, we only did the 'Two Hundred Cuts' once a year back home—just before spring planting." I was babbling, hoping to get myself off the hook. "I

suppose Grandfather always meant to have me start doing
it, but he never actually—"

"*Atoto!*" Drago said. "Enough! I see that I shall have to
perform the ritual on this sacrifice myself. You have evaded
this task successfully, Isaiah." He turned away from me
shaking his head in apparent disappointment. I took a deep
breath of relief.

Then, just as I felt I'd been spared, he spun and faced me
again with a knowing leer, as if he had timed my reaction.
"Very well. I will perform the ritual myself. But you—and
all the others here—will watch." As always, the discs of his
eyeglasses reflected light so that they looked like two bright
headlamps coming at me fast down a dark highway. But I
was learning to tell when he was pleased with himself by
watching his hands. Such as now, when his fingers fluttered
their soft dance up and down the *ofo*, like spirits of the
forest swaying to a melody that no human could hear.

"And at the end," he said quietly from behind his
glasses, "you will administer the Final Cut for me."

My heart ran back up into my throat again. For a
moment, the only sound in the sacrifice room was the
Colonel's greasy chuckling. It was the same laugh men use
when talking about their first time with a woman.

"I trust you can handle that?" Doctor Drago asked.

"Oh, yes, sir. That is, I . . . I guess I can. But. . . ."

His *ofo* rattled softly, like an annoyed snake. "Why do
you hesitate, boy? Is there some reason why you don't want
to give the Final Cut to our sacrifice?"

I shook my head mutely. I could hear the Colonel in the
background, giggling like a girl with an inexplicably deep
voice. It was becoming impossible to believe that this was
going to be an ordinary, everyday ritual. But I kept trying to
fool myself nevertheless, denying the evidence, as one will
when reality begins to look unacceptable. I told myself that
we would soon go outside into the grounds where a lamb or
a calf would be tethered. That's how it would have to be, I

thought, because there was certainly no sacrifice in sight in the Power House.

At last, I cleared my throat. "Doctor, I . . . I see no sacrifice here; what animal will we use?"

"Ah." He beamed the lights of his glasses on me again. "Well, as to that, we shall sacrifice the animal that eats salt."

I put my head down so no one would see my face. His use of the phrase "the animal that eats salt" had confirmed my fears: He had spoken in "the hidden language." Although the practice of juju is protected as a civil right in most African nations, some individual juju acts remain against the law, which makes it prudent for jujumen to adopt the habit of being indirect when speaking about rituals. And the Doctor had used one of our most well-defined code words: The animal that puts salt on its food is *man*.

The Colonel stepped forward. He seemed impatient, his big, round face cleared for once of its customary smile. "We start now, yes?"

"As you wish, Colonel." The Doctor turned to a surgical tray next to the stainless steel table. In the short time I'd been with him, I'd become accustomed to his somewhat westernized ways. So I was not surprised to see the tray laden with surgical implements rather than the homemade knives more traditional *babalawos* would use. He laid his *ofo* aside, took one of the scalpels and turned back to the man on the table. He peered down the edge of the blade with a squint, as if judging the instrument's sharpness. The white man became even whiter as he watched, utterly helpless.

The Doctor leaned toward the table, his eyes unreadable as always. Slowly, he brought the knife down toward the white man's throat. The white man's eyes followed the blade until it seemed they would go down into his cheeks. The tennis ball was heaving in and out of his mouth with the exertions of his breathing. And the air was filled with that peculiar sharp scent that a man's body gives off under extreme fear.

At the first touch of the scalpel, the white man urinated on himself. Drago slid the flat of the scalpel along the white man's neck, as if he were shaving him. My testicles tightened as I watched, as if they were trying to pull themselves back up inside me. The blade slid under the leather thong just below the white man's left ear. And Drago slowly, lingeringly rotated the scalpel, bringing its razor-sharp edge to bear.

Then, with one quick motion, he slashed the thong holding the tennis ball and the white man spat it out.

"Oh, thank God," the white man said breathlessly. "Thank God."

Drago returned the scalpel to the tray. He looked at the white man solicitously. "Do you understand what is happening here?"

"Yes! I mean, no. I mean. . . ." He had a British accent and must have been one of those holdovers from colonial days because he recovered himself in a matter of mere seconds. In fact, although he lay there tied up, naked, and wet, he spoke to Drago as he might have spoken to a house boy. "I was simply standing about outside the Club, waiting for my transport, when a local military vehicle pulled up. Well, I naturally assumed the Embassy had asked them to come collect me."

The Doctor's fingers swayed like reeds in the wind. "But not so, eh?"

"Certainly not!" said the white man. "Rather than taking the road toward the Lake, which they should have done so I could rejoin my unit, the buggers headed for the airport!"

"The airport? My, my. Then your trip must have been a long one."

"Yes. Six hours on the metal floor of an old Dakota, me trussed up like a Christmas goose! When we finally arrived here—wherever 'here' is—they threw me in some sort of old ambulance and . . . well, here I am!"

"Tsk-tsk. Your story is most sad."

"Yes, well. Now, you appear to be an educated man, not like the rabble that kidnapped me; I should be grateful if you release me at once. There's no point to holding me because I'm really not worth much in the way of ransom."

Drago made a surprised look. "No? Hmmmm. Then it appears we shall have to find some other use for you." His fingers caressed each other like lovers.

The white man's face began to lose its confidence again. "Now, see here. This is most irregular; I shall be missed, you know. Now unless I am released immediately, I refuse to answer for the consequences."

"You do, eh? Well, sir, Africa is a dangerous place. Disappearing here is not the same as vanishing from your Trafalgar Square at high noon, is it? Is it not likely that your countrymen will feel you've met with some unfortunate mishap?"

"Nonsense! I am an 'old hand' in Africa. *I* know my way around; *I* know how to take care of myself here."

"Indeed? You'll forgive me if I point out that you've not done well recently."

"None of your cheek, now, Boy-o!" the skinny white man said. "When word of this outrage gets back to my unit—"

Drago held up one of his elegantly swaying hands. "I regret that your unit will never hear of any of this. I think they are very far away."

The white man considered. "Nonetheless, I feel it safe to say that my Embassy—"

"I think, sir, that you should try to understand that you are quite alone here. 'Here,' by the way, is Lagos. We *do* have a British embassy, of course. Rather close by, in fact. But since they have no reason to believe you are anywhere within two thousand kilometers of Nigeria. . . ." He shrugged.

The Colonel's voice boomed out. "Doctor, please: Is time to begin no?" For the first time, he stepped into the white man's field of view.

"*You!*" the white shrieked.

The Colonel grinned down at the white man. "Is good of you to reco'nize you ol' frien'."

"'Old friend,' indeed! What is your part in all of this?" the white man demanded.

"My part? I am the man you will serve."

"Not bloody likely!"

The Colonel roared with laughter. "Oh, but yes. *Very* bloody likely. Is not so?" he said to Drago.

"Yes, indeed," the Doctor answered. "You see, sir, you will truly become the Colonel's servant, his representative. Not here, but in the Invisible World. You will become his messenger, his Spirit Slave—what we call *iko-awo*."

The white man's eyes showed that this was not the first time he'd heard the word.

"Ah," said the Doctor with pleasure. "I see you know *iko-awo*. That is good. The more you know about this ritual, the better. Because then, the more you will go to the *orisha* in a 'charged-up' condition. Yes, I think you will make a very strong messenger for the Colonel."

"Please," the white man said with an unexpected whine in his voice. "Please, let me go. I won't tell anyone, I swear I won't! Do all the juju you want, just let me go. I'll make it worth your while, both of you."

Drago looked as if he wanted to taunt the white man some more. But the Colonel seemed bored by the change in his attitude. "Begin," he ordered.

"No, look, I've got some money saved up. English money, sterling! It's yours, all of it. Only you can't do this thing. Especially you, Colonel. Why, you and your troops are the reason I am in Africa, don't you remember? I came here to help you!"

"Good," said the Colonel. "Now I give you the chance to help me ver', ver' much." He suddenly grabbed up a scalpel and thrust it into the white man's side to a depth of several inches.

The white man screamed and flecks of blood flew from his mouth all the way to the ceiling.

The Doctor grabbed the scalpel out of the Colonel's hand and threw it to the tile floor with a clang. "Do you wish this man to go to the *orisha* having died an ordinary death? Can you afford to indulge your anger if it creates such *waste?*" he shouted. The Colonel instantly looked regretful and almost abashed.

Drago bent to study the wound. He examined it critically and made the kind of quick, competent judgment that only a man who has inflicted thousands of such wounds can do. He sighed. "Four hours. No more. We shall have to work faster than I'd planned."

He went to a cabinet against the wall and brought back several packets with red crosses on them. Within minutes, he'd expertly cleaned and dressed the white man's wound. Then he pulled a chair alongside the table and leaned to the white man's ear.

"Listen to me. You will go to the spirits in pain. They will hear you above all others because your pain will be so great. You will plead for good fortune for the Colonel. If you fail him, he will burn your body and scatter your ashes to the winds. Is that clear?"

He snapped his fingers at the Colonel. The Colonel looked insulted, though I didn't know whether it was because of the Doctor's attitude or because he was being obliged to do something for himself. But in any event, the ritual required the Master of the Spirit Slave to bring forth by himself the vessel in which the remains of the sacrifice would be imprisoned. So the Colonel bit off his anger and went through the doorway into a small room in back that was always kept dark.

He returned puffing under the load of a portable clothing wardrobe. He set it down just beyond the foot of the sacrifice table, where the white man could see it. It stood almost as high as the ceiling, and was made of pressboard. It was the same color blue as a cloudless sky and it had a label on it: Sears, Roebuck & Company. Such cabinets were a common sight in Drago's *ile-agbara*. There were probably a dozen or more just barely visible through the doorway to the darkened room. I'd always before assumed they were just shipping cases for juju, because sometimes one of the men with fancy cars would take one of them away with him. I'd never looked in any of them because Drago had never told me to; it wasn't any of my business. Besides, it always *smelled* so bad back there.

Drago pointed to the cabinet. "This is your 'hostage home,' " he said to the white man. "Look upon it and know fear."

But the white man was moaning and tossing his head from side to side, though whether from the pain of his wound or from the terror of what was to come, I did not know. Drago chose not to repeat himself to the white man. Instead, he reached into one of the packets he'd brought from the cabinet and produced a little white cylinder wrapped in gauze, about the size of a peanut. He twisted it in his elegant fingers and the astringent smell of ammonia spread instantly through the sacrifice room.

But rather than simply waving the smelling salts some distance under the white man's nose, as would have been normal, he jammed the capsule up one nostril.

The white man's head thrashed wildly in an involuntary attempt to escape the noxious fumes. His screams nearly drowned out the popping noises that came from his over-taxed neck muscles. If the stainless steel table had not been bolted down, I'm sure it would have been dancing in place from the white man's exertions.

It wasn't until the smell began to dissipate that the Doctor removed the capsule. "Now," he said calmly, "you have had a lesson: You must understand all that will happen. You must pay attention to me and you must answer when spoken to. Do you understand?"

The white man glared at Drago in defiant silence. The Doctor was still holding the broken ammonia capsule, massaging it sensually between his fingers. When the white man failed to answer, he dropped it to the floor. With a sigh, he took a fresh capsule out of the packet.

"Yes!" the white man shouted, his eyes large. "Yes, I understand!"

Drago smiled and patted the white man on the head. "That's good. Thank you for responding to me."

Then he broke the capsule anyway and shoved it up the white man's other nostril.

I looked around the room. The two soldiers seemed to be as shocked and unsettled as I was. But the Colonel was vastly amused by the incident. He was holding himself with laughter, leaning backwards with his face toward the ceiling. I was surprised to see an erection bulging under the sharply creased pants of his uniform.

When the Doctor finally removed the capsule, he said to the white man, "Now you have had another lesson: Pain will be your constant companion for the remainder of your life. There is no way you can change this fact. Think on this and know fear."

He dropped the capsule on the floor and turned to look at his collection of scalpels on the tray. "It is right that you should be afraid," he said over his shoulder. "That is the purpose of this ritual, to send you to the spirits in a state such that they cannot help but notice you. Only then can you be effective in pleading the Colonel's case. I will put you into such a state by using pain. Think on this and know fear." He turned back to the table, his fingers stroking the handle of a gleaming scalpel. "You are alone," he said to the white man. "You are lost. There is nothing you can do. Think on this and know fear."

The white man was gasping for air. He still had a defiant look on his face, but much milder than before. Perhaps the Doctor's urging for him to "think on this and know fear" was working.

The first cut made by the Doctor was much more disciplined than the Colonel's wild stabbing. He set the blade just above the sternum and a bit to the left. He let it sink into the white man's flesh to a distance of perhaps a centimeter or so, just enough to separate the top layer of skin from the underlying tissue. He drew it downward evenly in a perfectly straight line until he got to the pubic hair. I could see the skin spread back behind his knife; it reminded me of plowing a furrow. But it would have had to be a furrow in a place like Georgia, where the soil is red, because a thin trickle of blood oozed up behind the blade as it passed. Without pausing, Drago went back up to the starting point. He moved his blade a little farther to the left and proceeded to cut another track, as straight as the first.

Then he made a short cut up at the top of the man's chest, connecting the two long parallel cuts. He turned the blade toward the foot of the table and undercut the meat to an extent of maybe ten centimeters, just enough to provide a flap of skin which could be grasped by a man's hand. This was all done so skillfully that the skinny white man never even cried out.

Cutting the tracks and creating the flap had taken only seconds, during which there had been silence in the room, except for the sound of heavy breathing from the white man and the Colonel. Drago set the scalpel down gently and took up his *ofo*. Then he turned to me.

"Isaiah," he said, "please remove the first strip from the sacrifice."

I'd been so fascinated by his work that my horror had subsided momentarily and I nearly forgot what would come next. This isn't as crazy as it sounds; remember that I'd been studying juju for years and this torture was actually a demonstration of my craft by a master. But now, it suddenly hit me: This was no innocent ritual, culturally enriching us through "traditional" religious observances. The white man, for all the pale and sickly ugliness of his skin, was a human being.

"Doctor, I . . . I . . ."

Drago said nothing to me, but the glare from the flat plates of his glasses was burning a hole into my very being. I knew I was disgracing myself, my grandfather, and all my ancestors. Not to mention my village and my whole tribe. But even knowing all this, all I could do was stand there, stammering like a frightened child.

The Colonel stepped forward. "I see this before. When we hunt zebra, back home. Often, young man afraid to kill first time. We call 'buck fever.' Is easy to fix." He grabbed my skinny arm in his hammy hand and pulled me to the table. With great precision, he pushed my hand forward toward the flap of skin hanging from the skinny white man's chest.

I tried to resist, but it was useless; the Colonel was twice my weight, maybe more. In spite of how badly I was shaking, he guided my hand unerringly to the bloody flap of skin hanging off the white man's chest. "Oh, God," the white man was muttering. "Oh, God, please don't!"

I tried to clench my fist, but the Colonel easily pried it open. He positioned the palm of my hand directly under the dripping flap. And then he squeezed it closed.

The flap was just the right size for my grip. As the Colonel painfully compressed my hand around it, the skin exuded blood and bits of marbly fat, which oozed out from between my clenched fingers. I felt my stomach revolve and then I vomited.

The Colonel didn't even seem to notice. He just leaned back, pulling my hand along with him. Slowly. The soft, squishing sound as the flap of skin unzipped itself from the white man's body was nearly drowned out by his pitiful screaming. I was transfixed by the sight of the flap, becoming longer and longer at the end of my arm, until it was a bloody, rubbery-looking strip. We pulled at the lengthening piece of bloody skin—the Colonel laughing and me weeping with horror—until the resistance of the attached flesh finally ceased just above the white man's penis. I would have fallen over backwards if the Colonel had not been there to hold me up.

The white man stopped screaming then and fainted from his agony. The Doctor revived him with more smelling salts while the Colonel laughed in that hearty, yet threatening, way of his. When no one joined in, he turned to scowl at his men. Even though he looked somewhat younger than they were, the soldiers clearly feared him. One of them was so unnerved by the possibility of the Colonel's displeasure that he even tried to force out a weak laugh of his own. But he only succeeded in producing a kind of breathless sound. The other soldier couldn't even try; he just rolled his eyes back into his head, slumped against his fellow, and slid quietly to the ground.

This seemed to amuse the Colonel anew and he roared again, holding his shaking stomach. His face was as round as one of our local pumpkins and he was missing two teeth in front. When he laughed like this, it made him look like a leering, jack-o-lantern of the sort that American children carve. The same look of plump, obscene menace was there.

I kept staring at my hand—the one that had pulled the strip of flesh from the man's body. Drago looked down at me with what was almost a look of kindness. "Did it feel any different than any other skinning you've ever done?"

I couldn't speak, but I shook my head. The fact is, it had felt just like all the countless times I'd pulled strips of skin from calves and from lambs to make the leather thongs with which we attach spear points to their shafts. The only differences were that this time the animal was alive. And, of course, this time it was "the animal that eats salt."

"If it is the same," said the Doctor, "there is no reason you should not continue to remove the strips while I make the cuts." There were tears in my eyes, but he was as cool as ever. His fingers twined sinuously through my hair as he tried to comfort me, just as though he were my grandfather.

"I *do* need your help, you know, Isaiah. There is much to be done and little time to do it. I know this ritual can be difficult the first time. But remember your Grandfather; do it for his honor if for no other. . . ."

"Grandfather?" I said. "Surely my grandfather could never have carried out this kind of ritual!"

A slight smiled cracked the Doctor's face. "No? Who do you think taught it to *me?* Of course, the old man only did it for your village, because he thought it would bring your people power and good fortune. I don't think he ever did it for a client, in fact, I doubt if he ever made ten *naira* in his whole life from his juju."

The vague air of sympathy disappeared and he became all business again. "Now," he said, "let's finish the job. And remember, Isaiah: You can no more change what will be happening here today than that poor white man can." He made a motion to the Colonel, who slid into the chair up alongside the white man's head.

For the next three hours, the Doctor cut and I pulled. As we did, the Colonel talked to the white man, which was difficult at first. But it soon became easier: The white man screamed his voice hoarse and made very little noise after the first few minutes.

I don't remember much of what the Colonel said to the white man; I felt like I was in one of those dreams in which you work all night and wake up tired in the morning. But I remember the Colonel's main objective because he repeated it to the white man over and over again: to eventually take over his country. He said he knew it could take ten more years, but that he was prepared to wait. Esu himself had appeared to him in the form of a monkey, he said, and had told him that it was his destiny to become the supreme ruler of his country. This the Colonel said again and again until at last, inevitably, the white man became the Colonel's *iko-awo*.

It took a little less than the four hours the Doctor had anticipated. By the end, the floor was almost carpeted with the little capsules of ammonia, as well as with empty syringes. These had contained the drugs that the Doctor injected into the white man as the ritual entered its later stages, when it became harder and harder to bring him back each time he passed out from the agony of his ordeal.

I have always told myself that the unknown white man was probably dead anyway by the time I administered the *coup-de-grace*. Or that he wouldn't have wanted to live in the kind of shape he was in and that I actually did him a kindness. Those are the things I've always told myself about that 201st cut, which I had to administer.

After a break during which the Doctor had coffee and the Colonel drank some French wine from a squat bottle one of his men carried, we removed the white man's entrails. That was a trivial procedure compared to everything else: a couple of quick cuts and done. The Colonel saved the liver in a plastic box that had a blue flower on its side and had a matching top which snapped in place; it looked very festive. Everything else was discarded. The hollow, skinned corpse was much lighter than it had been in life. We washed it and shoved a big iron hook through its back. Then we hung it up in the sky-blue wardrobe, like a butcher might hang a chicken in the window.

The white man had been tall and his toes nearly dragged on the floor of the cabinet. The Doctor told the Colonel they'd need to be "trimmed back" as the now-empty body stretched out over time. I have since heard florists advise people on the care of houseplants in much the same tone of voice.

The Colonel had his men carry the wardrobe out to the ambulance. I was detailed to carry the big carton of spices and herbs that he would have to apply to the body weekly, to keep the insects and smell under control, until it was fully "ripe," which would take about a year or so.

Then the motorcade set off for the airport and the long trip back east, leaving me a day older.

17

After that, I was ill for some time. I'd apparently caught some sort of fever, because I was unable to keep my food down.

It very much disturbed the Doctor for me to be sick. For one thing, he now seemed enthusiastic about my prospects to become a *babalorisha*, as my grandfather wanted. I think this was because, in spite of obvious misgivings, I'd still been able to carry out the Final Cut on the white man in the *iko-awo* ritual. I got some hints that my predecessor, Mustafa, had failed to perform when he was called upon in a similar situation. Drago told me he was going to send a glowing report about me back to Grandfather.

But at the same time, he was annoyed that my illness made me unable to "go and fetch." This was one of the duties he always demanded of the boys who studied under him. There was a rigid schedule of visits through the surrounding countryside which had to be made on time or else the Doctor's operation suffered. They involved his money juju—picking up fresh ingredients or delivering prepared products.

Some of the tasks were boring: About five days of each month were spent just delivering the Doctor's various aphrodisiacs, always to the same fancy address. And of course, while I was running around doing the deliveries, my duties in the sacrifice room of the Power House piled up on me. So I seldom looked forward to "go and fetch" days.

But on occasion the errands were fascinating. For example, one rainy day toward the end of my first month in residence, an unusually quiet and grim Speedy drove me out to a distant swamp in the forest. The way was marked by big, leathery-looking trees with trunks as gray as the day was. When we came to a marshy clearing surrounded by yellowish reeds, he turned off the engine.

For a long time, nothing happened; we just sat there. I asked him several times to tell me what we were waiting for, but he acted as if he hadn't heard me. Finally, he just rolled up the window between the sedan and his open compartment. We waited for the better part of an hour like that, not speaking, staring insensibly straight ahead out the windshield.

Finally, some of the bushes around the car stood up. They were men covered from head to foot with garments made of reeds. They also wore masks made of reeds that had only slits to see out of. They walked slowly toward the car and stared in through the windows at us for a few minutes with what I took to be a mixture of curiosity and hostility.

"Don't look at them, Boss!" said Speedy's voice over the speaking tube from the front compartment. "Just ignore them. Pretend you don't see nothin', Boss!"

Following his lead, I continued to look ahead fixedly, as if the frighteningly silent men weren't there. They didn't exhibit much in the way of interesting behavior anyway; they just stared and stared, cocking their heads at times as if to get a better look. Finally, one of them rapped with a spear in the hood of the car, at which signal Speedy pushed a button on the dash, popping open the big trunk of the Rolls. The silent men stepped to the rear of the car and filled the trunk with a number of sacks, so many that I felt the car lower toward the rear. Then I hard the trunk slam behind us and, by reflex, I looked back in Speedy's mirror to try to see what they would do next.

But they were all gone. They had just evaporated into the forest like morning mist. Only a few birds broke the damp silence of the marsh.

Speedy started the engine and we drove slowly out of the clearing. I had no idea what it had all been about until I heard some hoarse croaking sounds from the back as we pulled away.

"Frogs, Boss. Stinkin' frogs. Once every couple months, we gotta go see those creepy guys and get their stinkin' frogs. You know what my trunk smells like after I carry frogs in it? Huh, Boss?" He shook his head, but then he laughed loudly, his gold teeth glinting in the rear-view mirror. "That's right, Boss—it stinks! It smells like being right down inside a great big ol' stinky frog, is what it smells like."

And on he went, griping and laughing at himself at the same time. It was a relief to hear Speedy's rapid-fire monologue of complaint after the silence in which we'd passed the previous hour. But the croaking from the trunk kept getting louder and louder during the trip back, eventually drowning him out altogether. It had almost driven me to distraction by the time we finally reached the Doctor's palace.

The Doctor made me decapitate the toads while Speedy cleaned out the trunk. There were thousands of them and it took me several hours. Only the heads had value, the Doctor told me, so I enlisted Lucien and several of the other servants to carry away the bodies, except for a few dozen of the biggest ones, which I held out for that night's dinner. We took all the bodies to a spot in the western section of the grounds, toward where the Sun goes down, which is where the Doctor had instructed me to bury them.

The Doctor killed a piglet and sprinkled its blood over the pile of toad heads. Then he had me shovel them all into a big vat of salt water along with leaves from the *peregun* evergreen tree and several handfuls of white beans. He added eleven pieces of iron and boiled the mixture for three hours. He decanted the liquid that came off into a big flat pan and dehydrated it over a fire. It produced a dark slag which he covered with a paste made of mashed fresh fish and bananas. This he let "breathe" overnight—out in the yard, much to my relief.

The next morning he directed me to scrape off the paste, rinse the slag well with red palm oil, and then grind it up in a mortar. After a morning's hard work, the slag yielded about a kilogram of a dark reddish powder which the Doctor called *eru oku* ("spice of the dead"). This he caused Lucien to put in large salt shakers. I understand the spice was always taken at meals by every one of the principal members of his staff, except for me and Speedy.

But during my illness, I was too sick to "go and fetch" the toads on the appointed day. The Doctor was cranky about it, but all he could do was wait until I recovered enough to go, which wasn't until four days later. We found the toad men were still hiding in the clearing, just as they had been the last time, apparently having waited there unmoving for the four days.

By the time we made up a new batch of *eru oku*, the Doctor's whole staff was getting restless. Work around the palace was being done sloppily. And noisily: Lucien had begun to speak without provocation. And in words of more than one syllable. One of the housemen had even dared to question an order he was given. Things were getting out of hand. But the usual quiet routine of the household was restored as soon as the spice was put on the table for that night's dinner. From the mesmerized and lackadaisical way servants at the compound always acted, I always figured that the Doctor had some secret way of making them cooperative and docile. But this was the first time I realized

how dependent Doctor Drago was on his own money juju to
maintain control.

Of course, during the time I was so sick, I made the same
assumption that jujumen always make: that I was suffering
from "juju sickness." So I asked the Doctor to work a
charm on me and to turn the curse back on whoever had
placed it on me. But he declined; like most of our root
doctors and herbalists, he was able to distinguish quite
reliably between disorders caused by juju and those brought
on by other causes. For example, a compound fracture of
the arm sustained in a road accident clearly requires the
techniques of Western medicine. So even the most devout
jujuman today will demand modern treatment for such a
condition, although he will probably require that it be *in
addition to* traditional (i.e., juju) treatment. In many local-
ities, the local root doctor has had at least a minimum of
Western first-aid training and may be competent to stop the
bleeding, clean and suture the wound, set the bone, and
immobilize the arm in a cast. But he will also charm the evil
spell that caused his customer to break his arm in the first
place. So instead of working a juju cure on me, Drago sent
to town for Doctor Sese, one of the medical doctors who
practiced in Lagos.

Dr. Sese gave me some medicine that tasted worse than
any juju medicine I'd ever had. He told me to stay in bed for
at least two weeks. His instructions depressed me, since I
had no desire to be alone, with nothing to think about but
the Colonel and the recent *iko-awo* ritual.

But Dr. Sese also told Drago that it was a good idea to let
me read the books that Speedy offered to bring from the
library. And for this I was indebted to him, because Drago
looked on Western books with almost as much suspicion as
my grandfather did.

Drago assigned his most junior wife to tend to me during
this period. She was almost fourteen years old, a girl from
one of the more isolated regions that belong to the *Egba*

people. People from that region tend to be stumpy and muscular, with a corresponding lack of alertness and a perpetually sleepy look. They are referred to among townsmen as *omo igi*—the sons of sticks. They are considered by most of us to be old-fashioned; they are considered by some of us to be good-for-nothing. And, no matter how harshly they are characterized by the rest of us, they never seem to object.

The girl was representative of her people. As far as I could tell, she was totally uncontaminated by modern ways. She wore the traditional garb of the juju wife and was so festooned with cowries and beads and charms that she literally clanked when she walked. She was a strong girl, big-boned, and I estimated that she was wearing about three heads of cowries (six thousand cowry shells). In the old days, when cowries were used as money, it would have been a fortune, exchangeable for the heads of three enemies. But in modern times, when cowries have lost all but their decorative or symbolic value, it was only thirty pounds of junk. She also kept her face fully chalked at all times, after the old custom. This was a good idea in her case, because she was the most homely young woman I'd ever seen. Her looks and temperament notwithstanding, she was several months pregnant.

For the first several days of my illness, she refused to speak to me. She would bring me my broth and my medicine, and would fetch my books and so forth, as she was supposed to. But when she had no specific assignment from me, she would simply sit scowling on the floor in the farthest corner of my room. Occasionally she would flash one of the various juju hand signs that ward off danger. It wasn't until the Doctor struck her with his *ofo* and ordered her to speak that she finally did so.

Even then, her story came out only in short and grudging portions. But I eventually understood that she'd had a very hard life. Her mother had been a minor noblewoman among her clan while her father had been only a casual worker on the Lagos docks. He had been thought socially beneath the family and, as if in fulfillment of those opinions, he ran off before his child's birth.

The mother returned to her family, humbly asking them to take her back in. But they refused, saying that they'd never approved of her choice of man in the first place. Had she not gotten pregnant, they said, it might have been a different story. Their attitude could have been summed up by the popular American expression, "You made your bed; now lie in it."

The child was born friendless and into abject poverty. Her embittered mother named her Oba-bunmi, which means "the god of smallpox gave me this." Rather than simply abandon her, though, her mother was clever enough to sell her for a few coppers to a childless woman.

But, almost immediately, the woman died of unknown cases and everyone said that little Oba-bunmi was cursed and would bring bad luck to anyone foolish enough to buy her. After that, of course, selling the child was out of the question. But so was abandonment; the townspeople forced her mother to take her back, lest evil befall the village.

But that didn't mean her mother had to treat her well. Oba-bunmi was beaten regularly, for little or no reason. As she grew older, her mother repeatedly tried to sell her to people passing through town who didn't know her history. But the child had been so disfigured by abuse that there were no takers, even for free.

Oba-bunmi ran off as soon as she was able. For a while, she lived in the bush. As soon as she began to menstruate, she offered herself as junior wife to an extremely old man and woman. She made it sound unlikely that it was he who put her with child. But in any event, he died soon after taking her in. She must have thought she stood to inherit his land, which amounted to several hectares, because she began to lord it over the other women of the town. But

instead of inheriting, she found herself willed to Doctor
Drago, much to her surprise, as payment of some long-
standing debt. The Doctor would rather have had the cash,
it's safe to say.

That was the way the Doctor got most of his fifty or so
wives—through inheritance. Which points up one of the
commonly misunderstood aspects of African polygamy:
Not every juju wife need be a sexual partner to the
babalawo who owns her. Actually, it's only commonsense:
Most men can deal successfully with (at most) three or four
"mat wives." This innate physical limitation is recognized
even by Islam, which limits the number of a man's wives to
four (although modern Moslems frown on any polygamous
practice at all).

But an important man in the tribal society—an *oba*, an
olowu, or a *babalorisha*—might have dozens or even
hundreds of wives. It is even said that the semilegendary
founder of the Yoruba people, Oduduwa, had over a
thousand wives. The obvious question is, how could he
possibly have dealt with them all? And the obvious answer
is that he *couldn't*.

That gives rise to the distinction of a "jujuwife": a
woman owned by a man with whom she does not necessar-
ily have a long-term sexual relationship. In actual practice a
man will probably take a jujuwife once or twice before
going back to his regular mat wife. Although the new
jujuwife becomes an official part of her husband's harem
after that, any infidelity is conveniently unnoticed, unless
she is betrayed by pregnancy. And of course, the inheritor
of a wife may choose to have no relationship with her at all,
as was almost surely the case with Drago and Oba-bunmi.

Oba-bunmi was not exactly pleasant to have around; her
hard life had taken its toll on her personality. She was
morose in her behavior and morbid in her outlook. She even
told me that she thought the child in her womb was an
abiku, a child born only to die. We believe that the *abiku*

children are possessed by members of an evil fraternity of demons who live out in the forest, in the largest of the *iroko* trees. Each *abiku* who comes into the world arranges beforehand the time he or she will die, thereby breaking the poor mother's heart and amusing all the other evil demons.

The object of an *abiku's* mother must be to persuade the spirit in her child to stay beyond the time he or she has agreed to return to the forest. Only if the spirit is convinced to stay away from the forest too long will the demon forget the company of his or her fellows. He or she is then free to become a normal, loving child.

Needless to say, this puts an incredible burden on the mother of an *abiku*. She has to devote her full energies to spoiling the baby, living only for him or her, so that the spirit will be enticed to stay on. And, since humans cannot know the time the spirit planned to depart the child's body, the spoiling must go on for the rest of the mother's life.

Oba-bunmi did not seem to be the type of woman who was up to the formidable task of raising an *abiku*. She understood this, I think, and was resigned to whatever fate might bring; she even told me she intended to name the baby Akuji, which means "awake, and then dead."

By the time I recovered, with only modest help from Oba-bunmi, it was already June and time for the *egungun* festival in town. My people were never strong followers of the *egungun* cult and neither was the Doctor. However, a good friend of his was the *alagba* (master-of-ceremonies) for the big *egungun* festival in Lagos, so the Doctor and his staff of lesser priests were expected to participate. Actually, *egungun* is another of those demonstrations of how easily the West fools itself about Africa.

The *egungun* cult believes that spirits of ancestors can come back and inhabit our bodies. Just like all other forms of juju, *egungun* celebrates with festivals. Because they are so colorful, these festivals have been the subject of numerous books and travelogues in the West. You've probably seen the pictures: The celebrants wear masks and dance through the streets of the town to the accompaniment of drums and whistles. Western anthropologists comfort themselves that *egungun* is nothing more than a public party; a carnival; a fun-loving *mardi gras* staged by innocent primitives.

But *egungun* is a full-fledged African religious festival. And it has this in common with the other religious aspects of Africa: There's only so much we're willing to tell white people.

Which is reasonable because there's only so much they're willing to believe. The reality is that all of our "masked festivals" share the well-documented juju penchant for blood and lust.

Egungun begins with a night of prayer and fasting during which there is much sacrifice and blood is poured over the graves of our ancestors. This is so that they can participate in blood ritual in death, just as they did in life. This night of prayer and sacrifice which we call *ikunle*, meaning "the night of kneeling," is the *real* justification for *egungun*. Yet, I doubt if any Western visitors have ever paid attention to it.

What they notice are the next seven days, which are filled with visits from departed ancestors, those we call the *egungun*. They take over the bodies that are closest in physique to those they had when they were alive. They also cause the host to cover his head with a mask, so that no one will make the mistake of thinking that a mere mortal is in the body.

It is thought to be obvious that no man is responsible for what he does when the spirit of an ancestor is in him: His will is no longer his own, after all. So rape, looting, and murder are common occurrences, and no man possessed by an *egungun* may be punished for these crimes. Only the *spirit* that inhabits the man deserves the punishment; catch him if you can.

Like most aspects of juju, *egungun* has become more serious and widespread in recent times. One reason is that our people—just like people everywhere—have discovered chemicals. It used to be that our people could only become drunk on palm wine or on *ogogoro*, the local whiskey. Both liquors are weak, compared to Western standards, and you have to consume them in large quantities to get inebriated; relatively few people go to all the trouble to get really drunk. Most Nigerians, of course, were unable to afford Western whiskey or cocaine, so a relative sobriety tended to be the rule among us.

But oil money has changed all that, as it has changed so much in the coastal part of our nation. Now the *egungun* weave wildly through the streets day and night, often waving a whiskey bottle in one hand and a machete in the other. Both cocaine and marijuana are considered "sacraments" and are taken in large quantity, as are others of our indigenous hallucinogens, all of which become more powerful when mixed with alcohol. These days, the number of deaths in large cities after every *egungun* festival is in the hundreds.

The civil authorities have found it impossible to stop *egungun*. The best they can do is arrange a sort of "safe conduct" for innocent citizens: For one hour during each of the first six days of the festival, women and children are allowed on the streets to tend to normal business and police do their best to protect them. During the rest of the time, curfew is imposed. Then the streets belong totally to the *egungun*—the same ones Westerners laugh at in the travelogues—and even the police have learned to stay out of their way. By the seventh day of an *egungun* festival, even this modest effort at civil control is abandoned and curfew lasts all day and all night.

And the situation as described by the *Lagos Times* has deteriorated recently. The *Lagos Times* is our national newspaper of record, equal in the eyes of Nigerians to *The*

Times of London or the *New York Times*. Among the many stories about the excesses of the *egungun* cult is one that appeared on February 19, 1988. It said that the governor of the state of Kwara felt he could be forced to impose an indefinite curfew *throughout the entire state* because of the number of *egungun* killings there.

Of course, at the time I accompanied Drago to the Lagos festival, *egungun* had not reached the level of fever pitch toward which it is tending today. Besides, we spent most of our time at the various state and social functions that are given because many educated Africans pretend that *egungun* is a purely cultural activity. Even so, it was pretty rough and the Doctor recommended that whenever we had nothing scheduled we should all stay indoors just like the women and children.

I felt uncomfortable all the time we were in town and was glad to get back to the compound. For a couple of days, anyway. Then Oba-bunmi's water broke and the Doctor told me to bring her to the sacrifice room because she was "ripe." I suddenly understood that her dread about her future and that of her child had not been misplaced after all, but only premature.

18

Westerners find it difficult to believe just how important the products of money juju are to the daily activities of the tribal peoples of Africa. The notion that substances so common and trivial as water or oil can be empowered with potent spirit magic is almost laughable to the Western mind. Yet, consider the jujuman's view of life. He believes that *Olodumare* intended for his favorite creation—us human beings—to be happy. Nonetheless, our world is full of danger that subjects us to great pain and misfortune. How can these two ideas be reconciled?

It's obvious to the jujuman that evil can exist only because forces from the Invisible World are interfering with the happy fate that has been intended for us. So he seeks power to control all those evil forces. Pacifying them in order to restore his natural, happy condition is what the religion of juju is all about.

But if an evil influence comes into our lives anyway, we're taught that it can be cleaned out with the products made available by the practitioners of money juju. So all sorts of everyday items can assume enormous superstitious importance to us. This is particularly true of items that suggest power, like anything with a sharp edge. But it's also true of household items like brooms and even soap that suggest the idea of sweeping or cleaning away the evil that the spirits have dumped on us.

Because juju artifacts are often so common and homely, the West finds it easy to ridicule them. And so money juju thrives, even when scholars insist that the old traditional religion is dying out. It permits juju to be treated far too lightly, especially by Americans.

For example, it is not uncommon for an American who has been in New Orleans or in Haiti (where the variant of juju known as *voodoo* is practiced) to bring back voodoo artifacts. Other travelers to such popular vacation spots as Southern California and South Florida (where there are large Hispanic populations practicing another variant of juju known as *santeria*) invariably bring back some of the items they found in the "funny" little local store called the *botanica*. You've seen the kind of stuff: maybe a "saint" candle, a can of "Queen Oya's Good Luck Spray," a bar of "Gambler's Soap," a bottle of "voodoo water" or a vial of "Love Oil of High John the Conqueror." They pass this material around as a joke, sniffing it or spraying it or otherwise scattering it all over the office without a thought about what might be in it.

But consider *Doctor Drago's Gambling Soap*, which is sold in many cities in Africa. And elsewhere, for all I know. It's billed as "the soap that washes away bad luck." It starts out like the soap African householders have made for thousands of years. All you need is some fat which you boil along with an alkali. Our most common source of alkali is the ash from something that we've burned. Although ash from an ordinary woodfire is fine from the chemical standpoint, juju always burns the body of some newborn sacrifice, such as a chick, to produce "pure" ash.

Money juju always goes farther. It always corrupts traditional juju practice by emphasizing juju's most brutal aspects. And, in the case of soap-making, the form of corruption is obvious: If a newborn chick will make "cleaner" ash, how much more so will a newborn human infant make it?

On the day that Oba-bunmi gave her child over to the cause of Drago's profits, she could hardly have failed to know the purpose to which her baby would be put. After all, Drago made no secret of the viciousness of his rituals. To do so would have hurt his business; money juju entrepreneurs like Drago need a certain amount of publicity to prosper. Believers in juju generally accept that the more gruesome a ritual is, the more powerful it must be. So a man like Drago can use his reputation for brutality to convince his customers of the power embodied in his charms, potions, and other artifacts. And everybody knows that Drago's juju products are 100 percent authentic; if the recipe calls for a human baby, then a human baby is what's used.

As soon as we arrived at the compound from Lagos, Drago directed me to go and fetch Oba-bunmi. I ran to the Big House to get her, enlisting helpers from among the men who were always lounging around in the Doctor's yard, waiting to be assigned odd jobs. We carried Oba-bunmi, cot and all, out to the Power House. Her eyes were empty and glassy, though whether from the rigors of her labor or whether from *eru oku*, I couldn't say.

When we brought her into the sacrifice room, Drago was just finishing up his preparations. Two high stirrups had already been bolted to the foot of the stainless steel table and he was directing one of his junior priests in the drawing of juju symbols in bright lipstick on the white tile floor.

I don't know what got into me. But when the men and I had placed Oba-bunmi on the table and positioned her legs in the stirrups, I became dizzy. My mind filled with uninvited thoughts, most of which seemed to be shouting inside me, "I don't want this to happen!" Yet there was really no reason for me to feel that way. Nobody wanted Oba-bunmi's child, including the girl herself. It would wind

up in the dump outside town anyway if Drago didn't get to
it first. So why should I care?

But my thinking, for a jujuman, seemed to be going out
of whack. I kept remembering all those books Mr. Olungwe
had given me that talked about the dignity of human life. I
kept remembering the skinny white man whose name I had
never even learned but who I'd been required to kill. I kept
wondering if Oba-bunmi's baby would ever get to open its
eyes or if it would be murdered in darkness. And for the
first time in my career, I began to feel guilty. It flashed
through my mind for just a moment that maybe juju was
dirty and *cruel*, the way Western people always said it was.
That—at its best—juju was only a simple-minded and mis-
guided attempt to control nature. And that—at its worst—it
was a barely opaque cover for greed and for blood lust.
After countless sacrifices, I was losing my stomach for
killing.

I asked Drago if I could leave. To my surprise, he agreed.
Moreover, he appeared unbothered by my reluctance to stay
for Oba-bunmi's delivery or for the subsequent immolation
of her sacrifice. Maybe he felt that, with the death of the
white man, I'd already passed the test that had been set up
for me. Or maybe he saw me swaying a bit and thought I
was suffering a relapse of my earlier fever.

But I don't think so. Though I could not justify it, I got
the unmistakable feeling that the death and burning of
Oba-bunmi's child was simply no big deal to him. He'd
apparently performed the ritual so many times with other
unfortunate infants that he saw it more as a chore than as an
atrocity. He seemed almost bored. In fact, when I asked him
if I could be dismissed so that I could work on my notes, he
said, "Yes, Isaiah. There's not much for you to learn from
soap ritual. I'm sure you'll develop your own as you go
along; there's not much to it. Besides, have I told you that
it pleases me for you to write down so much of our lore?"

"It does, Honorable Drago?" He'd *never* said anything like that to me before.

"Yes, the Western people think they know such a great deal. But they do not even know which plants an old man can use to make his penis hard or which a woman can use to keep a wandering man at home. Someday, your writings will show them who knows what!"

I thanked him and started to back out of his presence, bowing as he always liked for me to do. "Wait," he said. He gestured at Oba-bunmi with his *ofo*, then set it aside. "Help me prepare this one before you go. She will be of no further use to me when we finish. Would you like her for yourself as a gift?"

"Me, Honorable Drago? Oh, no, thank you, sir." I automatically started to flatter him a bit, by commenting on his dedication. "Like you yourself, sir, I am much too busy for a woman."

He had been taking instruments out of the sterilizer that was against one of the white tiled walls; it seemed bizarre to go to such trouble for an infant who would be sacrificed before he or she could draw a second breath. But that was how the Doctor did things: to perfection.

"Indeed?" he said. He stopped removing the instruments and turned to beam the light of his glasses at me. "How strange. This is not at all the same story I hear from my eunuch."

I found myself too embarrassed to speak. The fact is, I'd been amusing myself with the daughter of one of his wives almost since the day I'd arrived. We used to meet out behind the compound's corn storage house, in a glade of fragrant lime trees. But I never thought the Doctor knew about it.

I stammered for a few seconds and then the Doctor laughed. "Calm down, my boy." He handed me some leaves from the "sandpaper tree" which we call *epin*. "You have done nothing to injure her bride price, have you?"

I started rubbing poor Oba-bunmi's stomach with the leaves, as called for when delivery is expected to be difficult. She still made no sound, even when the leaves began to rasp her skin slightly. "No, sir. I always give her a potion of *akara-aje* after."

He nodded, rolling his instruments to the sacrifice table. The root that we call *akara-aje* or "witch's bread" makes an effective, if unpleasant tasting, birth control potion. I always prescribed it because women could take it after sex, rather than before. The drawback to it, of course, is that it tastes so absolutely awful that many women only pretend to drink it. They toss it in the bushes when they get home, preferring to trust the whim of the *orisha*, rather than science, to prevent pregnancy.

"Good, Isaiah. You have behaved responsibly. But next time, use *imiesu*. Do you know it?"

" 'Devil's dung'? Yes sir, of course I know it. But I thought it was only for cancer."

"When chewed, yes." He kept working while he talked, laying out the same obstetrical tools a Western doctor would use to assist delivery. "But if you crush the nuts along with a few red tree ants and mix it up with a little sweetened *orombo* [lime juice] it prevents pregnancy. Furthermore, it tastes good, so you're sure your woman will take it. And there's something in it that makes the woman want to come back to you again."

He was full of tidbits like that. After my first week or two at Drago's compound, I wrote up several sheets daily about the remedies, rituals, and curses I'd learned that day, most of which proved remarkably effective over the years. He typified juju's hold on its believers: Just when you think nobody in his right mind could accept any more of its cruelty or silliness, juju shows you still another thing that *actually works*.

I stood there for a moment, marveling at Drago's practical knowledge of the natural world, until he asked, "Have you changed your mind? Do you wish to stay for the ritual after all?"

"Oh, uh, no, sir. Thank you. My writings, you know. I have to, uh. . . ."

He tested the big forceps a time or two. "Well, then be off with you, before I find some work for your idle hands." He was actually whistling as I left.

I never again saw Oba-bunmi nor, of course, her child. In fact, I almost never saw Drago again; a message was received early the following morning from my grandfather. He required me to return home.

I must confess to a certain relief. My confusion about myself and my place in the world had become even greater, I think, than that of most other adolescents. It made the warm familiarity of home sound especially good to me. I packed my few belongings immediately. These amounted mostly to piles of notes on Drago's rituals. I actually ran down the steps like a child when it was time for my last breakfast in the formal dining room.

The Doctor was wearing one of his three-piece suits from London. He looked up as I came in. "Ah," he said, "I see you received your grandfather's message."

"Yes, Doctor," I said. I bowed. "Please let me tell you how much I—"

"No time," he said briskly. "You must leave right now or you will have to wait another whole day." He got up from his breakfast and started pushing me out the door. When we got to the big front porch, he said, "My regards to your honorable grandfather, my boy." He shook my hand, as an American might do. His whole body was expressionless, except for his fingers which danced in my palm. Then, without any further ceremony, he closed the door on me.

The purple Rolls was waiting in the driveway at the foot of the stairs. The engine was running and Speedy revved it a couple of times to get my attention. I hurried down the

steps and jumped into the rear compartment of the big car.
Speedy was careful to pull away in the stately fashion he
always adopted around Drago.

"Well, Boss, you goin' home, huh? How long you been
here anyway? Oh, yeah, around four months. Well, that's
not very long, is it, Boss?" He looked somber, as if he
would miss me. "But I bet you're glad to be goin' back,
huh?"

He caused the wheels to squeal as we made the turn out
of sight of the Big House and I bounced back into the
leather upholstery. He immediately relaxed and laughed
loudly. "Yeah, Boss, I know what you mean. Always good
to be goin' home." His eyes looked at me in the mirror.
"You know, Boss, you look pretty good for a guy who just
been trained by the Doctor. Some guys come away from
there, they look like they been goosed by *Shango* himself."
He laughed again. "But, like you say, Boss—you weren't
there very long. I bet you still saw some stuff, though. Huh,
Boss? Sure you did. You really saw some stuff."

He paused. Then, without his laugh, he surprised me by
saying sadly, "I'm sorry you had to, Boss."

Suddenly, we were on the crowded main road again and
Speedy directed his attention to driving and horn-blowing.
His silence gave me time to reflect on the thoughts he'd
shared with me during our trips back and forth to Lagos. I
suddenly realized that he was the only one I would miss
from among the two hundred or so people who populated
Drago's compound. Perhaps it is a measure of the loneliness
of Drago's brand of juju that the only friend I'd made while
staying with him was this man whose face I saw mostly in
a mirror.

Nobody else could have gotten me to the bus terminal on
time; there were a few times when I thought even the sight
of Drago's purple car would be unable to clear a path fast
enough. But we roared up in front of the terminal, horn
blasting and lights flashing, with only seconds to spare.

There was no time for goodbyes, no time for me to remind Speedy to return my library books or to thank him for having been my friend. The only bus north to Ilesha that day had its engine running already, so I jumped on board. I pressed my face against the window, watching the dirt of Lagos go past. It was going to be very good to get back to the warm love of my village.

THE
WHITE MAN'S
JUJU

19

Some of the men from the village met me at the bus stop in our truck. They bowed and addressed me as "Honorable," which hadn't happened to me since I left. I admit that I enjoyed the attention. I had been kept so busy at Doctor Drago's compound that I almost forgot that I was a god of sorts.

I was concerned at the impatience this implied, though. A sense of urgency is not part of our lifestyle in West Africa and I worried that it might mean Grandfather was sick. But the men assured me that that was not the case, even though it was Grandfather himself who told them to come and get me in the truck, in order that no time should be wasted.

My first sight of Grandfather did little to reassure me. His descent into old age and decay probably went unnoticed by the village people who saw him every day. But to my eyes, four months made a noticeable difference in his appearance. He stooped a little now when he walked and the bones of his face were more prominent. He was not yet what I would have termed "an old man," but his feet were on the path to that sad, ultimate destination.

The Council of elders and lesser priests surrounded him like a protective shell. I saw that Joshua now stood scowling among them. He had taken the place of Moses Obuko, son

of my father's brother's son and father of many, who had
been killed by a fall while hunting in the forest. There were
those who whispered that it was a juju killing: Moses had
been a hunter of renown and they found it unthinkable that
he would stumble while running after a wild pig and fall
fatally onto his own spear.

Juju killing or not, the Honorable Obuko had to be
replaced and a general meeting of all the men of the town
was called. Joshua astounded everyone by rising and
putting forward his own name. He said that he should be
chosen because he was a "Man of Action." That seemed to
be his entire platform. It also conveniently explained why
he was bold enough to nominate himself. But it was
unlikely he could have found an elder to do it for him
anyway because, while it was not exactly taboo for a young
man's name to be placed ahead of the hundreds who were
older, it was a distinct violation of our social customs.

No sooner did Joshua, the Man of Action, propose his
own name as Council member than his friends, Yesufu
Owure and David Akuko, leapt to their feet. They showed
plenty of action on his behalf, yelling and jumping about,
exhorting the assembly to approve Joshua. So great was
their energy in support of him that some townsmen became
convinced that the two were possessed. A rumble began to
go through the crowd to that effect. If true, it would be a
momentous sign that Joshua's election was favored by the
orisha themselves.

And so, as his two friends shouted and leapt ever more
furiously, the conviction grew that Joshua should be the
chosen one. Yesufu sensed it and acted to push the decision
over the brink. At almost six feet, he was well-known as the
tallest man in the village and was highly visible. He drew
his machete and took a large slice out of his own left arm to
prove his frenzy for Joshua. He waved the meat aloft as a
token of his earnestness, which the crowd could not deny,
the way his blood was spattering down on them. First by

one voice, and then by dozens, the cry went up of *Mopade okorin na!* Translated, this means "I have met the right man!" Among us, it signals an affirmative vote. Within only minutes of convening, the meeting was adjourned, Joshua having been elected by acclamation. It had been the shortest open meeting in the memories of even our oldest chronicles.

A few of the more querulous old men let it be known that they felt cheated: Meetings to decide something as trivial as the ownership of an axe had been known to go on for days. Joshua and the younger men he represented, on the other hand, seemed pleased at the efficiency his rapid election had brought to an old process. Social implications aside, though, Joshua had carried the day and was now the youngest member of the Council by a good twenty years. It was rumored that he was also the most vocal.

But what surprised me most about the assembly that greeted my return was that *so many* people had turned out to welcome me home. Not only the entire Council, but hundreds and hundreds of our local citizens—maybe even the whole town—had gathered in the big square by Grandfather's compound. Grandfather came forward and saluted me with his *ofo*. It was not so big nor so grand as Drago's, but the crowd ceased its murmuring the instant he raised it. I bowed toward him. To my utter astonishment, he bowed back, just as if we were peers!

"We welcome home our brother, Isaiah Oke, and he has our blessing," he shouted. And the crowd repeated the phrase. I was moved and deeply honored.

After repeating his blessing loudly six more times, he stepped forward from the supporting circle of elders. I noticed for the first time that he was dressed in what could be called finery. His *girike* appeared to be of the silk we call *samayan* and it looked brand new. It was bright blue and much embroidered, extending down to his ankles and beyond his arms into ample, sweeping cuffs. Down below the hem of the garment, he wore brand-new sandals. And he'd even been shaved. Grandfather was never a man to pay much attention to appearances and I wondered what could be so important that he would trouble himself in this way.

He held his *ofo* aloft again and the crowd quieted. "People of Inesi-Ile," he shouted. "Today you will hear important news. I have had a report about our brother Isaiah. This report comes to us from Doctor Drago of Lagos." The crowd had been hanging on his every word. But at the mention of Drago's name, they became even more still, if such a thing were possible. They ceased to move, even to breathe.

"Doctor Drago," Grandfather went on, "reports that our brother Isaiah has distinguished himself. He reports that our brother Isaiah has faithfully recorded much wisdom through the juju of *reading* and *writing*. He reports that our brother Isaiah has brought honor to us, the people of Inesi-Ile."

The crowd went wild—cheering, stomping, whistling, and generally making as much noise as possible. After an appropriate interval of celebrating, Grandfather again signaled for quiet.

"Doctor Drago," he said, "has recommended that our brother Isaiah should continue to learn of Western ways. And so, we announce today an action never before taken by this village." Everyone remained quiet, even though Grandfather had made no further call for it. "Our brother Isaiah shall soon leave our village once again. Only this time, he will not go to Lagos, to study *our* juju, as he has for the last season. No, this time, he will go away to Oyo."

I couldn't believe my ears! Oyo had been the capital in the legendary "old days" before the British came, back when we were the proud nation of Yorubaland. Much smaller than Lagos, but far nobler in its traditions, Oyo transacted little in the way of international business, so Westerners seldom went there anymore. Yet it had a fine

university and was thought by many to be the cultural
center, the honorary heart, of all Nigeria.

Grandfather kept right on. "And in Oyo, our brother
Isaiah will study at the Normal College where he will
master . . . *the white man's juju!*"

The crowd "ohhh'd" and "ahhh'd" because this statement was beyond its understanding. Most of them knew that
my tutor, Mr. Olungwe, had already taught me reading and
writing; what more could there possibly be?

"Not only will our brother Isaiah learn more reading and
writing, but also . . ." Here Grandfather paused and
peered dramatically around the circle of anxious faces. "But
also . . . *accounting*—the secret of the white man's increase!"

The crowd went mad with pride and delight. They had no
more idea than had my grandfather what "accounting" was
all about. But if it was, as he had said, "the secret of the
white man's increase," it must be powerful stuff indeed.
Besides, it had a grand sound about it and they began
chanting it: "Ah-kown-TING! Ah-kown-TING! Ah-kown-
TING!"

Only when some of the men began to throw their spears
in the air in glee did Grandfather once again signal for quiet.
He waited until the last echo of the last yell had died away
before continuing. Finally, he looked around and said
calmly, "And there is yet more to be told."

More! Was there ever such a day in Inesi-Ile? Several of
the women were suddenly possessed by ancestors who
wanted to be present on this most auspicious of all occasions.

"My youth," Grandfather said, "is spent. Soon, age will
be heavy upon me. I must begin readying myself to become
an ancestor." There was a sudden, shocked roar of disbelief
and disapproval at this announcement. Some of the men
rent their garments as they cried, "No, *Babalorisha*, no!"

He let it wash over him briefly; there is probably no

greater pleasure than hearing the grief of one's people over one's death while one is yet alive to enjoy it. After a bit, he held his *ofo* aloft again and the crowd quieted, although there was still some weeping to be heard. "But the *orisha* have told me that my death will not come for some years yet."

The people erupted into spontaneous cheers. Some of the men ran forward and began turning somersaults, demonstrating their joy at this happy news. The women wept and raised their eyes and their palms to heaven in thanks.

Again, Grandfather calmed the crowd. "But a prudent man lays plans for his death, just as the tree ant lays up food for the rainy season." Many of the elders of the Council nodded their gray heads at this saying. "It would not be good for you to be without an intercessor between you and the gods. And so, I will name to you today the one who will succeed me as *babalorisha*."

The crowd caught its breath and held it. Even though I had been fated since birth to the position, it could never be official without Grandfather's blessing. But he had become disappointed in me when we faced Esu together. And I was always writing up notes on juju cures when there was ritual to be performed, so that Joshua or some other junior priest seemed always to be filling in for me. The truth is, I had long since despaired of ever having Grandfather's mantle transferred to my shoulders.

And, to be candid, I wasn't sure that would be so bad.

So, even though it would shame me, I expected (and hoped, to be honest) that Joshua would be named. And I think much of the crowd did, too. Joshua even moved forward a bit from the ranks of the elders. His chest was big and his mouth was hard in a sneer, as befitted his reputation as a Man of Action. He knew there were grounds to justify his appointment. After all, he was a Council member now as well as being the seventh son of Grandfather's seventh son, whereas I had never been more than a disappointment—a coward and a bookworm.

The only thing in my favor, besides my skill at reading and writing, was Drago's praise. And that was only because I'd found it in myself to put an unknown, skinny white man out of his misery.

"You must be protected," Grandfather told the villagers, solemnly. "For terrible times are coming; the *orisha* have told me so. And you must have a protector who is fit to lead in terrible times. Therefore, when I rejoin my ancestors, you will be protected by . . ."

Joshua's friends, Yesufa and David, started shouting and congratulating themselves.

". . . our brother Isaiah, a Man of Learning."

20

The Normal College at Oyo could not be confused with Oxford or Harvard. It is, in fact, what Americans would call a "junior college." There are many such institutions in West Africa because, even though we modern Nigerians are a very literate people, our educational system is somewhat spotty. That is, our city children receive their primary education in schools that are no different from ones in Pittsburgh or Pasadena. And today, our oil wealth has made our secondary schools more or less the equal of modern schools everywhere. They have well-trained teachers, up-to-date textbooks, and computers. But many of our rural children are still taught in the old "one-room schoolhouse," where books are outmoded and methods slow to change. So, for us, reading and writing are not in themselves enough to justify moving our children on to the next level of education. We need a common educational experience if all our young people of widely differing ages, cultures, and levels of preparation are to attend the same university. And that's where our junior colleges come in; they are "the equalizer" for our students.

Normal College is built on a site that is especially rich in history; it is said to be the location of the original military college for the warriors of the semilegendary Oranyan.

Oranyan was an important character in Yoruba history. He was the first *Alafin*, or "supreme king," of the Yoruba people. He was our version of George Washington and is said to have unified 1,060 separate kingdoms into the one vast empire known as Yorubaland. Some estimates put the territory under Yorubaland's control as an area larger than the United States, although this has never been proved. It is generally accepted, though, that eight of the independent nations of contemporary West Africa were eventually carved from the Old Empire.

Even though we now live in modern republics, many Yorubas remain loyal to today's *Alafin*. But he is less a political authority these days than a cultural figure. He is also a religious symbol, because the *Alafins* have always been hereditary priests as well as kings. In fact, if juju could be said to have the equivalent of a pope, it would be the *Alafin* at Oyo. To this day, the dynasty that Oranyan founded holds court in and around Oyo, where the modern *Alafin* lives in regal splendor.

The same, however, could not be said about students at Normal College in the early sixties. Conditions for us were just short of wretched. Normal College was started just after World War II and several of its buildings when I went there dated from that time. Most of them were prefabricated, so the campus did not make a favorable aesthetic impression. Nonetheless, it was a chance for genuine formal education and most of the students took it as seriously as they would have taken Cambridge, me included.

My room was in a dormitory (actually a mobile home) that we called "The Palace of the *Ejo*." *Ejo* is our word for the number "eight" and eight of us shared the place. As for the word "palace," that was an example of youthful sarcasm. Actually, it wasn't as bad as I make it sound; West African homes tend to have very small rooms anyway, so I was used to cramped quarters.

Besides, when they heard who my grandfather was, the

others all voluntarily turned over to me the lion's share of
the space. This worked out well for me because, like all
babalawos, I took my juju with me wherever I went. So I
hung a cloth between the plywood partitions that defined
our individual rooms and the space behind it became my
own *ile-agbara*.

I immediately began to use what I'd learned from Doctor
Drago—not his strong and brutal rituals, but his marketing
know-how. From the moment of my arrival at Normal
College, I let it be known that I was a *babalawo* of great
power. I could manufacture charms that would assure good
grades. I could prepare potions guaranteed to arouse the
interest of the girls of Oyo. I could recite chants that would
bring money from home by the very next post. In short,
through the power of my juju, I was prepared to supply all
the necessities of college life.

There were already two senior students vying to be
known as the head *babalawo* when I arrived. But neither of
them was the grandson of the great Aworo Oke. Neither of
them had studied under the dreaded Doctor Drago. Neither
of them was fated by birth to become *babalorisha* of all
Yorubaland as soon as he graduated from college. And, of
course, neither of them was the incarnation of the god
Orisha-Oko. When I let all these distinctions be known,
both men dropped prostrate before me and offered to be
junior to me.

Except for two Europeans and one Asian, our teachers at
Normal were all West or Central Africans. And, regardless
of their educational attainments, they carried juju in their
hearts. So they treated me with almost as much deference as
did my roommates and my fellow *babalawos*. One of my
professors, the Honorable Omo, even became one of my
best customers.

The Honorable Omo was a man of extreme years, having
received his education in England back in Colonial days just
after the turn of the twentieth century. He came to me the

second week I was in residence. With much embarrassment, he told me that he had not experienced an erection in over twenty years. (What he intended to do with one at his age he did not make clear.) But he had long sought both Western medical treatment and traditional juju treatment for his condition. The doctors he consulted simply shrugged and told him it was a part of growing old, that it happened to all men, and that he must learn to accept it.

The answer to his problem was simple, of course. At first, he was frightened when I showed him the *ishin* nuts I'd collected for him. Westerners know the *ishin* as the "king tree" and call its fruit "Bligh's cashew," because it is said to have been first described scientifically by Captain Bligh of the HMS *Bounty*. The Honorable Omo did well to be afraid of it; the unripe nut is one of the deadliest poisons known. Fishermen on the Osse River extract its oil, a few drops of which in the water returns a plentiful harvest of dead fish within minutes. It is a curious detail to the study of juju medicine that the plants we use to help men increase their sexual powers all seem to have use as poisons as well. Consider *akato*, which means "the executioner." It is said to be even stronger than *ishin*, whether used as a poison or as an aphrodisiac. But when used as an aphrodisiac, it must be administered as an enema, which cuts down on its popularity.

I had no wish to be the death of my professor, so for the Honorable Omo I made certain to collect only *ishin* nuts that were fully ripe. One handful of them—marinated, dried, ground into paste, and mixed with vinegar and the pulp from an *ejirin* (an African cucumber) would make even a piece of cooked macaroni hard. The Honorable Omo looked doubtful as I explained how it was to be rubbed on, left for half an hour or so, and then throughly washed off with juju-water containing peppercorns. After all that, I promised him, he would be his old young self again for the following two days.

Of course, I also warned him about how the mixture would burn. I told him to apply it to himself out in the forest because people might hear him yelling and, for just a moment, I thought I saw his resolve weaken. But then he said it would be worth it if the potion worked as promised. I again assured him that he would find the results satisfactory but, because of the undesirable side effects I'd just explained, I gave him the first treatment free.

When he came rushing back to me three days later, I informed him that I would not accept payment in the traditional (but now valueless) form of cowry shells. Rather, I required compensation in good, hard *naira*. He pointed out that my two predecessors had agreed to accept cowries. But I pointed out that I had made him as hard as *iki* wood and they had not. He stopped grumbling and handed the money over. He quickly became one of my best customers, calling on me twice weekly from that time on.

I made sure that everyone I helped told his friends about me. Just like Drago, I profited from word-of-mouth notoriety and business boomed. By the end of my second month at Normal College, I was able to hire a manservant from the town to see to my needs. He was reputed to be a worthless fellow. He had no land and no trade and lived on handouts. He kept moving around the town continuously, never standing in one spot long enough for anyone to get really angry at him and chase him away. So he was called *Akunyun*; that is, "one who wanders to and fro."

I changed his name to Speedy. He lived under the Palace of the Ejo and turned out to be a decent servant; all he'd ever needed was somebody to tell him what to do. He was a slow and clumsy fellow, it was true. But he was cooperative. He turned out to be a good helper at the many blood rituals for which fellow students paid me handsomely every time exams drew near.

Naturally, I was enjoying my advantages. Money came in freely. Teachers and students alike feared me. People who

met me in the road on my way to classes bowed respectfully. Now, this kind of treatment may be common for
college basketball players in the American midwest, but it is
extremely rare for a student in Africa. The result was that I
very quickly became what Americans refer to as a "big man
on campus" and my head grew large with pride.

Best of all, classes at Normal turned out to be almost
easy, compared to Mr. Olungwe's intense tutelage. I
breezed through my first term effortlessly and with quite
creditable marks. I went home during the midterm break,
astounding everyone in my village with my erudition. Some
of my townsmen kept pestering me to "say something in
accounting," while others asked me to "work some accounting" on behalf of their ancestors or for a sick baby.

It was on that first trip home that I rejoiced to see the dour
Mr. Olungwe happy at last. Grandfather had gifted him with
two hectares of land, an ox, and a wife as a reward for
having helped make a man of me. The Honorable Olungwe
was now a gentleman farmer as well as a scholar, and he
took to strutting around the town with a self-satisfied grin
all the time, as if he were the father of many.

And so my life went for nearly three more years: Pleasant
schooling was punctuated by rewarding trips home. It was
almost perfect. The only sadness was Grandfather's increas-
ingly great burden of age. The advancing years had a
peculiar effect on him: Every time I returned home, he
seemed to be lighter and smaller than he had been the
previous time, although his health otherwise remained
good, except for a persistent cough. I began to think that he
would not die, after all; he would simply shrivel up to
nothing and disappear one day. I'd never before seen
anyone become quite that skinny and sick just from age and
I couldn't shake the feeling that he had some terrible,
unknown disease.

A couple of days after I returned to Normal College for
my last term there, I was eating with some of my friends in

the building where we all took our meals. I suppose I could call it the "cafeteria" but that might be stretching the truth. At Normal, every student prepared his own meals; we simply consumed them in that common place.

But I was always popular in the cafeteria because the new Speedy prepared my meals for me. I'd even taught him to make a pretty fair replica of my mother's "palaver" sauce. No one else at school had a personal servant and I always made sure Speedy prepared enough that I could invite friends to dine with me.

This particular evening, I was sitting with my friend, Simon Meji, when a new group of freshmen was ushered through on their orientation tour of the campus. They were every bit as scared-looking as Simon and I had been three years earlier. So naturally we hazed them by throwing bits of *fufu* at them and yelling, "Better save this; the only food for you in this place will be *ayan* and *ekun* (cockroaches and tears)." Of course, this frightened the poor nervous newcomers even more, which Simon and I enjoyed immensely. Some of the young women among the group even sniffled a little.

The temptation to give them a really bad time was too much for Simon. "Look at the women in that mob, will you?" he asked loudly. "Have you ever seen such an ugly bunch of worthless women in your life? I'm glad we're going on to university before we get desperate enough to think they look good." He flipped three or four quick juju signs at them. Then he cursed them with a phrase that means, roughly, "May you be rejected, even by the bush"—"*Igbekoyi!*"

Some of the youngsters literally shook. I didn't know whether they shook with fear of juju or with the simple tension that is part of being a freshman. But their reaction amused Simon, who nudged me in the ribs and laughed.

I shook my head and tried a gentle expression. "Aw, leave them alone, Simon. They're just scared kids. Give

them a break." I smiled benignly up at the group. As soon
as some of them looked a little relieved, I yelled, "Even
though they really are ugly!" Simon howled with laughter
and slapped my hand in congratulations.

None of the boys in the tour group had the nerve to tell us
off. As for their guide, he was one of our teachers; he
certainly wasn't about to mess with *me*. As I said, I was a
"big man on campus," *plus* I was a powerful *babalawo*.
And besides all that, I was a senior, too.

But one of the girls looked more scornful than scared.
She was young, no more than sixteen or so, and dressed
after the fashion of the West: blue jeans, sneakers, and
tee-shirt. Her hair was very full, not plaited into the small
strips that unmarried women displayed. She stepped out
from the group and approached Simon and me, just as bold
as anything.

She put her hands on her hips and glared at us as a man,
even a warrior, might do. Then, in a most unseemly
fashion, without being first addressed by one of us men, she
spoke to us. "You know, you're not very funny, either of
you. That's not nice—throwing food at people. And I think
you've been calling us names; that's not nice, either." She
spoke in English with the most peculiar accent I'd ever
heard. Her speech was full of growls, like the language of
the wild dog.

Simon was shocked at her behavior and again leveled his
curse at her: "*Igbekoyi!* Be gone, Woman."

"Be gone yourself," she said to him. She seemed not in
the least frightened, as she should have been. Or at least, as
she should have given the *appearance* of being; that's what
would have been appropriate for a woman, especially one of
her tender years.

The freshman group was staring at us with big, round
eyes, eager to see what was going to happen next. This was
doing no good for my image as the strongest *babalawo* on
campus.

"Woman," I said gently, but firmly. "You forget yourself."

She turned from Simon to me. "Stop calling me 'Woman.'" She showed no more fear of me than she had of him; she probably hadn't been on campus long enough to know who I was.

I smiled at her, although Simon looked as if he thought I should lay an *epe* on her for her insubordination. But one thing I've learned: Some people respond better to friendliness than they do to threats. So I always try friendliness first. It's like that old saying in my village: "You can catch more termites with honey than with you can with vinegar."

"We address you as 'Woman,'" I said, "only because we do not know your name. What is it that you are called?"

She relaxed a little. "My name is Janet."

It was a strange name. I rolled it over in my mind. *DJA-net*. It sounded vaguely Arabic, but she didn't look like an Arab. "Are you Fulani?"

"Am I what?"

"Fulani. Are you Fulani, *DJA-net?*"

She wrinkled her brow. "I don't think so. What is it?"

I saw Simon roll his eyes back in his head. He was probably thinking that such ignorance could only come from an Ijesa. "He means, Woman, what tribe are you?"

"'Tribe?'" she said. "Oh, you mean what African tribe. Well, I'm just over here for a year while my father gets your new power plant built. But I'm not African; I'm an American."

"*Hepa!*" I said happily. "I have always wanted to meet one of your tribe. I know of all your great men."

She looked startled. "You do?"

"Oh, yes." I puffed up a little, pleased at being able to show off such esoteric knowledge. "I admire greatly your President of the clan of Kennedy." I signed on the tabletop the sign for good fortune and then raised my face toward the *orisha* and added the exclamation "*Kabiyesi!*" This is really a juju prayer we offer on behalf of royalty and it means, "May long life be given to him." Several people in the room who had been listening in (there being no such concept as "privacy" in tribal life) picked up my prayer and repeated it so that it became a chant: *"Kabiyesi! Kabiyesi! Kabiyesi!"*

She was a strange girl: Here I was praising her *oba* and yet she looked uncomfortable about the signs and juju prayers I offered.

"Ah," I said. "Perhaps you wish to rejoin your group and finish your tour? Very well, we will talk later. For now, you are dismissed."

She looked as if she were about to say something again, but thought better of it. Instead, she smiled wryly and shook her head. Then she turned to rejoin her group. I nodded my permission to the group's teacher/guide, who looked relieved and immediately ushered the group out.

"What is your interest in this woman?" Simon asked as they filed out. "She is too young for you. Besides, she is very plain and she behaves badly. Why, she is even more arrogant than a *babala* . . . I mean, her behavior is a disgrace."

"Yes, but she knows things you and I do not."

He put on a pious and conservative look. "If we do not know a thing, Isaiah, then our ancestors did not mean for us to know that thing. We know only what is good for us to know."

"Tell me, Simon, do you never wish to discover new things, to consider new ways? Do you never wish to look beyond our rigid social customs, to look beyond juju?"

"Never!" he shouted. He immediately began to ward off the evil my words might bring.

"Well, I do" I said. "I am interested in hearing the words of this foreign girl."

He gripped my arm, tightly. "Isaiah, my brother: No

good can come of it. Foreign ideas are not for us. They lead only to trouble."

I laughed and pushed him away. "I will hear her words, Simon, but I will not fear them. After all, what could a foreign child like her possibly do to hurt a powerful *babalawo* like me?"

21

A day or two later, I planned a feast in honor of the new student from whom I would learn so much about America. First I went into town and bought a choice pig and a large jug of the local maize beer. While I was at the market, I also spent much of my previous month's juju fees on the ingredients for a side dish of *Jollof* rice, which many people consider to be our most aristocratic dish.

At the little Shrine I'd built in the nearby forest years earlier, I sacrificed the pig and ordered Speedy to butcher it into small cubes. I discarded all the entrails, sparing only the kidneys; these I planned to present to my guest as a special treat to take home with her. As long as I was in the forest anyway, I took time to gather some mint and other herbs for the sauce. I was never able to get my *ragout* to turn out quite as good as that we used to have at Doctor Drago's; I couldn't get that musky taste in my meat that his had. But my guests always complimented me on the quality of the mint sauce I served with it.

That day, we took over the cafeteria just after midday for our principal meal (which, among us, is lunch). Also present, in addition to Janet and a freshman girlfriend of hers (an Egba girl whose name I didn't catch), were my friend Simon Meji, three of our teachers, and the headmaster of Normal College, the Honorable Doctor Abraham Olubiwi.

Speedy, of course, served the meal, though not without considerable grumbling. It is customary among us for servants to take their meals with their masters. The number of people present was such, however, that Speedy knew he probably wouldn't be sitting down to eat until everything was cold.

In spite of all my planning, we got off to a rather rocky start. After introductions, everyone sat and I blessed the assemblage and our food with a juju chant. Such a thing is not really customary, but this was a special occasion and I wanted my ancestors to observe how actively I was seeking enlightenment. Janet had only the slightest familiarity with our language; she couldn't possibly have understood more than a few words of what I was saying. But she appeared uncomfortable nonetheless.

She only picked at her food, trying to be polite, I think. But it was clear that she liked it not at all. As for the maize beer, she never even tasted it. The only aspect of the feast that really interested her was the fact that I'd worn my *ejigba*, the knee-length necklace that I brought out only on special occasions. Mostly, *ejigbas* are worn by kings or high public officials as a badge of rank. They are usually made of very costly beads, including even precious stones and the rarest of pearls in the case of the *Alafin*. Of course, the *ejigba* of even the most important jujuman is far less grand than those worn by our secular leaders. But it is more powerful.

Janet stared and stared at my *ejigba*. Finally, as I ran low on small talk while Speedy was clearing away after the main course, I asked her whether there was a problem. "Those bones you're wearing," she said, pointing to them. "What are they?"

"This one," I said, proudly showing her the biggest, "I

inherited from my grandfather's father. Where he got it, I don't know. This next one is the sternum of a hyena which I killed myself; he was possessed by an evil spirit at the time. Then there's this whole row: the backbones of a serpent, which is our most sacred animal. Here, of course, is the finger which I use for divining purposes. This next one—"

She stopped me. "Did you say 'finger'?"

I looked up. "Yes. It is the forefinger of a man who was a famous soothsayer; I am extremely fortunate to have it. See, the joints are glued together, so the whole thing makes a kind of pointer. Now, when I want to divine something— say, if I want to find water, or if I want to know whether today will be a good day to hunt—all I have to do—"

She offended me by interrupting yet again. Headmaster Olubiwi had enough presence of mind to turn toward Simon and comment on the quality of the meal, as if her behavior posed no problem. But I could see the three teachers peeking out from their lowered gazes, watching. "You mean to say it's the finger of a human being? A regular *person?*" Janet asked.

I paused for a second to collect myself. Her voice had an accusing tone about it that I didn't like. "Of course. What else would a soothsayer be? A horse?"

Everyone laughed and I saw her make an effort to pull her attention away from the bones.

"But you must tell me more about America," I said, seizing the opportunity to change the subject. "I understand that many children of Africa live there. Tell me, is it true that they all live side-by-side? Yorubas and Ibos and Hausas, all together?" *That* got Headmaster Olubiwi's attention. He looked shocked by the idea that such different peoples could possibly live together.

"Well, I don't know about that," Janet said. "I don't think there are many of us black Americans who can trace our histories all the way back to Africa. The fact is, most of us don't have any idea where our ancestors came from. Or even who they were."

It was my turn to be shocked. *Not know who one's ancestors were*? I could not conceive of the possibility. Knowing and honoring one's ancestors was only the most important duty of one's life, that's all. How could her people go on living under such conditions of depravity?

"Ah, yes," I said nervously, trying again to change the disgusting topic. "Because of the disruption brought about by slavery, is it not so? A very bad thing, slavery. Especially the way the whites practiced it, which was much different from the way we did. But I have heard it said that the adversity of slavery gave you black Americans some of your great leaders."

"Like who?"

"Well, like . . ." I remembered the only black American I'd ever heard about—probably the only black that white Americans at that time had ever heard about, too—and I thought to dazzle my guests with my extensive understanding of faraway America. ". . . like George Washington Carver!" I finished triumphantly.

She rolled her eyes in what was almost a juju gesture. "Oh, puh-leese! Don't drag up those old names from a hundred years ago. Get with it, Isaiah! What about all our modern leaders? What about Ralph Bunche? What about Martin Luther King? What about . . ."

I could take no more of it. She'd spurned my food. She'd gawked rudely at my juju. She'd interrupted me repeatedly. Now she even ridiculed my knowledge. I rose to my feet and slammed my hand hard against the table. "*Atoto!*" I shouted. "Enough of your noise! Will you continue to shame me before my guests? Do you not know meekness?"

She jumped up and slammed her own hand against the table, just as loudly as I had. My other guests jumped at the boldness of the child. " 'Meekness?' " she repeated. "How can you—a Nigerian—say that women have to be meek? Nigerian women have more power than any other women in Africa—maybe even in the world!"

It was true. The economic power of Nigerian women was only just beginning to be felt in those days. But already the message was clear to anyone with the wit to read it and it was becoming a sore point among our men. In southern Nigeria, buying and selling has always been thought of as "woman's work"; men here have always believed that commerce is unmanly. So women have always been the ones to take any extra produce of the family farm to market. Women have always transacted the sales and women have always handled the cash. The inevitable result, especially when petrodollars began to flood the country, was that the economic power of the nation would tend to flow toward women.

And so it happened. Many of the major international companies of Nigeria are owned, or at least controlled, by women, including some of the big oil interests. Even the office towers of Lagos and Ibadan are often owned by women's "clubs."

But Nigerian women still knew how to behave meekly, keeping up appearances in accordance with our customs. And that's what this little slip of a girl from America was *not* doing.

I controlled my rage. I tried to make my voice icy as I told her, "I bear you no ill will. Simply admit that you have behaved shamelessly and apologize to me and we will say no more about it."

I really felt I was being more than fair.

Janet did not seem to share my feeling. "Apologize to *you?* Well, I like that!" She picked up her purse and grabbed the arm of her Egba girlfriend, who looked as if she was about to faint. "Go try to make conversation with some guy who's wearing soup bones around his neck!" she said to the girl.

So now, she was belittling the sacred juju of a *babalawo*! Really, it was too much. It had gone beyond even insolence; this was sacrilege!

I fully expected that *Shango* would unleash one of his thunderbolts on her and split her in two. But for some reason known only to himself, the god refrained from taking this perfectly justifiable action; strange are the ways of the *orisha*.

"Stop!" I commanded. "You cannot leave. You must apologize; I am a *babalawo!* You must apologize!"

She stopped in the doorway and turned back toward me for a moment. She said, "Oh, drop dead, creep." She spun on her heel and left, dragging her hapless friend behind her.

Simon grabbed my arm and squeezed it in fear. "You heard her, Isaiah? You heard her? 'Drop dead,' she said. It is an *epe*, a curse on you!"

I reached under my tunic and clutched my *ibante* reassuringly. "We shall see about it," I said grimly. "Who this 'creep' is, though, I don't know—maybe one of her gods."

Then I understood why *Shango* had not struck her dead; he had left that task for me. "Soon, Simon," I said, "we shall see if her 'creep' is a match for my *Shango*. We shall show all the world who has the stronger gods!"

Headmaster Olubiwi knew when things were too close for comfort. He rose, bowed, thanked me, and took his leave immediately. We did not even go through the usual charade in which I would beg him to stay and he would decline and we would do this again and again until finally we would agree on just one more mug of wine for each of us.

The three teachers did not even think to add their thanks to the headmaster's; they just took to their heels, leaving the cafeteria free for me and Simon to plot our juju revenge on the American girl.

The only one who seemed happy about the way things

turned out was Speedy. He sat himself down at the end of the table and took a big swig of Janet's untouched maize beer. He followed it up with a huge chunk of *ragout* dipped in mint sauce.

"Good sauce, Boss," he said cheerily.

22

Simon urged me to turn Janet's curse back on her, to cause her to "drop dead." And I suppose I should have; turning a curse back on its originator is, of course, the jujuman's version of justice.

But I wanted to teach her a lesson more than to destroy her. After all, she was only a child. And an American, at that, totally ignorant of our ways. So the first curse I put on her was a mild one. It's a popular one, though, among the *babalawos* where I come from:

> Call upon *Olofin-Aye* (the *orisha* who controls famine and food) to witness. Sacrifice a pigeon. Then insert two pins or needles into its stomach. Tell *Olofin-Aye* to "sour all fruit and meat in the stomach of" your victim. Then transfer one of the pins to a piece of any fruit or vegetable, leaving the other pin in the belly of the bird. Bury the carcass of the bird. Place the piece of fruit on top of the burial spot and let it rot there.

This is a well-known curse, for which success is often claimed. It produces symptoms indistinguishable from those of common food poisoning. Its power to induce real sickness is taken for granted by most *babalawos*. This is despite all the unbelievers who argue that, in a land where refrigeration is uncommon and where Western standards of hygiene are not always observed when food is prepared, frequent bouts of mild stomach problems are to be expected anyway.

I laid the "belly curse" that very night. I did not go out of my way to look for Janet or to get news of her for some time after that. There was no trick to avoiding her because she didn't live at Normal with the rest of us. She lived in town with her father who dropped her off every morning on his way to work on the power plant. But even if she'd lived in the next dorm, I would still have avoided her. It's always best to give one's *epes* time to work. In fact, sometimes months elapse before one gets to take credit for the belly-ache every victim experiences sooner or later.

When I finally did see her, it was purely by chance. Simon and I were walking to a class and spotted her across the central square.

"Huh! She looks okay!" Simon said, shocked.

"Give it time to work," I reminded him.

"Yeah? Well, it's been weeks now. Maybe something went wrong. Why don't you go talk to her, see how she's been feeling?"

"Me? Not a chance. I don't ever want to talk to that girl again after the way she behaved."

He stopped walking and stared at me, hard. "Is Isaiah, of the Oke clan, afraid of a girl's juju?"

I laughed. "Don't say ridiculous things, Simon. I just don't see any reason to start up with her again, that's all."

He thought about it a second before he said, "Okay, then. I'll see to it myself." He trotted across the open square to challenge her.

From where I stood, I couldn't hear what they said. But it clearly wasn't friendly because, after a few words had been exchanged, he raised his hand as if to strike her. She put her hands on her skinny little hips and said something that made him freeze like a statue. Then she shook her finger at him and he backed up, as if she were cursing him as well. He turned and ran, a man being chased by an invisible lion. He slid to a stop and tried to hide himself behind me, just like a child hiding behind its mother.

"Now she has cursed me, also! She told me to 'drop dead,' just like she told you. Only she shook her finger before my face as she said it. Right in my face! This is some powerful American juju, I know it! Oh, Isaiah, will I die?"

He was panicking while Janet walked away toward her class as if the incident was trivial. Others around the square stood looking at us with open curiosity. It was mortifying.

"Stop that!" I hissed at Simon, pulling the hem of my garment out of his hands. "You will not die. Have I died because the witch cursed me? No! Therefore, you will not die, either."

He came out from behind me and faced the spot where Janet had stood. "Forgive me, Isaiah. But I am not a *babalawo* like you; I cannot face up to juju by myself. Protect me!"

"Come," I told him. "We need not attend our class. Instead, let us prepare to destroy her."

As we went back toward the Palace, I thought I saw where I had gone wrong: I had neglected to let her *see* what I was doing to curse her. With another Yoruba, it would not have been necessary to go to such trouble. Often, the very knowledge that one has angered a *babalawo* is enough to cause intense physical pain, even before a curse is laid. But this young witch apparently had a background so different from ours that she failed to appreciate power unless she saw it for herself.

So this time, we laid our plans more carefully. I sent Simon to the market square with some money and instructions to buy a young monkey and some other items. Meanwhile, I went into the forest to begin gathering the other necessary materials. It took several trips over the course of two or three days until I was able to gather together everything that would be needed. Then I invited Simon and two other men, whom I did not know well but who came well recommended, to accompany me out to my shrine in the forest. They would act as my seconds during the ritual.

It took place at night, naturally. While Simon and I got the monkey ready for sacrifice, the other men started a rhythm on the *sekere* drums I'd brought. Both of them had the reputation of being good musicians and they justified it. In perfect unison, they snapped the sleeves of cowries that surrounded the calabash bodies of the drums. I could have enjoyed it purely as music; the fact that every beat was putting power into the ritual I was about to perform was an added bonus.

I passed around several of the hollowed-out fruits of the *osuigwe* plant which I'd filled with palm wine. The British used to claim that *osuigwe* and alcohol was a remedy against malaria. But we West Africans know it as the kind of mild hallucinogenic that plays a role in both our public ceremonies and, to a somewhat greater extent, in our secret rituals. Today, of course, some jujumen use street drugs for their rituals. Such traffic is usually ignored by our law enforcement authorities, because the drugs are said to be for devotional rather than recreational use. But in fact, the drugs they buy are often resold.

For our ritual, I needed to heighten the effect that *osuigwe* would produce. I considered having everyone chew raw seeds of the candlewood plant. But I've always regarded it as dangerous; I've known people to become so enamored of the seeds we call *ata* that they become addicted to the stuff.

So instead, I brought some thin latex which I'd bled from an *ayan* tree. I dipped a parrot feather into the powerful stuff. Then, very carefully and gently, I drew the feather across the eyeballs of each of us, starting with myself so the others could see there was nothing to fear. Between the two hallucinogenics—the *osuigwe* and the *ayan*—it required only the least suggestion from me that something was about to happen to the monkey. They stared toward where the little animal was tied up with a mixture of dread and excitement on their faces.

Simon was the first to see it. He'd never been to any but the simplest rituals before so it was no surprise that he was almost overcome by what he saw.

"Look!" he cried out in a shaky voice. "The monkey . . . it grows!"

The rest of us then saw that it was true; before our eyes, the monkey became taller. First to the level of a man's waist. Then to his chin. Then it was as tall as a man. "Keep playing," I said to the men, as I walked toward the monkey.

"Who is in you?" I asked it.

But the monkey just stared at me.

Again, I asked, louder this time, "Who is in you?"

It still refused to answer. I turned back and scooped up the pack of "bribes" I'd told Simon to buy in town: a string of brightly colored beads, a baby's rattle, and a can of snuff, which I opened before setting it down. To these items, I also added some bananas. I laid the whole before the monkey.

"Please accept these gifts," I told it, bowing. "Now, tell me: Who is inside you?" The monkey reached down (it was now taller than any of us men) and took up the can of snuff.

Aha, snuff! Snuff is a thing for men, not for animals or spirits. So it made sense, I thought, that he who was residing in the monkey must have been a man at one time.

The monkey looked at the snuff for a moment as if he was wondering what it was. Then he raised it to his nose and took a big sniff. He dropped the can abruptly, as if startled, and for the first time, I heard him: "Baba-Tunde!" he barked through his nose. And again, "*Baba-Tunde!*" rubbing furiously at his nose. "BABA-TUNDE!"

Tranlated, this means, "an old man."

So. The next question to be settled was, *which* old man?

Not my father, certainly. Nor my grandfather; he was living in *this* world still, as far as I knew. Could it be the father of my grandfather? Yes, perhaps that's who it was.

"O, great Baba-Tunde: A witch has cursed your servant. Will you not help the son of your grandson?"

Baba-Tunde took up the rattle, looked it over still rubbing at his nose, and then shook it.

"He shakes his *ase!*" Simon cried. "Hear it? What can this mean?"

"It means he will help, you fool! Now keep silence while I speak with this, my great ancestor!" I spat on the ground to show my displeasure. Simon put his head down, properly chastened at interfering with the work of a *babalawo*.

When I turned back to Baba-Tunde, he had grown to where his head touched the lowest branches of the trees. "O, great Baba-Tunde: What punishment will suffice for this witch? Please choose a scourge and visit it upon her. For by insulting me, she has insulted all our generations of the clan Oke."

Baba-Tunde threw the rattle aside. He shook his head, which was now up in the tree branches, and he rubbed his nose again. He barked out his name some more—"*Baba-Tunde!* BABA-TUNDE!"—and his eyes started watering heavily, the huge drops crashing to the ground around me like buckets of water dropped from a tree. For a moment I was reminded of the sneezing and weeping reaction of one unaccustomed to snuff. But I knew that couldn't be: My great-grandfather used it all the time and, having decided it was he in the monkey, it made no sense that the monkey would be sneezing from snuff.

Then Baba-Tunde reached up and rubbed his eyes, hard, shaking the tears off his paws when he was done. And at once, I understood.

"O, great Baba-Tunde, I understand: She has seen our shame. Therefore, she should see no more, ever again; you will strike her blind!"

I bowed respectfully in recognition of the favor he was granting me. At that moment, one of the men playing the drums screamed. I looked at him in time to see his head go back, as if he was watching a bird fly high in the sky. A look of maximum horror crossed his upturned face. Then he passed out, his mouth open and dripping spittle. I reflected that I should have warned him not to be afraid of learning the secrets of the monkey. Or of *anything* that might go on during the ritual, for that matter. But it all happened too fast for me to prepare him.

Fear is contagious. The first man's fear spread to the man next to him, and then to Simon. They both looked upwards, screamed, and fainted, just as the first man had done. I offered a prayer of thanks that, as a *babalawo*, I was immune to such fear.

Then I turned back to find that Baba-Tunde had grown again. Now he had grown even taller than the trees. His feet filled all the clearing. His body was bigger than any mountain. He let out a roar so loud that it seemed to come from right inside my head. But I knew it was real because I could feel it shaking the earth I was trying to stand on. Then, even as I leaned back as far as I could to watch, his head went higher and then higher yet, until it became the Moon overhead, grinning down at me.

By the time we all came to, Baba-Tunde apparently had gone back to the Spirit World because the monkey was back to normal size again, tethered right where we'd put it earlier. I felt foolish momentarily because I'd forgotten to get Baba-Tunde's permission to sacrifice it. That would have been seemly in as much as it had been his host, however briefly.

But Baba-Tunde knew the rituals as well as I did; he would expect me to complete this one. So I drew my blade across the monkey's throat and caught some of the blood in one of the *osuigwe* cups. We all took a taste, even Simon, who took just enough to wet his lips. Then I removed the left paw and wrapped it in a banana leaf to preserve it.

Monkey is a delicacy among us, so I skinned it and butchered it quickly. I discarded the entrails and the head, which we buried in one of the pits in the little clearing. The meat I split with the two musicians because Simon didn't want any. He took the skin, though. Then we hiked all the way back to Normal College.

The others must have been as exhausted as I was. When we finally got to the campus, they all split up as fast as thieves and, without even a whispered word, they all ran to their rooms. I yawned, envying them.

But it wasn't until I completed my last remaining task that I finally tumbled onto my mat for a righteous, well-deserved sleep. After all, the whole idea was for the witch-girl to *know* she'd been cursed. Anonymously . . . mysteriously . . . mystically.

When I fell asleep at last, it was with a smile, wondering what the witch-girl's reaction would be when she opened her door the next morning.

23

But she didn't go blind. Nor did she ever get that bellyache. In fact, it was difficult to tell exactly *what* effect my juju was having on her.

Other than to make her quite angry, of course. She awakened me the next morning with such a pounding at the aluminum door of the Palace that it shook in its frame. I answered it myself; my juju fees had been dropping steadily while she remained so healthy, so when they finally fell off to nothing, I'd had to let Speedy go.

Janet stood defiantly in front of the trailer. She was accompanied by Mr. Agura, one of our younger teachers. It was a condition of his employment at Normal College that he act as "resident student advisor" in addition to his other duties. The title meant that, until a newer and more desperate teacher was hired, he had to live on campus, available at a moment's notice to any student who might claim his help. Times were hard just then and positions for educated Africans were few. But at that moment, with a *babalawo* looking down at him, Mr. Agura appeared unhappy that he'd ever accepted the job.

Janet held up a hunk of newspaper. She peeled back a corner and exposed the monkey's paw. The blood was dry and the paw had begun to look rather dessicated. "Is this your idea of a joke, you creep?" she demanded.

I blinked. Perhaps "creep" was not so good a word as to describe one of her gods after all. Then I smiled blandly in an attempt to recover. "I have no idea what you mean."

"No? Well, somebody tied *this* to the doorknob of my house last night." She shoved the paw toward me and shook it in my face. "I've asked around and they tell me it's more of your stupid juju." She flung it at me, newspaper and all. I ducked and it splatted up against the wall inside the Palace.

"Now you listen to me, Mr. Jujuman Oke: I don't want any more of your juju junk around me. I'm a good Christian girl, so save it for somebody who believes in it, okay? And Mr. Agura is going to see that you do. Isn't that right, Mr. Agura?"

Mr. Agura seemed unable to speak. He was so unnerved that I wondered whether he might be a jujuman himself. I rolled my eyes in the pattern that makes up one of our many juju recognition signals—the left, back, up, back, repeated very rapidly three times. It was the kind of thing that a non-jujuman would not be likely to notice. Or, if he did, to discount it as just a facial tic. But a jujuman, of course, would give another secret signal in reply. Among us, whole conversations take place in this way without a word ever being exchanged. But the only response in Mr. Agura's case was a rapid oscillation of that lump in his throat that Westerners call "Adam's apple." It wasn't any juju signal that I knew of so I concluded the poor fellow was not one of us; he was merely scared out of his wits.

His reaction was typical, though, of even educated Africans: We still find it difficult to confront juju. In fact, it's much easier to simply pretend it no longer exists. Admitting that juju continues to be such a potent influence on our people is an embarrassment to our determination to be modern. So the most sophisticated among us simply deny it. And, when forced to face it, we're as ill-prepared and uncomfortable as Mr. Agura was in the presence of a real, live jujuman.

Janet continued to accuse me. "If you didn't hang that disgusting object on my door, who did?"

I smiled at her condescendingly. There was no need for me to intimidate the child further; it was enough that she knew she was under a terrible curse. "Now, young lady, you accuse me falsely. I tell you I have no idea what you're talking about."

She shook her head in disgust. "You aren't even man enough to own up to it. Doesn't it bother you to lie like that?"

Actually, it didn't; there is no moral standard in juju against lying. What *did* bother me, though, was that a small crowd had begun to watch the exchange. They were waiting not to hear the truth, but to see my power. The problem was, I'd already used some pretty heavy-duty curses on Janet to no visible effect. She remained unharmed even though others had confirmed for her that she was the object of a juju attack mounted by one who was reputed to have access to overwhelming power in the Invisible World. Yet, here she stood: not only unafraid, but defying me—*challenging* me—in front of everyone.

And for the first time in my life, I saw the courage that comes from an independent will. This little girl didn't fear me because she didn't fear my gods. On the contrary, the fear had become all mine; I was afraid to try any more of my huge store of traditional curses on her. It wasn't that I was afraid she would turn them back on me, as I would if I were cursing another *babalawo*. It was even worse than that; I was afraid that nothing—absolutely *nothing*—would happen.

I continued to proclaim my innocence. But I knew that I no longer held any conviction of power or of faith in myself. I could feel it: I was becoming afraid of *her*, rather than the other way around.

She scolded me a while longer. I tried to bluster my way through, but I didn't fool anybody; even Mr. Agura dared to snicker toward the end. I glared at him and he choked off his laughter, so at least I still retained that much influence. But it was small consolation.

When she'd said her piece, Janet turned and left with Mr. Agura in tow. I tried to save face by saying loudly, "Yes, you may go; you are dismissed now." But there were some titters from the crowd and, embarrassed, I retreated into the Palace of the Ejo.

There was no denying it: It was time to get tough. I would have to use the Power that frightened even me.

24

I got ready to meet the Power. It was something I'd dared to do only three times previously in my life: Once when Grandfather told me to go into the forest and fast and seek out my own special spirit helper; again shortly after my initiation; and finally, after my encounter with Esu. It was not an experience I looked forward to; the Power helped me but that didn't mean it was my friend.

I journeyed in secret back to the forest around Inesi-Ile to make my preparation. Without letting anyone know of my presence, I hid myself near Grandfather's Shrine. For three days, I took no water when I thirsted, but drank only a mixture of palm wine, vinegar, and a little blood from a chicken I'd killed. I took no solid food either, but chewed only the yellowish root of the plant we call *iboga*. *Iboga* is a deceptively innocent-looking shrub of the family scientists know as *Tabernanthe*. The name by which we call it is designed to deflect suspicion that the plant might be important; it means only, "This belongs to the Ibo people." *Iboga* grows wild in the Ibo territory down in Gabon and probably originated there. But jujumen all through West and Central Africa have cultivated it since time immemorial for its narcotic effects.

I prayed continuously during the three days, demanding

help from every god I could think of, while I accompanied myself on a drum to get their attention. I slept almost not at all. Whenever I did drop off, my sleep was of poor quality, troubled by vicious, colorful gods who leapt from branch to branch in the surrounding trees, screaming and jeering at me.

The third night, a great serpent came to me in my sleep. It tried to crush me in its coils, just as it had at my initiation. Only it succeeded this time. After forcing all the air out of me, it opened its jaws wide and swallowed me whole.

There was a terrible pressure all around me, as if the hand of God was squeezing me like a rubber ball. I remember thinking as I was forced down the serpent's gullet, *Being born must be something like this.*

There came a moment of relief when I popped out into the comparative roominess of the serpent's stomach. But it was short-lived as I saw all the others the great serpent had eaten: a hyena, a parrot, a horse, a leopard, a giant spider, and many others.

They knew everything; they took turns reciting the secret doubts and fears that I had tried to keep inside me. They all kept telling me that they hated me because I'd shamed my people, whereas they never had: The spider claimed to have been a good spider, the leopard a good leopard, and so forth. But I had not been a good man, they said. Certainly not a good *juju*man, because I'd let myself be influenced by foreign ideas until I'd begun to doubt the ways of my own people. They were offended, the animals told me, at being compelled to share the serpent's stomach with such a traitor to his ancestors. They kept saying that they would like to kill me and eat me. But they couldn't since the serpent had already done that and now we would all have to be together in its stomach forever.

That dream was the worst of them. But all the others I'd had over the three days were of a similar quality. Yet, unpleasant though the period of preparation was, I dreaded its end. Because that meant going to face the Power. As the Sun's descent marked the beginning of my fourth day in the forest, I could put it off no longer. With dread pulling me back at every step, I walked the short distance to the mahogany grove.

Mahogany is the most noble of the woods produced by our forest. It is durable, yet not so hard that it cannot be worked. It is abundant and it is beautiful when finished. We have long used it as a primary building material. In addition, it provides a wealth of medical products to whomever is knowledgeable.

And in our forest, there is what we call a "grove" of mahogany trees, although it is really an entire section of forest—more mahogany than my people can use in one hundred lifetimes. And in that grove, there is one special tree, one sacred tree—a living giant, hollowed out untold years ago by one of *Shango's* lightning bolts.

I first found the sacred tree when I was but a boy. I had been training under Grandfather for just a few years then, so I was only about ten years old. He sent me into the forest to seek out my "special spirit," the private one that is unique for each *babalawo*. He promised it would become the ultimate Power in my life. But he warned me that this Power could only be experienced as the product of a long, hard, and lonely quest.

I'd been wandering alone in the woods, hungry, cold, and frightened, for perhaps ten days before I saw the hollow tree. *Struck by lightning*, I thought when I first saw it, *and yet it lives!* I was small for my age and the hollow was ample for my frame back then. I climbed inside, oblivious of the weevils and the other vermin, and called out to the Great Spirit who must surely rule such a magical tree.

A deep voice spoke authoritatively inside my head, demanding to know who dared disturb his repose. I said my name, but there was no further response. I brushed some of the bugs away from my face and said my name again, out loud this time. There was still no answer.

Then, trembling inside the tree, I whispered my Name, that secret word given to me the seventh day after my birth that identified me uniquely and forever to the residents of the Invisible World.

Immediately, the Power of the mahogany tree began to say *his* Name in my mind. It was more than just a label; it was a Name that embodied the Power's whole history and identity. His Name was so long that it took hours for the Power to tell. It boasted of the forces he could control and the demons he could command. It remembered what men he had possessed and it predicted who he would possess in time yet to come, even out to ten generations from now. It conveyed his hatred of mankind in general and of *me* in particular. It made me tremble and weep at the malevolence, the hatred, the sheer evil that were the sources of this Power.

And yet, when the recitation was over, the Power was under my control, because I had heard his Name. But the Power was so wicked, so vile, that I should never dare to call upon it, except in times of extremity. Now, as I squeezed myself into the hollow space that I'd long since outgrown, I cringed with the thought of what the Power would say when I confessed that a mere *girl* had caused me to come running for his help.

But, unlike the previous times I'd sought the Power, there was no answer in my mind. For hours I called, weevils nestling in my ears and nostrils, my skin rubbed raw from the tight, woody little womb, my bones sore from the cramped confinement. During all that time I praised the Power; I begged him; I pleaded with him; I condemned and cursed him. But all to no avail. My mind remained empty of an answer.

I called all night, while the *iboga* wore off and I started to become aware of how much physical harm I was doing to myself. With the coming of the dawn, the bugs became less vigorous in their attacks on my squashed, naked body. But that was the only difference. There was still no answer from the Power.

It wasn't until the Sun started heating the hollow tree like an oven that I finally tumbled out, sore everywhere and sick from the smell of my own sweat. I lay on the ground for a while, looking at the home of the great Power that had lived in a dark part of my mind since childhood. I was tired, hungry, and lonely. I was bruised and bloodied, achey and sore.

But I was also sober for a change, free from the narcotic effects of both *iboga* and religious ecstasy. For the first time, I was able to see that the mystical home of the dreaded Power was nothing more than an old hollow tree.

I picked myself up and washed in a nearby stream. I ate a breakfast of wild plantains and water from the stream. But it couldn't fill up the hollow feeling I had inside; my own private god had turned out to be a shadow of a starved, drug-numbed brain. For me, juju had turned out to be such a powerless joke that it could be jeered at safely, even by a child like Janet.

And, if all that was true of the supposedly omnipotent juju, what of *me*—the *babalawo* Isaiah Oke, a god and the son of gods? Did I have no special power over nature after all? Was I to be just another struggling human being, like everybody else?

I eventually made my way back to Normal and let myself into the trailer, ignoring all the notices taped to my door that, in the opinion of the headmaster, I was seriously truant and faced possible expulsion. But my need to act out my new resentment of juju was stronger than any concerns over school. The first thing I did was to dismantle my *ile-agbara*, my private "power house." Until I started to remove it all, I hadn't realized how much my juju collection

had grown over the years: an old perfume bottle with a
squirt bulb at the end of a long rubber hose, a piece of
somebody's grave marker, the rusty breech of a World War
I rifle, a colorful umbrella that I'd found on the grounds of
the Lagos Colony Golf and Country Club, the mummified
head of a lizard, a glass doorknob, a dried beef heart, and
on and on and on. I'm sure it would have filled several
boxes, had I troubled to pack it. But I just scooped it up,
armful after armful, and flung it out the front door of the
trailer. There was no reason for me to be ceremonious; I'd
begun to think of it as "junk" rather than "juju."

My last act of sacrilege was to cut off my *ibante*. I slipped
a knife under it, but then found myself unable to make the
cut. I had worn it for so long that removing it would be like
amputation. It had become the same color as my skin. It
looked like it was part of my body, like a small roll of fat
around my middle; I hadn't thought of it as anything other
than a part of me for years. In spite of everything, it still
took an effort for me to see my *ibante* for what it really was:
a source of rashes, a home for fleas and ticks, and a
generator of strange smells.

Pulling together my courage, I slashed through the *ibante*
violently, first at my waist and then on each thigh. It
crackled like dry dead reeds when the knife blade bit
through. I went to the door and threw the filthy, petrified
rag as far away as I could. Then I fell onto my sleeping mat
and, for the first time I could remember, I felt naked.

I wept and then I slept. At one point, one of my
roommates—Lazarus, a premed student—rapped on my
door and asked whether I was all right, but I ignored him
and he went away. I guess he told the others that I didn't
want to be bothered because nobody came by after that,
though I kept waking up at the sound of people coming and
going.

I must have gone off my head for a bit because they
eventually had to break my door down. I hadn't eaten

anything substantial in over a week by that time and I'd also suffered a series of very painful emotional shocks. I remember being tended by the school physician and by my friend Simon, who knelt at the side of my sleeping mat and fed me because I was too weak to do it for myself.

When I finally came out, I learned that I'd been expelled for unexcused absence. There was a time when nobody would have dared take such an action. But now, after witnessing the impotence of juju before the defiance of a little American Christian girl, everybody around me seemed to have found his or her courage. Nobody feared the future *babalorisha* of Yorubaland anymore.

It was at that point that I understood my loss was total, a loss of public status as well as of private faith.

And I went looking for Janet.

FREEDOM

25

I caught up with Janet in the school's cafeteria. She was chatting amiably with her fellow freshmen, just as if she'd not destroyed every belief that gave my life meaning. The group scattered when I sat down across from her, all except for Janet. She stood her ground, even though she looked frightened.

"Hey," she said, "I don't want any trouble."

"I do not intend any trouble for you," I told her. "I merely want to talk with you."

She looked suspicious. "About what?"

"About why you did not fear my juju."

She looked as if she really preferred not to discuss the subject. But, with an air of exasperation, she said, "I already told you, Isaiah: I'm an American. We don't believe in stuff like juju. We don't believe that it can hurt anybody. We think it's just silly superstition."

Then, as an afterthought, she added, "No offense."

I waved her apology off. "Whatever its source, I must possess this power of yours," I said. "I can give you some things of value. I own a nice piece of land, for example, near my village—it could be sold for hard currency. Also I have some jewelry, items I used to wear sometimes on special occasions for juju ceremonies. I no longer have any

211

need of it." I coughed to cover up my horror at what I was saying. "All of it is yours, if you will just sell me your gods."

At first, she looked confused. Then, after a moment, she shook her head and smiled. She said slowly, as if I were a baby, "There's nothing for me to sell. I mean, we Americans are the way we are because we're free. And nobody has to sell you freedom. It's what we call a 'right'; it belongs to everybody already."

"It does?"

"Sure. And if you don't have any, it's just because somebody took it away from you. So what you have to do is take it back." She nodded her head sharply, as if to say that everything was settled.

I stared at her in total confusion. What was the child on about? Nigeria had been free from Great Britain for almost three years. It hadn't made any great difference that I could see. Not in the lives of ordinary people, anyway, except maybe to make things worse. In fact, there was constant strife between our dozens of political parties. There were even those who said that a bloody civil war between us and the Ibos was inevitable. If that's what she meant by "freedom," she could have it.

"But what about your gods?" I said. "I have seen you Christians before and I have not understood you." I remembered the strange people in Ghana, who sang and performed their rituals in broad daylight, in white buildings with open windows, where anybody going by could see in. "But I did not know you Christians possessed a power greater than juju. Please," I said, "sell me your gods. I will worship them vigorously; I will feed them all their favorite foods. They will be happy if you sell them to me, you'll see."

She was beginning to relax a little in my presence, I thought. She even rolled her eyes up in her head the way I'd seen her do before when she wanted to express impatience.

"There are no gods to 'buy,' " she said. "Christians pray to *Christ*. And Christ is free."

" 'Free?' " I repeated. "Ah! Then he, too, must be an American, this Christ fellow. Is it not so?"

This time she even managed a little laugh. "Well, lots of us would like to think so. But no, we can't get away with saying that." She idly traced patterns on the table with her finger. *Juju!* I thought instantly and automatically. Then I mentally slapped myself for thinking it. I had lived so long under the spell of juju that it was going to take a while for me to learn not to be what this American child called a "creep."

Janet glanced at me from a lowered head, as if she were embarrassed. "Look, Isaiah, if you're so interested in Christianity, I can fix it for you to talk to somebody who can explain it better than me."

I was surprised. "Better than you? You mean, you do not know all? You are not one of the high priestesses of this Christianity?"

She showed impatience again. "Not hardly. I'm just an ordinary school kid. I mean, I go to church on Sunday and I read the Bible and all, but I'm hardly the one to preach to heathens. No offense. I mean, I'm nobody special."

"And yet, you speak of your religion openly," I said with wonder, "as if you did not even fear your god. You discuss him with strangers. You hide nothing."

"Yeah, well. It's that same freedom thing again, that I told you about before. If you become a Christian, you'll understand."

"*Me?*" I said, shocked. "Me, a Christian? It is so easy to become one, then?"

"It's a lot easier than becoming an American, that's for sure. Look, why not have a talk with Dr. Osborn? You'll like him—he's a wonderful man, very understanding and warm. He's our local pastor here."

" 'Pastor?' "

"Kind of like a, what do you call it, a *'babalulu'*?"

"*Babalawo*," I corrected. "He speaks to your god for you, this Osborn?"

"We *all* speak to God for ourselves. But a pastor is . . . well, he's kind of a teacher. Our spiritual leader, you might say."

So! A *babalorisha*. Just what I'd spent my own life preparing to be. Surely he and I would have so much in common that he might condescend to share some of his great secrets with me.

I felt myself perspiring with anticipation. "Do you think he might be persuaded to regard me as a colleague, this Osborn?" It was difficult to keep the excitement out of my voice. "Do you think maybe, if I worked hard, I also could be a *pastor?* This is the kind of work for which my grandfather trained me, you see, and—"

"Whoa, Isaiah! One step at a time. First, let me set up an appointment for you to meet Doctor Osborn. Then see what you think, okay?"

I liked Doctor Osborn very much and I have always flattered myself that the feeling was mutual. He was small and slight, but very strong-minded. He reminded me of Grandfather.

He must have had vast experience in relating to those who were troubled. He visited the headmaster on my behalf and asked him to check with the school physician to see how ill I'd been. It was only through Doctor Osborn's efforts that the decision to expel me was modified. True, I had to spend the rest of the year on probation, but that was quite mild compared to expulsion.

Doctor Osborn made a place for me in his beginning Bible class at the mission church. His classes gave him a chance to display one of the reasons for his great success as a missionary: his skill as a storyteller. That's an essential quality for anyone who wants to communicate effectively with African tribal people, given our oral traditions. He kept us all so spellbound with Bible stories interspersed with tales of life in America that some of us failed to notice he was also converting us to the Christian faith.

But Christianity did indeed answer a need in my life that juju had left vacant. The innocent spontaneity of Doctor Osborn's little church refreshed me after all the blood and the exacting ritual of juju. And Christianity's emphasis on love through faith cleansed me after juju's lust for power through fear and violence.

That's not to say that my decision to become a Christian was immediate; my renunciation of juju had made me understandably suspicious of all religions. So I spent as much of my final year at Normal as possible examining this strange, nonviolent, monotheistic faith. I took every break I could from my academic studies to pester Doctor Osborn to teach me the Bible. In fact, I spent so much time reading the Bible and then trying to explain it to my classmates that I nearly flunked out. You know how new converts to *anything* are, right?

But Doctor Osborn went to bat for me again and convinced the administration to give me one last chance. Thanks to his many reminders about "Rendering unto Caesar what is Caesar's," I forced my concentration back to academic work. In the end, I achieved such a healthy balance between religious and secular concerns that my final grades turned out to be quite commendable after all.

As I began making ready to accept my diploma from Normal, I also accepted baptism from Doctor Osborn. For me, it was the culmination of a process that had begun long before; maybe in the old hollow tree, when I first admitted the bankruptcy of juju. Or maybe when I came away to college and was exposed to ways of seeing the world other than through juju eyes. Or maybe even back when Mr. Olungwe first taught me to read and opened my mind to the existence of philosophies other than juju. But no matter when my process of rebirth began, it was fulfilled when I heard the words of the baptism ceremony about "renouncing Satan and all his works." I took them to be a formal renunciation of juju and I felt clean afterward.

I sent word home—not about my conversion (I was not yet independent enough for *that*) but about my graduation. I had been allocated four tickets for people to come and witness the ceremony. I knew Grandfather himself could not come, of course. Nor would he be likely to send any of our young people who might be contaminated by this strange Western idea, this nonjuju "ceremony of the graduation." In the end, he made the decision to send four of our bravest and handsomest warriors, all staunch jujumen.

They attended the graduation ceremony in full battle regalia—spears, shields, parrot feathers, and all. The problem was, several other tribes were represented as well, and they all displayed their chalked facial markings with as much pride as my own kinsmen did. I thought that a war would break out right on the spot, the way they started glaring at each other. But the administration of Normal College had grown accustomed to such problems in our culturally diverse society and were prepared. They had volunteers on hand to go through the crowd welcoming each delegation in its own language and thanking it for letting all the others live.

I received my diploma amid wild shouts of pride from my contingent. They kept carrying on the same way all during the headmaster's "farewell tea" out on the parade ground. Since they'd been convinced not to fight with anybody, they apparently decided they would out-shout another band of warriors over on the opposite side of the field. The other warriors thought this a good idea so the two groups hurled verbal threats and imprecations over the heads of the tea drinkers for a full hour. They were so disorderly and loud that I wanted to dismiss them. But they had been ordered by my grandfather to give me an escort home, so the decision was not mine.

At first, Doctor Osborn chuckled at the thought of how embarrassing it would be for me, now an educated man and a good Christian, to ride the train with these fierce warriors and their weapons. Then he grew more sober and said he hoped they weren't dangerous. I told him they weren't, and that the really dangerous part wouldn't come until I got home.

When I faced Grandfather to tell him that I was no longer a jujuman.

26

But Grandfather knew. I don't know how he knew, but he knew. This time, he had prepared no feast, no celebration, no homecoming welcome for me.

As soon as we entered the village, I figured out that the men who'd been sent to my graduation were not really my honor guard after all; they were my jailers. They took up positions all around me, boxing me in. I tried to turn off into the lane toward my mother's house, but they pushed me back into their midst with the hafts of their spears. They refused to explain themselves and continued trying to walk me in the direction of Grandfather's compound. When I became insistent, one of them turned his spear's point toward my ribs, which convinced me to go with them meekly.

The old man was hoeing his garden. I wasn't sure at first that it was him. He'd lost still more weight but he moved as if he were carrying heavy weights inside of him. Performing such an everyday task as gardening was a tribute to him. Not just because he was no longer the man he once was, though that would have been reason enough. But there was also the confrontation with me that he clearly knew to be imminent. He had planned for me to be his legacy to his people, to be his claim to immortality. But no one can live

another's life for him, and he somehow knew that I had
chosen otherwise. His disappointment must have been deep
to the point of despair. And still, he hoed his garden.

My guards came to a stop, boxing me in. I bowed and
greeted Grandfather respectfully. He looked up from his
work, leaned on his hoe and just stared at me. At first, I
thought it was the same dispassionate look with which one
might study a bug before stepping on it. But after standing
under his gaze for a long time, I saw a tear come down his
wrinkled cheek.

He shook himself and gestured toward his private quarters. Two of the men took my arms, resolving any doubts I
might have had that I was being welcomed home. A jug of
palm wine and two mugs had been set out on a little low
table. Grandfather and I squatted on opposite sides of it like
enemies across a contested field. I hoped it wouldn't turn
into a yelling match, the way the parade ground had for the
warriors back at Normal College. We both held our tongues
until the men left.

When Grandfather finally spoke, his voice was very soft.
"Our ancestors have been crying out to me. They say they
are displeased with you; can you say why?"

"Honorable sir," I said with lowered head, "I know you
will be hurt by what I have to tell you and for that I am
sorry. I hope you will understand. But please do not talk to
me about 'communicating' with our ancestors; I no longer
believe in such things."

"Indeed?" He poured some palm wine for each of us, a
good host in spite of the pain on his face. Behind his
naturally dark complexion, there were large spots of a still
darker hue on his hands. Age, I thought, was overtaking
him faster than it had ever overtaken any other man. Either
that or. . . .

But I could not think it. I told myself that he was no
thinner, that his movements were no less smooth, that his
cheeks were no hollower than they had always been. That I

was looking at the early stages of "slim" disease in my beloved grandfather was something I could not face. Nor could he, apparently; he waved aside all my polite, but sincere, questions about his health and returned instead to the topic of religion.

"What do you believe in now," he asked, "since you no longer believe in communication with our ancestors?"

"I believe in Jesus, Honorable sir."

He sipped at his refreshment. "This is an *orisha* with whom I am not familiar. What is his power? What forces does he rule?"

Responding was pointless and I should have known it; there was too big a gulf between us now for me to make him understand. But I was filled with the kind of consuming zeal that religious converts so often show at first. It made me feel that I had to size every opportunity to display how determined my new faith was. So, I answered him humorlessly, as if he were asking me sincere questions instead of baiting me. "He has all power," I said. "He rules all forces."

"So this going away to school has taught you much—you have discovered a new, very powerful *orisha* for us. This is good." He offered me a kola nut from a bowl beside him. As I reached out, he seized my arm and peered suspiciously at my new wrist watch. "Is this part of the juju of your Jesus?"

"It's not juju; it's a gift," I answered stiffly. "From a dear friend, Doctor Osborn. He presented it to me to honor my graduation."

"Hmmmm." He cocked his head to one side and listened. He nodded in time to the ticking. His hearing must have been exceptionally acute for one of his years and poor health. Either that or Doctor Osborn had given me less of a watch than I thought. But after a few seconds, Grandfather seemed to lose interest and dropped my arm back into my lap.

"And what of that?" He pointed to my Bible, which I now carried at my side always.

I lifted it and shook it above my head, as I had seen Doctor Osborn do so often when he preached. "This is the word of God!" I said in my best pulpit voice.

He leaned forward and cocked his head over again toward my Bible. Then he leaned back and shrugged. "I hear nothing."

"It is a *written* word, a word which *I* am able to read. If you like, I can read it to you, Honorable sir. It will help you see how Jesus can save you."

"Thank you. Perhaps another day." He was being painfully polite but clearly wanted to get down to the *important* matter. "Now, tell me—how shall we appease this new *orisha* of yours? What is his food? How shall we sacrifice to him? What blood does he prefer?"

I shook my head. "It is very difficult to explain. Jesus demands no sacrifice. He wants no blood other than his own, which he has shed for all of us."

"Really?" Grandfather sat back and thought about that a bit. "He sounds like a most generous fellow, your Jesus."

"Oh, yes, Honorable sir: He is!"

"He sounds much more pleasant than our other *orisha;* I certainly hope he will get along with them."

I wouldn't let myself consider that Grandfather might be taunting me. But even if I had, I probably would have welcomed it at that stage of my life: It would have made me a martyr, in a way. And that would have made me feel good. "There are no *orisha* for him to get along with," I said, a little stiffly. "Jesus is the *only* God."

Grandfather raised his eyebrows. He calmly took another kola nut and munched on it. "No *orisha?* This will be a surprise to all the spirits who serve them—the spirits of the forest, the spirits of the air and the water, the spirits of the rocks and the trees and the grain and the animals."

I took a deep breath. "There are no such spirits, either, any more than there are *orisha*. There is only Jesus."

He sat back on his haunches again and appeared to think about this for a while. "So. No *orisha*. No spirits of nature." He shook his head as if confused. "Next, you will inform me that you have discovered some new facts about our esteemed ancestors: Perhaps that they are *not* all around us, after all, watching all our doings as we have always believed."

"Yes," I said gravely. "That is so. Our ancestors are in heaven, with Jesus." I stumbled a little over this last statement. My grounding in Christian theology wasn't very firm yet. I didn't know at that time how to respond to the charge that our ancestors didn't know Christ and, therefore, hadn't been saved. But there was no way I would dare tell Grandfather a thing like *that*.

The appearance of an open-minded seeker of knowledge began to fade from his face. "No ancestors? Then, who is it that I talk to when I seek help? Who is it that I see when I make ritual at my Shrine? Who is it that shows me hidden truths when I divine the future?"

I took a deep breath before answering. "All these things," I said with a sadness that masked my insensitivity, "are imagination and superstition. They are what Western people call hysteria."

"I see. You no longer believe, then? You no longer have any faith at all in our traditions?"

"No. Not in juju, anyway." I was burning with the desire to Witness, even to this poor, sick old man who had not the slightest chance of profiting from my testimony. I raised my face heavenward. "The only true religion is Christianity; all else is idolatry and nonsense."

The look of shock on his face was painful to me. "I'm sorry to have to tell you that," I added with a slightly smug air.

But the funny thing was, I really *was* sorry. Saying it in

that superior way reminded me of Janet saying, "No offense," every time she insulted me. I suddenly realized that I was being pointlessly cruel to a dreadfully ill old man whose beliefs were as genuine as my own. And, even if his *ideas* were crazy, I had every reason to love *him*.

Instantly, I was ashamed of myself. Why is charity always the last of the virtues to be learned by Christians? And by everybody else, for that matter? All of a sudden, I wanted desperately to find some way to make things right with the old man; I didn't want him to go to his grave hating me. But my remarks about our ancestors had taken things too far. He was actually shaking with rage, no longer bothering to hide the anger that I had so carelessly kindled. "Very well," he said. "Bring on this Jesus of yours. I would meet him. We will match him against *my* gods; then we will see who is who! Show him to me!"

"I cannot. He is not like *your* gods—pieces of old junk that you pretend are sacred. He is different. If I could only make you understand . . ."

"You will not permit me to see him?"

"I *cannot*, I tell you. He is only in my heart."

"Then, that's where we shall have to see him, isn't it?" He got to his feet and kicked the bowl of kola nuts across the floor. He drew himself up to all the height he could muster. "Take yourself out of my home. I place on you this Obligation: Go right now through all the streets of Inesi-Ile. Go far and wide. Tell all the people to make ready for a sacrifice tomorrow at dawn. No one is to stay in bed. No one is to go to the fields at that time or tend his flocks or start the firing of a pot. All must come to my square outside and witness the sacrifice."

A sacrifice? I didn't want to believe what he had in mind. But I could think of no other interpretation.

"Pa," I said, "look. Let's start again. I really didn't meant to offend you—"

"Me? Worry not about how you have offended me; worry

about how you have offended your ancestors! Only this Jesus who you keep in your heart will appease them!"

"Aw, Pa. Can't we just—"

"Enough! You have been placed under Obligation. Must I remind you what that means?"

It was more than a request, more than a suggestion. More than an order, even. Being placed under an Obligation by an elder meant performing the assigned task no matter the cost. Even if one's life was endangered, an Obligation had to be met. It had always been so in our clan. Especially after the confrontation we'd just had, I couldn't bring myself to let Grandfather down any further.

"Yes, Pa," I said, and ran from the house to do as the old man wished.

I'd gone through only two or three streets, stopping before each house to call out Grandfather's demands, when I heard a heavy tread behind me. I turned and saw Joshua's cruel face grinning down at me. We are not a tall people, and Joshua would have been judged big even by the standards of Americans. Towering over me, face heavily chalked, he was a sobering sight. Especially as he was carrying his machete casually at his side.

"So," he said, "the great Isaiah Oke has returned from his *school*." He said the word "school" as if it were as bitter in his mouth as the *oruwo* fruit from the brimstone tree. "You have learned the ways of the *white* man well, have you not, son-of-my-father's-brother?"

I tried to overlook his obnoxious tone as I ran on toward the next house to fulfill my duty. "Why do you molest me, Joshua?"

"I do not molest you," he said. "I escort you. On the wishes of our grandfather."

So, Grandfather no longer trusted me enough even to believe that I would carry out his Obligation voluntarily. It was a bitter realization, made no sweeter by the fact that he'd chosen Joshua to be my shadow. I stopped before the

next house and yelled out Grandfather's invitation to anyone
who might be inside. It struck me as incongruous that I
should be clutching my Bible for comfort while I invited
people to my own juju execution. Logically speaking, it
made no sense.

But I had to fulfill the filial duty imposed on me by
Grandfather. It was something my whole tribal experience
had conditioned me to do. To ignore an elder's direct orders
would have been unthinkable. "It is not necessary for you to
watch me, Joshua." I told him as I set off again. "I will do
as I have been Obligated to do; I am not without honor."

He merely laughed and threw me the juju hand sign
which means, "May your lie choke you."

It took about three hours to go all through the town. I was
hoarse and my feet were sore by the time we finished.
Joshua had stood loftily behind me at every house, idly
slapping his machete against his leg. The impression he
gave was that he was my keeper. It augmented my shame,
and he enjoyed it.

As I started back, I again tried to turn off down the path
toward my mother's house. She had not come out when I
stood before her door, shouting out the shame of my coming
sacrifice. But it was almost dark now, and maybe she would
let me in if I snuck around the back. Or maybe not. But I
thought I would try.

Joshua stepped in front of me, making the hand sign that
means, "May you lose your way." He blocked the lane like
a big, grinning wall.

"Please, Joshua, I want to go see my mother. I've been
through the whole town, as Grandfather ordered. So you
can go back now."

"Yes," he said with the kind of leer one sees on old men
who covet young girls at a festival. "I will go back. But you
will come with me."

"Joshua, I told you: I want to try to see my mother now."
The look on his face became still more obscene, it

seemed to me. He was getting real pleasure from being Grandfather's watchdog. "It is forbidden," he said. "You may never see her again. You are to come directly to our grandfather's compound where you will be held in the storeroom. Until it's time for sacrifice." His chest puffed out. He was enjoying his assignment. "And Grandfather has chosen me to ensure all this, Little Man."

"But I don't understand, Joshua. Have I not done all that Grandfather asked?"

"So far, yes. But he wants to be sure you're present for tomorrow's sacrifice. He'd be very hurt if you happened to miss it." He laughed down at me. His breath had the smell of one who is too lazy to clean his teeth well.

It was true that I hadn't yet made up my mind as to what I would do. Part of me was afraid that reconciliation with Grandfather was no longer possible, that his decision to sacrifice me was unchangeable. That part of me kept telling me to behave intelligently—to run for my life.

But another part of me wanted to believe that I could still reason with him—that if we could just talk to each other calmly, I could make it all well.

Joshua laughed loudly again, as if he already knew what the outcome would be. And that helped me decide. "Now, Joshua," I said in a hollow voice, "prepare for your end. Today may be your last day."

He gave me a haughty look. "Oh? What will you do, Little Man? Can you overcome the best warrior in Inesi-Ile? Can you outrun the fleetest legs? Can you prevail against the strongest arms?" He laughed at me again.

"No, Joshua," I looked up at him and very deliberately closed one eye while keeping the rest of my face as immobile as possible. "But can you stand against the power of . . . MY EYE?"

The derisive laughter cut off with a sharp intake of breath. His mouth fell open and he let out a kind of frightened squeak. It was an incongruous reaction from such a big, strong, well-armed man. But that's what juju does.

He dropped his machete and threw his forearm across his eyes. He aimed his other hand in my general direction in the universal hand sign for protection against "the evil eye." I saw his index finger and pinkie quiver like the horns of a nervous bull in the brief instant before I hit him in the stomach with everything I had. His breath exploded out of him, but he didn't go down. He just dropped both hands to his midsection and looked surprised.

So I hit him in his slack jaw, which did the trick. His head snapped back and he went over backward; it was like felling a giant mahogany tree.

As he hit the ground, I turned and started running in a near panic. But I remembered that I had almost no money at all on me. What good would it do me to run?

I didn't dare go to my mother's house now. And I had nowhere else to go. So I went back to Joshua. He was out cold and there was a bloody space where one of his front teeth use to be, but otherwise he looked okay, for which I offered up thanks. I reached under his tunic and untied the money purse we wear around out middles. Then I grabbed up his machete and took to my heels again.

I ran without thinking for a few minutes before I calmed down enough to make myself stop and think of a plan. I was well into the forest that surrounded the town and headed south. Of course, that's exactly where they would expect me to go; back toward Normal College, territory that I knew well.

So I turned east, toward Grandfather's juju Shrine, the direction he'd least expect me to take. Somewhere well beyond it, I recalled, there was a road. I had to outwit the posse that would be out after me as soon as Joshua came to and reported. There was a time when I wouldn't have had that worry; I would have killed Joshua so there would be more time before the alarm spread. But I couldn't do that anymore. I had truly become, in the words of the scriptures, "a new man."

But I found myself praying fervently that the new, Christian Isaiah could still run as fast and as far as the old, juju one.

I made good time and, after an hour or so, recognized the area: I was close to Grandfather's Shrine. I ran into the clearing I knew so well and collapsed exhausted in front of the little corral where we penned the sacrifices. I promised myself to rest only long enough to catch my breath and then to go on again toward the distant East Road.

I set down the machete and opened Joshua's money purse. It offered no help: only some worthless cowries (and a few nearly worthless one-*kobo* pieces) fell into my hand. I tossed the cowries away and dropped the *kobo* into my own money pouch. I went to toss the purse away, but there was still something inside it. I shook it again and a key fell out.

Keys were uncommon at that time in rural West Africa and I'd only seen a few in my life. My experience with them was so slight that they all tended to look alike to me. And yet, there was something familiar about this particular key.

Suddenly, I recognized it: It was the key to the box that held all my juju notes of the past fifteen years, ever since I'd first learned to read and write.

Grandfather had given it to Joshua.

It hurt me more than anything else that had happened to me. I could deal with the loss of my faith in juju; I had something better to replace it. I could deal with disgrace in the eyes of my people; I had gone a different way by choice. I could even deal with the forfeiture of my grandfather's love; people will love whom they will and no one can force the love of another. But to give my writings to Joshua— *especially* to Joshua—was a pain that could hardly be borne.

My pain didn't last long; it transmuted itself into rage, the way a truly serious hurt always does. I ran across the clearing to the Shrine and kicked in the door. I dug up the big tin box from its burial place under one of the altar stones and used Joshua's key to open it. The papers were so tightly packed inside that the top of the box popped open as if it had been on a spring. I grabbed the pages, filling both arms, and ran outside. I left behind me a trail of yellow paper with green lines.

I sat, dropped the stack down on the ground, and, in the moonlight, squinted at what I'd written. Some of the pages surprised me with their childish scrawl; I would not have thought there was ever a time when I'd printed so poorly. Others surprised me for their length and for their precision of detail. Many of the pages were insightful, recording the reasons *why* jujumen believed certain things. Others had a certain semiscientific logic about them, as if there might be something to them other than simple superstition. Taken altogether, the record was more than juju recipes; it was, in its way, a window into the minds of my people. I sat there until the sky began to pink in the East, rereading it all and letting the pride of the accomplishment wash over me.

I heard a sound. It startled me out of my fixation; otherwise I might have remained there until I was caught. What should I do? There were too many pages, far too many, to take with me. But one thing I'd become sure of during the night's reading: Joshua was not to have them. In his hands, there was no telling the evil which could be worked.

Besides, they were mine. And they were too good for him.

I grabbed up as many of the pages as I could carry. It made a pile well over my head and individual pieces kept blowing off as I made my way toward the stream from which Grandfather always got his "juju-water."

I have no idea where the stream eventually emptied. Not that it was important; where it flowed behind the Shrine, it was straight and fast, though shallow, which was all that I needed to know. I flung the papers over the water with all my might, as if I were throwing them with the strength of my resentment toward Joshua. They separated and fell like dead dreams.

For a moment, they floated randomly, bumping into each other in the swift current as if they couldn't make up their minds where to go, same as me. Some of the pieces tumbled and sank, but some of them clumped together to form big mats, reminding me of the way tribal people cling to one another to survive. The mats became so big I was able to see them all the way down to where the stream turned and got drunk up by the dense forest.

I sat there for a bit, watching the empty stream. Then I went back to the Shrine and made trash of it. I kicked over the two little buildings and the sacrifice corral. Using one of the corral rails as a lever, I pried up the main altar stone, with its generations of caked blood, and rolled it toward the stream. I blessed the slight downhill stretch that made the job easier. It rolled like a wheel clear to the middle of the stream where it tipped and disappeared under the swift water.

Lastly, I broke and scattered all the juju: the strings of beads, the bones, the shells, the broken bottles, the old pieces of iron, the scraps of cloth, the jugs for juju-water and all the rest. I did a very thorough job and by the time I finished, it was full light.

I looked around at the mess and understood that it was not only the wreckage of juju, but of my tribal life as well. There was no way I could ever go back now, not even if, through some miracle, Grandfather were to have a change of heart some day. I was cut off forever from my people.

And yet, I was still a tribal man inside and that part of me wept. I stood in the midst of all the wreckage I'd made and asked myself the question that always comes at the turning point of one's life: "What now?"

FLIGHT

27

There was nowhere for me to go but onward, toward the faraway East Road, which more or less marked the boundary of our territory. I ran quickly, not knowing whether my fleetness was due to the rest I'd had at the Shrine or to the guilt that was pursuing me through the dark forest. If I reached safety and started a new life, that life would have to include some way to live with the memory of how much harm I'd done to my people. As I ran, I prayed through my tears that they would find something to replace their juju. In time, of course, they would. My people have resilient spirits, as do all people.

But for Grandfather there would not be enough time. He could not live long enough for the wounds I'd inflicted on him to heal. He would never find another form of security to replace his lost juju, nor would he live long enough even to forgive me. His death was certain; no one with "slim disease" ever survived.

The people of the West have not yet lived with AIDS long enough to know its true face. Movies are made about it and books written, and they think they know it. But, for most, the movie is about someone else's life and touches them only when the victim happens to be somebody famous, or if the story is especially poignant.

But we Africans have had to live with AIDS for longer than they. We were living with it in our very midst a whole generation ago. We watched our village people die without even the meager comfort provided by Western medicines. And they died just as inexorably, just as inevitably, just as painfully as people anywhere.

At first, the affliction was doubly mysterious and fearful because it was so unusual: Few villages of any size failed to see at least one brother or sister wasted by it, but those cases were still isolated and rare. To us, AIDS was indeed more like a curse than a disease, inexplicably singling out one person from a large village. But that aspect of AIDS, of course, was soon to change.

My personal experience makes the spread of AIDS more than just numbers to me. Some years ago, I attended in evangelical conference in the interior of Africa, well east of my native Nigeria. I decided to make a holiday of the long trip, so I stayed on an extra week to trek around in the bush country. One of the villages where I stopped was a particularly progressive little place, neat and tidy. It was located on the bank of a picturesque river and the people were extraordinarily pleasant. I stayed there only two days but I never forgot the beauty of the place nor the kindness of its people. They had no problems that I could see, except one: There were four cases of "slim" disease that nobody knew what to do about. This was a very large incidence for a village of that size. The people wondered who it was that had cursed them so. For only a juju curse, it was thought, could have brought on such a concentrated misfortune.

Last year, I found myself within fifty kilometers of the place and decided to look in on the friends I'd made there years earlier. The driver I hired to take me there refused to get out of the car when we arrived, but told me he'd wait, even though I hadn't asked him to, as if he expected that I would not be staying long.

I couldn't believe it was the same town that I had so

admired. Grass was growing in the street. Starving cattle, their ribs showing, tried to make a meager meal of it. Not one of the roofs in sight seemed to have been thatched any time in recent memory and several of the homes had crumbling walls as well. Flies were everywhere, crawling about in congealed masses like living carpets.

The few people who moved about did so listlessly and seemingly without hope. They looked weak, hungry, and . . . slim. The town square was nearly empty, except for several sacks of rags propped up in the shade of a wall. One of the sacks moved or I wouldn't have known that it was a man.

That made me look closer. I saw that all the rag sacks were *people*—people so bedeviled by the swarms of black flies that I wondered how they could even breathe. I tried at first to chase some of the flies away from them, but it was hopeless. I tried to ask them what had happened to them, but they obviously didn't want to talk and just turned away from me. And who could blame them, in the shape they were in?

I wandered around for a few minutes, but saw not one person who was healthy. Nor did I see anyone I recognized, although "slim" changes one's appearance so much that I could have walked right by an old friend without knowing him or her. The town, which I thought to have a population of about a thousand on my first visit, was now a ghost town with maybe fifty or so citizens.

And, so far as I could tell, every one of them was sick unto death with AIDS.

The mystery of AIDS in Africa versus AIDS in the West is that women and men in Africa get it in more or less equal numbers, while in the West, it's more common among men. Scientists have concocted many elaborate theories to explain this discrepancy, many of which depend on bizarre sexual habits on the part of the entire African population, children included. But one of the things I've wondered about is whether there couldn't be a simpler solution: AIDS is a blood disease, spread by contact with infected blood.

And who has more exposure to raw blood than a jujuman?

We cut ourselves and we cut others. We splash blood about. We even drink it. It's part of our ceremonies, part of our rituals, part of our everyday lives. Men, women, and even children drink blood—human as well as animal—as casually as Americans drink cola.

Could this be how AIDS was spread among us? How it was able to spread so fast and so far? And how it affected our men, women, and children so universally?

I haven't heard of any Western doctors or scientists who have seriously considered the possibility that our juju blood rituals are responsible for the unique pattern AIDS has made in Africa. In fact, those scientists to whom I've mentioned the idea dismiss it because they refuse to accept that human sacrifice is as common in Africa as I say it is. I can't blame them; scientists no more want the gruesome facts of juju to be true than laymen do.

And, unless you've been born and raised in Central Africa, it's easy to argue that I'm lying. That happened to me on an American radio show recently. The other guest was a very young anthropologist. The topic was "Traditional African Religions." She became so heated when I told the truth about juju that the host cut to a commercial earlier than planned so he could calm her down.

When we came back on the air, she had regained her control and said she could prove that jujumen no longer offered human sacrifice. Juju sacrifice these days, she insisted, was only *symbolic:* just a little corn or a handful of rice thrown on the fire. A chicken, maybe, a couple times a year; on rare occasions, maybe even a goat.

But humans? Never!

How did she know? Simple: She asked a jujuman, she said, and he told her so.

Besides, she reminded me, human sacrifice is against the
law, had been ever since 1886, when Her Majesty The
Queen of England directed us to "abolish the said abomi-
nable practice."

"Now, if that doesn't convince you," she said, "I don't
know what does."

Okay. Try some of my evidence, from the January 19,
1988 edition of Nigeria's *Daily Sketch*. A thirty-year-old
news vendor was found in Onitsha with his throat slashed
and his ears and his genitals removed. The report said that
his room had been "sprayed with blood" and that the
murder weapon was found hidden under a cushion: a
decorated machete.

Or how about this from the *Nigerian Tribune* of July 29,
1987: A man wanted a spirit slave and hired a "native
doctor" to create one for him. The victim was the client's
thirteen-year-old nephew. In this particular ritual, the boy's
head was severed from his body, which was then thrown
into a canal. There was no testimony as to what rituals
transpired prior to the decapitation. The head was preserved
in a small box in the client's room. It was subsequently
admitted as particularly gruesome evidence in his murder
trial. Two other participants who helped out with the killing
were tried separately: the client's mother and father—the
victim's grandparents.

It may be true that juju practice, including blood sacrifice, almost died out at one time in the more sophisticated
parts of Africa, just as "experts" would have us believe.
But lately, circumstances have conspired to renew its appeal
for the masses. Beginning in the 1950s a series of laws was
passed protecting and guaranteeing "the practice of traditional religion."

That seems to be the same principle one finds in the First
Amendment to the United States Constitution, guaranteeing
freedom of religion. But our governments in Central Africa
do more than take a "hands off" attitude toward juju. They

actively endorse and sponsor something called the "Festival
of Arts and Culture," known locally by the acronym
"FESTAC." This is supposed to be a periodic celebration of
our folk dances and, as a "cultural activity," it is paid for
out of government funds. But, its grandiose name aside, it
is really a thinly disguised promotion of juju, attended by
herbalists and *babalawos* from all over Africa.

Juju, in the guise of culturally primitive innocence, is
taking over all our institutions. We built a fine, new
school—the Benue Polytechnic—which we hoped would
help us move into the modern world. But in the Nigeria
Daily Times of August 1, 1987, a front-page report de-
scribes the court-ordered closing of the new school. The
judge who chaired the commission of inquiry on the matter,
Mr. Justice Eri, said that the staff practiced "juju and
witchcraft" on the premises to the point that the school
became unworkable. He did not identify the specific rituals
that were going on, but he referred to them collectively as
"nightmare sorcery." They must have been even more
grotesque than the rituals I used to practice because Mr. Eri
said they made the school "administratively bankrupt,
financially archaic, and intellectually emaciated and redun-
dant."

So there's really no question that juju, including human
sacrifice, is being actively practiced once again in Africa, as
shown by these current newspaper reports. The Nigerian
writer, Wilson Asekomhe, however, may have gone too far;
he states in his essay, "The Menace of Ritual Killing," that
"human sacrifice will soon become *the number two cause* of
accidental death in West Africa, second only to automobile
accidents" (emphasis added).

But just suppose that the ritual letting and consumption of
blood—including human blood—is a reality in today's
Central Africa, just as I have said. Could it explain not only
why AIDS befalls women as easily as men there, but also

why AIDS spread so quickly? And, if so, what are the implications for America?

Robert C. Gallo, of the National Cancer Institute (U.S.), and Luc Montagnier, of the Pasteur Institute (France), are the scientific investigators who discovered human immuno-deficiency virus. More easily referred to as HIV, this is the virus that causes AIDS. Gallo and Montagnier wrote an article entitled "AIDS in 1988" that appeared in the October, 1988 edition of *Scientific American*. They ask why the virus appeared so suddenly and spread so fast:

> Where was HIV hiding all those years, and why are we only now experiencing an epidemic? Both of us think that the answer is that the virus has been present in small, isolated groups in central Africa or elsewhere for many years. In such groups, the spread of HIV might have been quite limited and the groups themselves may have had little contact with the outside world. As a result, the virus could have been contained for decades.
>
> That pattern may have been altered with the way of life in central Africa began to change. People migrating from remote areas to urban centers no doubt brought HIV with them. Sexual mores in the city were different from what they had been in the village, and blood transfusions were commoner. Consequently, HIV may have spread freely. Once a pool of infected people had been established, transport networks and the generalized exchange of blood products would have carried it to every part of the world. What would have been remote and rare became global and common.

I call your attention to the statement that "blood transfusions were commoner" in our cities. Perfectly true, no doubt. But common enough to account for AIDS? From my experience, exposure to ritual blood is far more common among my people than is medical transfusion. But that's my

242BLOOD SECRETS

only quarrel with the statement. Perhaps adding a line to the effect that "Central and West Africans frequently and willingly expose themselves ritually to raw blood" would complete the picture. Recognizing ritual bloodletting as an additional source of exposure to contaminated blood makes the rapid and widespread distribution of HIV throughout Central and West Africa not only understandable, but inevitable.

At first, the rest of the world experienced AIDS only in certain well-defined segments of their populations. These were groups that science could have predicted were vulnerable to a blood disease: homosexual men, people who'd received transfusions, and users of shared intravenous needles. But there was one other group that seemed especially susceptible to AIDS, too.

Haitians.

Science never did come up with a convincing reason why Haitians should be singled out above all other peoples in the Western Hemisphere for the tragedy of AIDS. But, just as was the case with us Africans, nobody wanted to seriously consider the idea that Haitians practice ritual letting of human blood through the religion called voodoo, the New World offshoot of juju. Instead, theories were advanced based on tortured logic to suggest that the entire Haitian population—including octagenarians and infants, heterosexuals and celibates—made a habit of bizarre sexual practices.

Suppose it is more than coincidence that AIDS has hit hardest in Africa and on Africa's children in the Caribbean, both of whom are exposed to human blood during religious ritual. Are there implications for America's population, *as a whole?*

I believe there are. Satanism (a form of juju) is not unknown in America. On a recent "Geraldo" television show about Satanic cults (aired October 6, 1988), the guests were all former devil worshippers. They appeared—to my eye, at least—to be educated, articulate, middle-class American youngsters.

All of them were white, incidentally—another sign that juju practices are spreading. Every one of them confessed to having participated in human sacrifice, to having consumed human flesh and having drunk human blood.

And these nice, white, American teenagers knew of the "spirit slave" ritual—the *iko-awo:* One of them explained how he obtained power from the creatures he was killing. He confessed that the power was his motive for ritually sacrificing to Satan, whom we Africans know as Esu.

Another young man, identified only as "Kurt," admitted to ritually cutting and scarring his body, to drinking his own blood mixed with the blood of others during ritual, and to sacrificing goats and dogs.

Sound familiar?

Now, if Americans are beginning to practice blood ritual, we may see an increase in the kinds of diseases that follow from exposure to blood—including, most prominently, AIDS. And the disease would not be confined to the "risk groups" already identified. Rather, the disease would spread more evenly than in the past.

In other words, if I'm right, AIDS will break out into the general population. It will begin to look more like our African disease: It will infect women as well as men, heterosexuals as well as homosexuals.

Notice that this is a prediction for the future; we know that AIDS has not broken out into the general population in America *yet*. There is evidence to that effect from the state of Illinois, which conducts a mandatory HIV test for any person applying for a marriage license. According to the *Chicago Tribune* of October 11, 1988, 125,000 people were tested. Out of that large number, who are more or less representative of the general population of the United States, only fifteen were found to contain the virus in their blood.

So here's an easy way to know whether I'm telling the truth about human sacrifice in Africa and about how the practice is spreading to where you live: Look for an increase in the incidence of AIDS in the general population. It will begin to show up in women, in heterosexual men, in children, in older people. It will become an epidemic among you as it has among us.

That's the only way I was ever able to understand my grandfather's AIDS: I think he got it from exposure to blood during juju ritual. The certainty of his death was just one more burden for me as I ran away from Inesi-Ile that day. How long he would last, I didn't know; the disease seemed to work differently from person to person. But I was sure death would overtake him before he had a chance to forgive me.

Even so, I didn't dare turn back to apologize; running on toward the East had taken on the same inevitability in my mind as had Grandfather's death from AIDS.

28

I made it all the way to the East Road without running afoul of the search party that I was certain had to be breathing down my neck by now. They would be going slower than me, of course, because they were tracking while I was just running. But they would be pretty mad, too, and wouldn't be taking any rests. Fearing a spear through my back at any moment, I hid in the bush until I heard the cross-country bus come bumping along.

I stepped out into the middle of the road to flag it down because I could imagine the reluctance with which the driver would stop to pick up this dirty, sweaty vagabond. He apparently decided that stopping would be better for his rickety bus than running me down, because he squealed to a dusty stop just inches from my knees. He studied me with obvious distaste for a moment after I got aboard. He couldn't have listed himself as a bus driver anywhere else in the world: He had only one eye and the fingers of his left hand were missing. "Where do you want to go?" he asked gruffly.

I had run off with only a few *kobo* in the money pouch around my waist and had been able to add only a few more from Joshua's purse. I opened the pouch now and dumped the pitifully small collection of bronze coins into my hand. "How far will these take me?"

He sniffed disdainfully. "Just out of sight, maybe. But that's all."

"Look," I said, "I really need to get as far as I can. How about letting me ride for free? Please."

He shook his head and pointed to the door. "No money, no ride."

"I'm desperate, sir. If you take me with you, I promise to pay you back. Double."

"The company can't put your promises in the gas tank." He glanced at my watch. "Now, if you had something of value, something that I could give to the company that they could turn into money. . . ." The watch was worth many times the price of a fare even to Port Harcourt, the eastern-most city in Nigeria. But I pulled it off anyway and handed it over. He studied it critically. "Okay," he said, "this will take you as far as Benin City."

"But that's not far enough. That's one of the first places they'll . . . I mean, couldn't you take me farther than that?"

He held my watch as if it were a dead fish. "Farther?" he repeated. "For this?" Nevertheless, he slipped it over his wrist and held it up before his good eye. It looked incongruous next to the stump of his hand.

After a moment of study he shook his head again. "I only drive to Benin; I can't divide this watch up to share with the fellow who takes over from me," he said. "No, Benin City is as far as you can go for this watch, boy." He dropped his hand to the gearshift and depressed the clutch as if about to get under way again. But he was looking at the machete I'd taken from Joshua rather than at the road. "Unless, of course, there's something for the other driver, too."

So I handed over the machete. I hated to part with it; it was a good one, English-made. He appraised it as he had the watch. It met with his approval and he shoved it down between his seat and the wall of the bus. "Okay," he said with a grin that showed he knew I was in his power, "what else you got?" I noticed that he had dropped all pretense of "compensating the company"; I felt like I was simply being robbed. I again offered him the few *kobo* I had in my money purse, but he acted as if these were beneath his dignity. "What's that?" he asked, pointing at my Bible.

I held it closer to me. "It is only a book."

The eyelid of his one good eye narrowed. "The way you hold it so close, it must be worth something. Maybe I can find somebody who will give me money for it, eh? Give it here."

I stepped back. "No, Honorable sir, this is of no use to you. I've already given you everything I had that you might value."

"I said, 'Give it here,' boy!"

"Please, Honorable sir. It is only my Bible; I am a Christian."

"A Christian?" He spat on the floor near my feet. "Okay, boy, keep your book; who wants a thing like that, anyway? You can ride until somebody tosses you off, for all I care, but you don't ride in here with decent people who fear their ancestors." He jerked his thumb toward the roof. "Up top with you." He laughed raucously.

It wasn't fair, of course. The watch and machete I'd been forced to surrender were worth far more than the price of an inside ticket; they may have been worth as much as the frail old bus, for that matter, but I grabbed the edge of the roof and swung myself up without complaint, anyway; what other option did I have? The driver grated the gears when I was still only halfway up and tore off down the road in a cloud of dust.

The roof top was like a griddle. I spread my garments out as well as I could to keep my skin from blistering on the hot metal, but that let the Sun beat onto my exposed skin. Between the Sun and the dust from the road, it was torment;

I didn't know if I could take it for more than a couple of hours.

But I did. I hid up there hungry, thirsty, dirty, and tired through two dust storms and eight drivers until we eventually reached Port Harcourt. Altogether, it had taken four days hard journey from Ilesha. Following me would have been an enormous undertaking for my kinsmen. So at least I felt physically safe when we finally arrived at the absolute end of the line. What I could *not* feel, of course, was financially secure. So my first priority was to find a way to get some money in this strange and very unpleasant town.

I decided to get a job as an accountant. After all, I'd had good training at Normal College and the main business of Port Harcourt is shipping, an industry which requires lots of accountants, auditors, and so forth. So a job in accounting seemed a logical and potentially rewarding choice. But there were a couple of impediments.

First, although I really was quite skilled, I had no way to prove it: My diploma from Normal College was still back in Inesi-Ile. It wouldn't have been very smart to write and ask them to send it on to me. Besides, I told myself petulantly, Grandfather had probably found it and given it to Joshua by this time anyway.

Then there was the problem of my appearance: I didn't exactly look the part of a successful accountant. I'd slept outdoors for want of enough money to rent a room and my clothes looked about the way one would expect. And somebody had stolen my shoes while I slept.

I tried to wash in the public fountain but a policeman chased me away. If he hadn't been so muscle-bound, he might have caught me. But I gave him the slip and then went back and got the newspaper I'd used for a blanket the previous night. I figured out where all the offices were that had advertised for an accountant and then confidently set out.

The first place had a buzzer on their door; they looked me over through the window and refused to open up for me.

The second place was run by a huge Ibo man who chased me down the stairs when I admitted I was Yoruba.

The third place wouldn't let me in, either. In fact, when I kept insisting through the closed door that they give me a fair chance to interview for their job, they called the police on me. Then I wasted time trying to apologize until the policeman showed up—the same Hercules who'd chased me away from the fountain that morning. I had the pleasure of my second race of the day, barefoot and on an empty stomach. All in all, my first morning in Port Harcourt had not been a good one.

After a couple days of the same treatment, I was reduced to begging. But even that didn't work—there was too much competition. Some professional beggars beat me up and warned me to stay out of their territory. I had nothing left by then but my Bible and I was beginning to get too weak from hunger to read it. I could have asked help from the nearby Christian church, of course, but that was something I avoided as long as possible; the church in Africa has burdens enough without adding my hunger to the list. But in the end, hunger overcame my scruples and I went around there, begging a handout.

The pastor, Reverend Mervyn, was a gaunt and distracted young man, laboring under the guilt of not having saved all of Africa single-handedly. He had given away everything he had until his own appearance was not much better than mine. He invited me in.

He turned out not to be a real missionary, after all; he was only serving two years in Africa before going back home to a place with the beautiful name of "Forest Hills." Just hearing it spoken made me homesick. There was little he could do for me because he'd stretched the meager funds of his little church past the breaking point already. And he'd tried to stretch his personal energy the same way. The more

I studied him, the more it seemed good to me that Pastor Mervyn's "hitch" was almost up: He was tormented by our endemic poverty. He'd come to us, as so many young missionaries do, full of plans to feed every hungry belly in Africa. Some Westerners learn to live with the realization that it can't be done; some, like the Reverend Mr. Mervyn, never do, and if that kind stays too long, Africa consumes them.

He scrounged us some stale bread and a few *kobo* for me, anyway. I had the feeling that they were to have been for his own supper that night and I felt very guilty about taking them.

But I took them anyway.

He listened to my story while I chewed the hard bread; to this day, I think the listening may have been more important than the bread. He suggested that I go to the hiring halls down at the docks because many members of his congregation had found work there.

I hadn't considered that before because of a problem that I share with other contemporary Nigerians: Since oil has brought so much easy wealth and corruption, no one wants to labor anymore. Everybody wants to be an entrepreneur, an agent, a middleman, or a go-between. Anything but a *laborer*. Many of us would rather stand in the hot Sun all day to sell one *kobo's* worth of matches than swing a pick or lift a shovel, because that would be "dirty" work. The work at the hiring halls was for porters, cleaners, stevedores, and so forth. Not accountants.

But the luxury of looking for a professional job was one I could no longer afford. So I joined the flood of men who converged on the waterfront sheds each morning, just before dawn. Each shed contracted a certain type of work and men who wanted that type would go there to apply. We had to show up in person every morning because the jobs were awarded only for one day at a time. "The hiring master" sat up in the front of the room on a high stool behind a big desk and called out numbers apparently chosen at random from a jug by his side. If the number he called matched the number a man received as he entered the shed, that man got a day's work.

I went to the shed for common laborers, declaring myself to be available for any type of work. But my number didn't get called the first day, nor the second, nor the third. By the end of the week, the few bronzes Mr. Mervyn had given me were gone, spent on food of the very meanest sort just to keep myself alive, and I was on the edge of despair again.

I went back to the church but found that Mr. Mervyn had been recalled in disgrace to his beautiful Forest Hills. He had bankrupted the little mission church through his excesses of charity. His fate back home was uncertain because his failure had done little to endear him to his American parishioners. They had agreed to foot the bill for his mission and had expected a going concern for their money rather than a soup kitchen. As for the church building itself, some men were boarding it up when I went by to beg another handout. They said there were no plans to reopen it.

It was then that I hit bottom. I just sat down in the street outside the little church and wept. I was unmindful of my safety, and oblivious to the calls of "Get out of the road, fool!" I was broke and alone, a stranger in a strange land. I had no one to lay claim to the title of "friend," no one to acknowledge me as family, no people to accept me as one of their own. I had nowhere to stay, nothing to eat, and no hope for the future. Even the comfort of the little mission church had been denied me. It was the low point of my life. I just rocked back and forth on my heels, hugging my Bible close to my chest and asked quietly, "My God, my God, why hast thou forsaken me?"

The next morning, I walked down to the hiring halls, more out of habit than for any other reason. They gave me my number when I went in, like always. I dragged myself up to the hiring master to plead, like always. He called out the first batch of numbers and mine was not among them, like always.

I almost didn't even care. I turned back to sit down and spend the day staring passively into space along with the other hopeless men. I bumped into someone and dropped my Bible to the floor. When I picked it up and brushed it off, the thin coat of reddish dust it picked up from the floor went all over my hand, so I rubbed the back of my left hand with the palm of my right, making a clockwise circle as I did.

I looked up and saw the hiring master watching me intently. He stared at me for a second, as if making a silent judgment of some sort. Then he popped his eyes to the left, then back, then up, then back. He did it three times, rapidly. It could have been a facial tic.

But I knew it wasn't.

The hiring master looked around the shed quickly, as if to see if anyone was watching us. Then he yelled at me, "Hey, you. Country boy. Come here!" I approached his desk warily. "Give me your ticket!" he barked and I handed it over.

"So! Here's my 'missing man,'" he said, loud enough for everyone to hear. "Why didn't you come up when I called your number, fool? You tryin' to throw my reports out of balance?"

"N-no, sir," I said.

"Well, be sure it doesn't happen again. Now go out back and report to Mr. Luganna; he'll give you your day's assignment." He turned back to the papers on his desk, apparently having lost all interest in me.

"Oh, and one more thing," he said as an afterthought. He took another quick glance around the room. When he spoke again, his voice was as soft as the forest nights around home. "Don't line up with those sheep anymore. Come up with the other goats no matter *what* number I call. Got it, Country boy?" He winked and went back to his paperwork.

I stood in shock for a moment. This was my first insight that juju is more than just the old-fashioned, out-of-date, rural superstition that good people like Pastor Osborn think it is, but is alive and thriving in our modern cities. In fact, it exists even among literate people in positions of power and influence.

I wasn't sure what to do. On the one hand, a day's work meant food, shelter, money. All I had to do was pretend to be a jujuman. In fact, I didn't even have to pretend; all I had to do was keep my big mouth shut.

On the other hand, that was the same as denying my Christianity. Wasn't it?

Maybe I had become even more deeply religious than I'd realized. Or maybe I was delirious from hunger. In any event, I walked up to the hiring master's desk and cleared my throat. He looked down at me.

"Honorable sir," I said courteously, "I am grateful to be chosen for work. But I have no wish to deceive you."

"Deceive me? How do you mean?"

I thought about the food. About the chance for a warm room and some clean clothes. I thought about all these, and then I blurted out, "I am a Christian."

He just looked at me for a while, unmoving, as if he expected me to say something else. "Yes, and . . . ?" he prompted.

"That's all, Honorable sir. I cannot accept work under false pretenses. I am a Christian."

He blinked a few times, then started to shake as if he were trying to hold in a laugh. After half a minute or so, he wiped his eyes with a rag. "So am I, boy," he said in a shaking voice. "So am I. And so are most of us. Except for those who are Moslems, of course. We have to be *something*, don't we? Why, I'm in church every Sunday without fail. Right down front, too!"

"But, sir, you called me a 'goat,' a jujuman, and I am now a . . ."

He dropped his amused look. "Shhhh!" he hissed. "Listen, Country boy, if you don't want to work, that's fine with me, but don't waste my time with nonsense about religion. Anybody who's ever been a jujuman is one of us, no matter what he pretends for the bosses and the whites. Now, if you're too lazy to work, I can always give the number to somebody else."

"Oh, no, Honorable sir! I'm happy for the chance to work."

"Then get out back like I told you and stop wasting my time." He shook his head and muttered to himself, " 'You can take the boy out of the country, but you can't take the country out of the boy,' " and sort of chuckled quietly once more. Then he started moving his papers around again as if I no longer existed.

So I walked out back in a kind of stunned condition and reported for my first day's work. The job I got may not have been much by some people's standards (scrubbing out the hold of a big cattle barge), but I thanked God for it. I worked so hard that some of the other fellows took me aside at the midday break and told me to take it easy so I wouldn't make them all look bad.

I ate like an *oba* that night: *three* bowls of rice cooked in coconut milk and laced with juicy hunks of antelope meat. I was too worn out to go all the way into the "native quarter" of town so I took a room in what passed for a hotel just off the business district. Being in the "international" part of town, it was segregated, and the room that I got was only marginally better than sleeping in the bush. But at least it was dry, and with the rainy season just around the corner, that was a blessing indeed.

The hiring master, who I found out was Mr. Mamuyo, seemed to remember me with fondness after that first exchange, though whether for my honesty or for my naivete, I never learned. When he found one day that I could read, write, do sums, and balance books, he took me off the boats and gave me a try as his clerk. After a few days, he made the position permanent, and at a handsome salary, too.

A few months later, I rented a small two-room house for myself on the outskirts of the town. It was one of a series of little houses all owned by the same landlord, a short Moslem man. He acted as if he were renting me a Fifth Avenue penthouse, the way he questioned me. But that was good; I wanted peace and quiet from my neighbors and this landlord seemed the kind of fellow who could provide it.

The long walk from the house plus the long hours spent clerking for Mr. Mamuyo kept my days very full. What time I had left I spent at the mission church in the neighborhood where I was living. I began to teach Sunday school and enjoyed it very much. I organized a social group, set up the men's club, and started a youth choir. It was the kind of socially conscious leadership I'd been trained for by Grandfather and I turned out to be pretty good at it. So much so that the pastor recommended me to his bishop. A new "daughter" church was being planned for the future and the bishop was kind enough to consider me to be its lay-pastor. My life was beginning to fill up.

Mr. Mamuyo was so pleased with my progress after a year that he introduced me to his daughter, an attractive and pleasant girl of marriageable age. I did not have time to court her but my pastor agreed to act *in loco parentis* on my behalf in arranging a marriage with Mr. Mamuyo. The pastor and the jujuman began to meet on a regular basis to hammer out the details of bride price and so forth. They seemed to like and respect each other and would linger over their palm wine and kola nuts far longer than was necessary. The two men were the closest I had to family now, so the fact that they enjoyed each other was a source of delight for me.

I'd been in Port Harcourt for nearly two years and everything was going beautifully. I don't remember ever

being happier. Best of all, my conscience was clear: Mr.
Mamuyo never raised the issue of juju again. As time went
on, I all but forgot that such a grotesque thing as juju even
existed.

Until the morning that I found a monkey's left paw tied to
the doorknob of my little house.

29

The Honorable Mamuyo was visibly shaken at my news that someone was trying to curse me. We sat and reviewed my life since coming to Port Harcourt, but we could think of no enemy I'd made who would want to take such an action against me. Finally, he leaned back and shook his head. "I do not understand," he said. "You say juju has been worked against you. And yet, it is no juju that I know."

I sipped the palm wine of his hospitality. "We call it 'monkey hand.' It has long been used by my clan; how popular it is with others, I don't know. It's an *epe* that is supposed to produce death gradually and after much suffering."

"How do you mean?"

"Well, the victim's brain is supposed to deteriorate. His hands start to shake and his memory fades. His understanding fails and he may even begin to act like a child. All this goes on for a long time, getting worse and worse, until the victim finally dies."

"Hmmmm. It is powerful, this *epe*."

"So it is said. But it has always claimed its greatest success against older people. That's the way juju works—it takes credit for something that would have happened anyway." I remembered how angry I was at Janet's immu-

nity to this same *epe* when I used it on her. Looking back,
I realized that no really clever jujuman would have tried that
particular curse in her case. It would have produced a result
only if she was a true believer: Then she would have started
to hobble around, shaking like an octagenarian. Or, if she
had been an elderly person, those same symptoms might
have eventually manifested whether she believed in juju or
not. But in either of those cases where the outcome was
what he'd wanted, the astute jujuman would claim credit
loudly. His credibility would be enhanced in the eyes of all
potential victims. And that would put more people into the
"true believer" category, improving the probability of his
success with future curses.

But the Honorable Mamuyo was having none of my
explanation. He made a hex sign that showed he disclaimed
my words. "You say that this *epe* is a powerful one, Isaiah,
and popular with your clan. But around here. . . ." he
shrugged. "So it must be that your enemy is someone from
your past rather than your present."

I nodded. His words made sense: My enemies had found
me at last. And a lump of dread began to grow in my
stomach from that moment. It wasn't the juju that threatened me. Rather, it was the thought of a hatred so
implacable that it could drive my kinsmen for years across
half of Nigeria just to seek me out for vengeance.

But the Honorable Mamuyo, a typical jujuman, was more
concerned with the *epe* itself than with its implications.
"How is it that I, who have travelled much in my life, have
never heard of such a ritual?" he asked.

"Have you ever been west?"

"Yes, of course." The Honorable Mamuyo took great
pride in the exploits he had performed when he was
younger, including serving in World War II. He puffed up a
bit now. "I have been to Lagos itself, and even beyond."

"Well, I've studied in Lagos and my people are from near
there, though a bit farther north. A little place, just the

estate of my grandfather, really. Inesi-Ile: You probably never heard of it. . . ."

He froze, a nut halfway to his mouth. "Are you . . . are you part of *that* clan Oke?"

"Why, yes," I told him. "My grandfather is Aworo Oke."

He dropped the nut from fingers that suddenly began to shake like river reeds when the winds of the rainy season blow. His mouth fell slackly open. He thrust his hands toward me and began to sign for the various *orisha* to protect him: "*Shango*, protect me. *Oduduwa*, protect me. *Osanin*, protect . . ." I reached out and took his hands to stop him.

"Honorable sir, please do not fear me. I would never harm you. You know I am a Christian; I no longer work juju. Besides, you are my benefactor and I have come to look on you as my father. Why would I harm you?"

"*You?*" he shouted. "Who fears *you?* It is your clan I fear! Your grandfather is," he gulped audibly, "a *babalor- isha!* Think what mischief his juju can do here!"

"None!" I said. "Surely you cannot believe in this non- sense!"

But his face made it clear that he did.

"You have said," I reminded him, "that you consider yourself also a Christian. Is this any way for a Christian to behave? Even when I studied under Drago, I never—"

He seemed suddenly unable to get his breath. "Did . . . did you say, 'Drago'?" he gasped.

"Yes, Doctor Drago of Lagos. Grandfather sent me to him some years ago."

The Honorable Mamuyo was managing to back away from me, even though he'd not gotten to his feet: He was kind of walking on the cheeks of his buttocks. He stopped only when he bumped against the wall. Instead of juju hex signs, he was now repeatedly making the sign of the cross at me, something he must have picked up from watching the

Roman Catholics at their worship. At the same time, he was muttering, "In the name of Allah, the compassionate and the merciful," something the Moslems were always saying. Our African penchant for syncretism seemed to have reached new heights in him; he was taking no chances on ignoring any of the religions that were popular among us. I'd never seen a man so afraid.

"You . . . you never told me all this, Isaiah! I mean, Honorable Oke!"

"But it is all nonsense! I never even thought it worth mentioning." That wasn't strictly true, but my suppression of my past *was* more out of shame than any other reason. "There is no cause to fear juju," I said. "It is only silly superstition."

He had flattened himself against the wall like a leech. "Please, Honorable Oke," he burbled, "please, I did not know of your power; how could I know? I do not want to be in the middle of a battle for power between *babalawos*. Please, please: Take your juju feud elsewhere, I beg of you!"

I was becoming impatient with him. "I am no longer a *babalawo*. Besides, the whole thing is nonsense: I'm not involved in any 'juju feud.' And there is no 'power' to battle over!"

"No, no, of course not, just as you say, Honorable Oke." He was on his knees now, back against the wall, shaking and weeping. It was pointless to continue. I bowed respectfully, as one should to his future father-in-law, and let myself out.

There was blood smeared on the left post of my porch when I got home. Inside, the head of a small dog was on my sleeping mat and the air was full of the wretched smell of burned camphor bean plant. This juju, of course, was trivial and laughable; I could have just ignored it and gotten a good night's sleep anyway. But the fact that someone had been in my house left me feeling the way I imagine a woman would

who has been pulled into the bush by an *egungun* and forced
to have sex against her will.

The next day, Mr. Mamuyo failed to show up for the first
time since I'd come to work for him. I tried to take over his
duties as hiring master temporarily, but I was far less
efficient at handing out the assignments than he was and the
men grumbled at my slowness.

That afternoon, a strange man came and sat on one of the
benches in the back of the shed. He spoke to no one,
apparently content to wait around for quitting time. There
was nothing distinctive about him: sunglasses, khaki shorts,
a yellow tee-shirt, and a New York Yankees baseball cap.
Except for his dreamy, almost beatific smile, he looked like
any other unemployed local man looking for work. But
from the way the other men moved aside to make room for
him, it was obvious that he was important, though exactly
why wasn't clear until his shirt rode up a little, exposing the
pistol tucked into the waistband of his shorts. The fear on
the part of the other men, the gun, and the unwavering smile
meant that he was probably a member of the Ogboni
"Fraternity." And there was no way that could mean good
news for me.

The Ogbonis are our most politically powerful cult. They
started out as another of our homegrown religions, a
mixture of Christianity, Islam, and juju. But where the
Ogbonis differed from all the rest was in their political
astuteness. They invited practitioners of all other religions
to join them on a nonexclusive basis. Because they seemed
to welcome everybody equally, they developed a reputation
for being diplomats, negotiators, "fixers." Soon, it became
important for even *obas* to join this "fraternity" of like-
minded men. The local Ogboni "House" became the
political nerve center—the "Tammany Hall"—of every
sizable town in Central Africa.

It was inevitable that the political power of the Ogbonis
would extend to activities of an even more lucrative sort.

Today all our officials can tell you proudly and honestly that we have no such thing as "organized crime" in Central Africa. We do, however, have what we refer to as Ogboni "Business." It includes all the usual: prostitution, drugs, big-time gambling. Of course, the Fraternity controls the unions that operate the hiring halls on the waterfronts, as well; in effect, the unknown guy sitting quietly in back was my boss.

Finally, the last man gave up any hopes of getting work that day and shuffled out of the hall to fend for himself as best he could on the street. I pretended to busy myself with my paperwork. The Ogboni man walked casually to the front, hands in pockets. He stood by the side of the desk, humming almost inaudibly. When I felt I could no longer safely ignore him, I looked down. "Yes?"

He pulled off his cap and twisted it in front of his stomach, the way a nervous man and humble of the town might do. "I beg leave to speak with you, Brother Goat."

"You are Ogboni?" I asked him.

"Yes, Brother Goat, I have that honor. The Fraternity has sent me to discuss a matter with you." He smiled ingratiatingly, then hastened to add, "with your permission, of course!"

I pushed my work aside. "I am always pleased to have the council of the Fraternity."

He twisted his cap some more and then said, "Well, Brother Goat, to get to the heart of the matter . . . it is said that someone has something against you. It is said that there may be a juju feud."

"There will be no feud," I said with dignity. "I no longer take blood. I am no longer juju. I am Christian and only Christian. But I admit that some jujuman seems to have something against me."

"Ah! But you will not fight back? You will not turn your enemy's *epes* back on him?"

"I will not. Now, let me guess: For a fee, you will find this *babalawo* and 'reason' with him. Is that your pitch?"

He looked shocked, as if the idea had never occurred to him. "Why, you know, perhaps we could at that; perhaps we could. I would be most interested in discussing whether we could help you in that way, Brother Goat. But first, we must dispose of the matter that brings me here."

It was my turn to be surprised. "That is *not* why you wanted to talk to me?"

"No, Brother Goat, the matter involves a brother of ours who is deeply grieved. He is too embarrassed to face you; he fears your wrath. He fears trouble. And the Fraternity's first duty is to preserve peace among the brothers, is it not?"

"Whether that's so or not is not the point," I said testily. "I am not a member of your Fraternity. I am not one of your 'brothers.'"

He gave me the kind of peaceful, dreamy smile one sees only on those who know they are in control. "All men are brothers, Brother Goat. So I have offered to act on behalf of both of you. The Fraternity's only wish is to see everybody happy."

"And I can help this 'brother' be happy?" I asked.

"Ah, yes. You see, according to our brother, your work here has been exemplary, above reproach, perfect in every way." His smile broadened as he recited my virtues until he was positively beaming. He paused and his face fell, as if with regret. "That's why it's all the more difficult for him to let you go. He hopes you will understand."

I blinked. "You mean . . . I'm fired?"

He only twisted his cap harder and stared at the floor, mangling it with shame and regret.

I slammed my account book shut. "This is ridiculous," I said. "I cannot believe it. The Honorable Mamuyo would never be afraid to face me himself. Besides, how can he fire the man who is to wed his daughter?"

He wrenched his cap so hard the little button on top flew

off. "Ah, well, as to that, Brother Goat . . . a man without a job, with no prospects, really ought to reconsider getting married, wouldn't you agree?"

I felt myself getting angry, but there was nothing I could do against the well-acted humility of an Ogboni. "Very well," I said, "you may tell your Fraternity that there will be no trouble; Oke is leaving."

I grabbed up my few personal effects and strode out, leaving him, his gun, and his smile in sole possession of the hiring shed; what happened to it was no longer my responsibility.

I arrived home to find my landlord on the porch.

"Out," he said. "Take your filthy juju and get away from my house. I won't have people like you living here."

"Wait," I said, "you don't understand—"

"I don't understand?" he shouted. "I don't understand that juju is the scourge of Africa? I don't understand that you people with your blood lusts and your drugs and your cruelty to animals and children keep us all in the dark ages? I don't understand that you jujumen would spread disease and killing around the world if you weren't penned up here?"

"But I—"

"No more talk!" he screeched. "You pretend to be a good Christian man, so I figure, 'Why not? Why not take a chance on him; he seems a nice fellow, even if he is a Christian.' Then, this!" He pointed to the blood on the porch post. "And this!" He toed the dog's head with disgust. "And this!" He tore down a cloth banner that hadn't been there that morning. It was covered with hex signs and excrement and blood.

I didn't know what to say. Neighbors all up and down the block were leaning out their front doors. They were all listening to him lambaste me, and several of them were throwing hex signs my way, as if to ward off the evil I might bring by being around. Even though I'd not done anything,

I felt intensely ashamed. I just hung my head and nodded mutely.

"Here." He shoved a big sack at me. "Your clothes and belongings."

"My books," I said, "what about—"

"I'll send them on. Just get yourself and your poxy juju feud off my property. And don't ever come back. I'm not afraid of your mumbo-jumbo magic tricks, so you'll answer to me if you ever come back and molest any of the good people hereabouts."

I shouldered the pack and trudged off. My neighbors, who had asked me only the week before to run for the town council, watched me leave with a mixture of hatred and fear. It was impossible to tell which emotion dominated. To the landlord, they were all good Moslems: believers in one, true God and enemies of demonic possession and witch-craft. But they all signed juju curses at me as I went by.

I saw no reason to look back.

30

I spent that night in a pew of the mission church, even though I could have paid for lodging. But the hotel said they were "full up," in spite of the dozen keys dangling in plain sight from the board behind the desk. I also went to the houses of friends I thought I had made among the church congregation, looking for a place to stay. But no one was at home, at least not to me. Even though it made me feel paranoid, I couldn't shake the feeling that word had spread about me: "Have nothing to do with Oke. He's a *babalawo* involved in a juju war."

The feeling was reinforced the next morning when I started looking for a new job. Even though I was known around town as an excellent employee, none of my contacts seemed to be hiring. In fact, one man who had tried to hire me away from Mamuyo only a few weeks earlier refused to see me when I called at his office.

It didn't take long to figure it out: These city people still believed strongly in juju. No matter how modern they wanted to appear, no matter how devoutly they claimed to embrace other religions, they were as much enslaved by fear of juju as the simple villagers back home had always been.

I stayed about another week in Port Harcourt, trying to

put my life back together. But it was no good. My friends from church all found things they had to do and couldn't talk to me. The Honorable Mamuyo and his daughter were nowhere to be found. Even my pastor and his bishop were uncomfortable in my presence; the day after I asked them for help, there was a new lock on the church door. And they both refused to see me after that. I wondered if maybe there wasn't some basis in fact for what I had always before regarded as only a vicious slander: That in order to rise to the top in the Church Mission Society (which is the dominant Western church in Central Africa), one must be a secret jujuman.

Only one person spoke to me for more than a few seconds and he was a man I barely knew. He hunted me up, told me he'd heard of my plight, and asked after my health and well-being as a friend would do. He sympathized with me and offered to help me in any way he could. I was so happy I almost hugged him.

Then he asked me to work some juju for him—to curse his wife, who had become burdensome, so that she would die and leave her money to him. When I declined, he turned his back and walked away from me forever. The episode showed me that I probably could have made a rich living there as a *babalawo*. Selling potions, hexes, and charms from dark doorways. Taking money from guilty-looking patrons to curse their friends for them in secret. Letting blood at forbidden rituals in cellars while a few *naira* convinced the police to look the other way. Working black magic from the shadows, just as jujumen do in other cities of the modern world.

I finally gave up and left town for good, disillusioned and feeling the need to "shake the dust of that place from my feet." Unlike the last time I had to run from juju, I had some money this time, so I was able to ride *inside* the bus.

But, just for the record, the inside of a cross-country Central African bus isn't a whole lot more comfortable than the outside. The ruts and potholes we kept hitting were like my tormentors: They made my life miserable even though I never saw them. Typical of all jujumen, my unknown assailants had done their work from the shadows and under cover of darkness. The only consolation I had was the knowledge that they must be tearing their hair out: None of their juju had worked on me. At least, not the way they planned.

I went up to Enugu, a good-sized place just south of our foothills. No one there knew me and I had a pouch full of *naira* notes, so I easily secured good lodging at the little hotel. It took me a couple of weeks, but I finally ran down a decent job with one of the international companies that exports the excellent tea and coffee grown in the highlands. I joined the local church and resolved to melt myself into the local scene so thoroughly that my juju enemies would never find me. I even assumed a new name: Nnaia Ojike, the given name of my old pal Speedy.

As time went on and I remained safe, my confidence grew. All I wanted was to live peacefully, free of juju's bloody interference in my life. And this time, I felt I could rest easy; I had gotten away clean. Besides, why would my tormentors want to pursue me? Hadn't they lost me my job? My friends? My fiancee? My whole contented life in Port Harcourt? I mean, even though their juju couldn't work on me the way they wanted it to, still, hadn't they done enough to satisfy their need for vengeance? Hadn't they?

Of course they had.

I went about the business of making a new life again. I became so busy and so confident that I almost forgot my unknown juju enemies. Until the morning a couple of months later that I woke up to find blood and tadpoles in the water pitcher in my room.

I flung open the door to the hall just in time to see a figure move out of sight into the darkness around the corner. Stark naked, I ran out into the second-floor hallway of the

International Hotel and gave chase. I rounded the corner fast and flung myself wildly in the direction of the figure. I may have yelled something like "Aha!" or "Oho!" But then again, I may simply have jumped in sinister silence.

In any event, the person I jumped onto turned out to be this little old gray-haired white lady from Boston. She screamed, fainted, and hit the floor with a loud thump. I'd only met her once before, in the lobby, when she told me she was in Enugu to help set up the new municipal library. So I figured right away that she would be justified in treating the present encounter as a diabolical liberty.

Feet started pounding up the stairs immediately so I decided that going for help was unnecessary. Instead, I knelt down by the poor lady's side, patting her hand to see if I could bring her around. She seemed to be breathing poorly, so I started to undo her blouse.

That, of course, was the exact moment when her traveling companion popped her head up over the top of the stairs. She was an equally gray librarian lady who also screamed and went over backward. She did not hit the ground, however, because her son was right behind her to catch her. He had told me when we met that he was something called a "middle linebacker" at Boston College. I had no idea what that was, but it clearly called for a great deal of size and strength. A certain quickness to anger also seemed an asset to that activity, judging by the look that came over his face.

I immediately sized up the situation. Seeing that an explanation might prove difficult, I dropped the old lady and ran into my room. I locked the door and barricaded it with a chest of drawers. Even so, I began to doubt it would stand long against the barrage of blows the son started laying on it. I tried to explain to him through the door how innocent it had all been, but I made a poor job of it. Under the circumstances, what could one expect? I just rambled on about juju and the "hit squad" that was after me and so forth.

Fortunately, someone came—the manager, I guess—and calmed him down. I couldn't hear everything that was said but I made out the words "juju" and "witch doctor" over and over again. After a while, the hall became quiet. I wondered briefly whether even college-educated white people from America could be scared by the possibility of juju black magic. Though it seemed more logical that the manager had simply been able to talk some sense into him. But in my heart, I still felt that he had been given the shameful message: "Have nothing to do with Oke; he is a *babalawo* involved in a juju feud." It was the whispered message that would ensure I stayed lonely and feared and hated as long as I lived.

I got dressed and packed my bag. But I waited until it was daylight before I dared move the chest of drawers. I opened the door just a crack, fully prepared to slam it at the first hint of any "middle linebacking," but all was quiet.

I hurried down to the desk, but the clerk hid behind the counter when he saw me. He refused to come out, even though I told him I simply wanted to pay my bill. I insisted loudly that I was no jujuman, that he should not fear me and hate me just because of vicious rumors. But the more I protested, the more he cringed back there. I finally counted out an amount that I guessed was about right and left it on the counter.

As I crossed the street, I looked back and saw the woman's son behind the curtains of their room. He no longer looked fierce and angry. In fact, he looked relieved, as if he was glad to be seeing the back of me. It was the same kind of look I'd gotten from my neighbors back in Port Harcourt.

This time, I took a train, hoping that train engineers talk to nosey strangers less than bus drivers apparently do. I took the first train north, into alien territory. Oh, it was still Nigeria, all right. But it was alien to me nonetheless.

The north of our country is as different from the south as it is from another country. For one thing, we in the south are a river and forest people; our terrain compares with that of America's Gulf Coast, especially around Louisiana. The north is much higher in elevation and receives only about a tenth our rainfall. It is, in fact, the border of the great Sahara Desert.

But there are more fundamental differences—the northern people are almost unanimously Moslems. They speak Arabic more readily than they speak our indigenous languages and their customs are similar to those of the Mediterranean peoples. Had the British not decided we were one country, we would happily be two.

The train stopped first at Kaduna, but only for a few hours. Then it went on to Kano, the end of the line in more ways than one. It is as far north as one can get and still say one is in Nigeria, and it is a dreadful place. I did not even leave the train station, wretched though it was. There was really no reason to: I was only running to confuse my tormentors, to "put mud across my trail," as we say back home. I stayed in the squalid, ramshackle station, sleeping on the filthy floor for two days until I could get a train going back south.

Finally, six long, miserable days after I left the International Hotel, I arrived back in Lagos. I knew it was uncomfortably close to home. But it was the only place in Africa anonymous enough for a man to lose himself, especially in the very heart of the city.

I knew I had to lay low, not only to prevent my identity being discovered, but also to avoid being accidentally spotted by any of Drago's people. That was the only part of building a new life that wouldn't present much of a challenge: How hard could it be to stay out of the way of a purple Rolls Royce? So, on the whole, I thought my decision to hide out in Lagos and make a new life there was a good one; Lagos was so crowded and so mobile that there was no way for my juju enemies to get to me, even if they knew I was there.

A week later, as I was walking to my new job at the big asbestos factory, I nearly tripped over two crossed *iki* wood branches somebody had laid in my path. Where the two joined together, a broken pop bottle filled with smelly juju-water had been set out. It startled me momentarily, but that was all. I kicked the assemblage apart, and the bottle bounced into the road, throwing its vile contents everywhere. I got through the day at the factory by telling myself that the juju had been laid for somebody else. That my juju tormentors had no idea where I was. That I was safe. And that juju was silly and harmless, anyway.

I had to stop telling myself all that, though, when I got back to the hotel that night. The dead dog just inside the door to my room had a rusty iron pipe shoved all the way through it—in at the anus and out from the mouth.

The ritual must have been done right there in the hotel room because the dog was laying in an pool of blood and other fluids, boxed in by black candles set at each point of the compass. There were scorches on the body, presumably from the same black candles. It must have been horribly painful for the poor beast. It must have been noisy, too, even though a bloodstained strap in the corner showed that they'd gagged the dog in an attempt to keep it quiet. And, yet, no one seemed to have complained.

Were all the other occupants of this big, international hotel jujumen? Or were they simply good people—Americans and Europeans on business—who just "didn't want to get involved"? Who found it easier to ignore those "strange noises" from down the hall? Who said, "It's none of *my* business what people do behind their own doors"? Juju depends on that kind of apathy; as it has truly been said, "All that is necessary for evil men to triumph is for good men to do nothing." And good people today find it more convenient to believe that juju does not exist than to confront it.

That was not so for me, of course. I was aching to confront my tormentors; it was just that I had no idea who or where they were. They had found me in three different cities now, these "hit men." Very well, there must be an underground network of some sort. And they'd obtained access to my hotel rooms, so they must have ways of coercing people, even Westernized people like the desk clerks in major hotels. They used juju that was favored by my clan, so they had to be kinsmen of mine from Inesi-Ile. And, of course, they worked in secret, out of shadows. Just like all jujumen.

Beyond that, I knew nothing. It wasn't much to go on. But it told me one thing: They had come and gone from the private parts of my life at will and there was no reason they should not do so again. They would follow me forever, to whatever place I tried to build a life for myself, and would ruin it. So I decided I had to figure a way at all costs to confront them and end their harassment of me. I decided I was through running from juju.

The next day, I went down to the factory as usual. But instead of going in the double doors marked "Laborers Only," I ducked into a nearby alleyway and returned to the hotel as surreptitiously as I could. It was a good thing my savings were still ample, because I missed a lot of work: I had to repeat my routine for about ten days before I finally caught my enemies in the act.

RESOLUTION

31

Even from out in the hall, I could tell that someone was in my room. There were faint scuffling sounds from inside, and a smell like burning leaves hung in the air. I slipped my key in the lock and turned it so slowly that even I couldn't hear it. Then, with all my strength, I flung the door open.

One of the men was someone I'd never seen before. Before I could react, he bolted out the door, an obviously frightened hireling. The other man, the one in charge, was startled but not frightened. He looked up from the live rat he was tying, squeaking and spread-eagled, to the floor at the foot of the bed. It took me a moment to recognize him.

"Joshua!" I said.

The two years since I'd last seen him had not been kind. He was much leaner, and the loss of weight on his formerly muscular frame made him look gaunt. His cheeks were hollow and his eyes were shiny and fevered, like those of a bird. Not a fierce proud bird of prey, but perhaps an injured buzzard. The hot rage that had filled me so quickly out in the hallway disappeared, to be replaced by an almost tearful pity: One cannot remain angry with a man who has the "slim" disease.

He stood, and the smoke from the dishes of herbs he was burning swirled around him like a fog. The look of him

reminded me of the last time I'd seen our grandfather, the
same slack expression, the same exhaustion. And, when he
spoke, the same flat tones.

"So," he said. "At last you know who is responsible for
all your woes, son-of-my-father's-brother."

"Yes. And I'll make sure the authorities know, too. I'll
make sure they see you red-handed." I didn't want him to
make a break for it, as the first man had done, so I slipped
the key into the lock, twisted it, and pulled up on it,
breaking it off. "Now," I said, "you can't run."

He straightened his back, as prideful as though he'd won
some great victory over a powerful foe. "I have no wish to
run; I am not ashamed. For I am he who is responsible for
all the evils that have come upon you. For your illnesses,
for the flesh that rots off your body, for the worms that
consume you from the inside out."

" 'Worms'? I have no 'worms,' Joshua; never felt better,
in fact." I taunted him, patting my stomach in a self-
satisfied way. "Your juju can no longer harm me, Joshua."

"Yes, yes, yes!" he cried. "Juju is deadly! Juju kills!" He
insisted the way a child does, as if saying something loud
enough, long enough, or often enough could make it true.
"Terrible things have happened to you. I know!"

"Yes, Joshua. But there was no magic to any of it."

"No? You have no family. You have no friends." His
confidence began to return. "Whose doing was it, if not
mine? Tell me you do not fear the power of my juju."

"I've thought about that, Joshua. And you know what? If
my friends ran and left me at the first sign of trouble from
somebody like you, maybe they weren't worth much to
begin with." His face clouded over again. " 'Fear' your
juju, Joshua? Maybe I really ought to be grateful to you
instead." And I experienced the immense pleasure of
laughing at him.

He moved toward me and actually stumbled a bit under
the weight of all the juju he was wearing: a heavy necklace

of old iron doodads that hung almost to his ankles, stacks of
iron bracelets all the way up both arms, an iron chest plate
that seemed to be the floor pan from some old car or truck.

He looked ridiculous and I laughed at him again. Yet,
there was a time when I couldn't have laughed, a time when
I would have been frightened into a cringing silence. All the
iron paraphernalia meant he was preparing for the "iron
ritual," in which iron, the hardest material known to our
ancestors, is endowed with the essence of *Ogun* himself.
The iron that a jujuman wears when he performs the ritual
is supposed to act like an accumulator of supernatural
energy, which then is focused into one very special iron
artifact: his *ida-agbara*, or "sword of power."

Every juju family has one. Usually, it's just an old knife
that some ancestor long ago decided was sacred to *Ogun*,
probably because its edge was especially sharp or because it
was used to kill the family's meat animals. Or maybe just
because he liked it.

But, sometimes, as was the case with the clan Oke, the
ida-igbara was something much grander. Ours was said to
have been the personal property of His Excellency Gilbert
Thomas Carter, Esq., Governor of the Colony of Lagos.
The grandfather of my grandfather is said to have stolen it
during a treaty-signing ceremony in Abeokuta in 1893. It
would be more glamorous, of course, if I could say that he
won it in battle. But like most Central Africans, the Okes
have always been farmers rather than warriors. Still, stealing the Governor's sword took its own portion of courage
during the often harsh days of British rule.

And it was clear why my ancestor wanted the sword
badly enough to risk stealing it from the British Governor:
Long and thin, with a gracefully flared guard around its
handle, it must have been a truly beautiful thing in those
days. Of course, that was back when it was polished and
oiled daily until the countless layers of beaten steel in its
blade glistened like fresh running water in the Sun.

They say one could see the engraved hallmark of the
Wilkinson Company on it for the longest time. But then, the
corrosion that is a natural consequence of being buried in
earth all the time finally made it illegible. Every "sword of
power" must be buried when it's not in use because, as the
babalawo tells it, "Only the Earth is fit to be your
scabbard." To ensure that the sword does not go hungry
during its long sleeps in the ground, the blade is fed male
blood just before every burial."

The Oke *ida-igbara* lay beside Joshua now. He did not
take it up, for there was no need to; the sheer power of the
hatred directed through the metal was supposed to kill me.
He just glanced at it and then looked back at me with a
smile, as if I were supposed to fall down, paralyzed with
fear, which was *exactly* what I was supposed to do,
according to juju belief.

When I didn't keel over, Joshua looked surprised for just
a second, as if he was wondering what could possibly have
gone wrong with such powerful juju. Apparently he decided
that the sword needed to be fed because he grabbed it up and
swung it at the rat.

It was a big rat, a dull sword, and a sick man. I heard the
rat's back break when the sword struck and then its head
began thrashing around in agony. But the sword was so
corroded that the blow didn't even draw blood. At this
point, a Westerner would have recognized the old sword as
useless. But Joshua couldn't give up on his juju: Rather than
discard the ineffective sword, he squatted and half-cut,
half-sawed, the poor rat's head off.

Then he rose and faced me. Slowly, almost lasciviously,
he drew the flat of the rusted blade across his tongue,
savoring the rat's blood. This was the kind of thing that
always struck horror in a naive, uninitiated audience.
"Now," he shouted, "see the all-powerful *ida-agbara* of the
clan Oke! Look upon it and die!" He turned the point of the
sword toward the floor and held it out in front of him

stiff-armed, the same way my pastor back in Port Harcourt used to hold the big cross on Sundays.

He looked so preposterous standing there over his dead rat—mouth fouled with blood, clanking with iron like a living junkyard—that I just had to laugh again. I know it wasn't very charitable of me, but I couldn't help myself. I wasn't laughing only at him, of course, but at the whole pointless and silly history of juju.

Joshua did not take kindly to it. His nostrils flared in fury and he shook the sword in my direction a few times. It only made me laugh all the harder. "Just like a jujuman," I hooted. "Put a sword in his hand in the presence of his enemies and what does he do with it? Kills rats!"

He lowered the sword and studied it for a moment. Then he raised his fevered eyes and smiled at me. "Perhaps you are right, son-of-my-father's-brother," he said. "Perhaps there are better uses for a sword." His right hand went to the handle.

I backed away, no longer laughing, as he began to clank toward me. I grabbed at the doorknob and had only an instant to regret having broken the lock before the sword crushed the wood of the door frame just inches from my ear.

Joshua grinned at me maliciously while working the blade back and forth to free it from the wood and have another go. But there was a dull *snap*, like the sound of green firewood. Joshua turned away from me to gape numbly at the little stub of broken blade left in the handle of the mystical *ida-agbara*. The rest of the broken sword was still stuck in the door frame.

He blinked a few times and then staggered back, stunned at what he had done to the "sword of power." The useless remains of the sword slid from his grip. He fell to the floor, twitching as if possessed by a juju demon. He lifted his face toward the ceiling and his mouth and eyes opened wide.

I don't know the cause of what happened next. It could have been that he was overwhelmed with the guilt of what

he must have regarded as sacrilege. Or it could have been
simply that his disease had impaired his lungs and that stress
had finally caused them to fail. But either way, he seemed
to have lost the capacity to breathe.

Not that he couldn't take air into his body; he was gulping
great heaving chestfuls, in fact. But he appeared unable to
take oxygen from what he inhaled. He thrashed around the
floor, gasping like a fish that had been pulled from the water
and left on the dock. It almost seemed as if the harder he
breathed, the less good it did him. He reached out toward
me and I believe that, in spite of everything, he was looking
to me for help.

"Joshua!" I yelled, going to his side. I had read somewhere of a way to force water from the lungs of someone
who has drowned. That didn't seem to be Joshua's problem,
of course, but I couldn't think of anything else to do. So I
rolled him over and kneaded his back hard, working his
lungs for him. It did no good at all. I rolled him over again,
fearing that I might be doing more harm than good. After
that, I didn't know what to do except kneel by his side,
praying, but feeling otherwise helpless.

His agony lasted longer than I would have thought. It
took several minutes for him to die before my eyes, still
starving for air. Whether it was hysteria caused by breaking
his sacred juju relic or whether it was his "slim" catching up
with him, either way, juju had claimed still another victim
in its long history of misery.

32

There wasn't much of an investigation. That's not to say that my people attach so little importance to the law that Joshua's death could be taken lightly. Rather, it demonstrates how common ritual-related killings are in our part of the world. Had Joshua been found dead in an alleyway of a gunshot wound and with an empty wallet, there's no question that the District Police would have been called in. But the local Town Constable who came round needed only one look at the accouterments of juju—Joshua's ritual "armor" and his shattered *ida-agbara*—to convince him that he needed no help in solving this case.

I spent that night under guard at the local clinic where they treated my injuries as well as they could. But I was suffering more from mental shock than from physical distress; time would have been the right medicine for what ailed me. Nonetheless, I was taken before the magistrate early the next morning.

Everything seemed to have been arranged in advance, as if there was a separate and well-defined procedure for dealing with legal problems involving juju. There were no preliminaries and no one asked me to speak. The magistrate just banged his gavel immediately and said I was guilty of "creating a public disturbance," during which an "innocent

bystander" unfortunately died of heart failure; his words
were dutifully recorded by his clerk. He then fined me ten
kobo—about the same penalty as for a parking ticket. But
he offered to tear up the official record if I would agree to
clean up the room so that "there remains no trace of the
nature of this most regrettable disturbance."

Shortly after, word reached me that Grandfather had
died. Some say he died on the same day as Joshua. They say
that he died just as I feared he would: with a juju curse for
me on his lips. With both men dead, I should have felt
myself beyond the long reach of juju, which had chased me
all across Nigeria. Nevertheless, it was only after another
full year went by without any further juju harassment that I
dared to return to my home.

Inesi-Ile had grown considerably during the years I'd
been away; there were strangers everywhere. It was the
beginning of a population trend that eventually would
extend through our entire society: People were starting to
desert the country in favor of towns, even small towns like
ours. The newcomers tended to be rootless. Not having the
same ties to the land that we did, it was easy for them to
pick up and move elsewhere. So the good opinion of their
neighbors was of little value to them; they had no reason to
fear the consequences of behavior that our more established
families would find unacceptable.

Some of the social changes brought about by this influx
of strangers were readily apparent, like increased prostitution and public drunkenness. Others were more subtle and,
perhaps, more troubling for our society in the long run. For
example, I noticed that locks began to appear on our doors
for the first time. That may seem a small thing, but always
before, it had been enough among us to simply to lay a stick
on the ground in front of the doorway when leaving the
house. It was not the stick that provided security; it was that
everybody knew what the stick *meant* and respected it. But
the newcomers didn't know our ways and had no reason to

trouble themselves to learn them. If they disgraced themselves among our society, they thought, what of it? They
could always move on.

I felt some of that same social disorientation when I first
went back home, almost as if I'd never been there before. It
certainly didn't feel the way home is supposed to feel to a
prodigal son. Even my mother was more reserved toward
me than I might have expected her to be. Her attitude hurt
me at first, even though I vaguely understood that I had
become somewhat of a stranger to the community. I knew it
wasn't simply because I'd been away for so long; it was also
because of my split from juju, the spiritual common ground
of all the diverse people of Central Africa. Still, my
mother's coldness confused me. Then one day, I found her
crying alone.

"*Iya*," I said, much the way an American adult might try
to cheer his or her mother by calling her "Momma."
"What's wrong, *Iya*?"

She dabbed at her eyes. "You know my friend Akamba?"

I nodded without enthusiasm. Akamba was the town's
self-appointed soothsayer and therefore an important per-
sonage. But in my view, she was little more than an old
busybody, spending most of her day in gossip down by the
river and going into a "trance" on the least provocation.
Like most of our older citizens, she was distantly related to
our family. So it was certain that her opinion about things
would be very important to my mother.

"Well, Akamba says you are a thief."

"A thief? Me?" In our simple society, where there exists
so little that can be owned personally, thievery is an odious
offense. So I was stunned by the accusation, even though
I'd picked up numerous hints that I was unpopular around
town. That's our way: We Africans tend not to speak bluntly
about personal matters. But I'd assumed all the dirty looks
and hidden whispers were because Joshua had been a
popular figure in the community and some people blamed

me for his death. So there were many things that Akamba
could have called me that wouldn't have surprised me. But
to be called a thief was astonishing: There was absolutely no
basis for such a charge. "How can she say such a thing,
Iya?"

"Akamba says that Inesi-Ile was once a pleasant place,
prosperous and happy, like a family, where everybody knew
everybody. One knew one's place, then. But now," she spat
on the floor, showing her displeasure, "now we fear each
other. We take each other's goods without leave. And one's
words can no longer be relied on to be true." She shook her
head, clearly bewildered by the new problems of modern
times. "The land has been bought up by the Ogboni so that
we no longer own our own farms, as our ancestors did. Yet
there is not enough work for our men. They drink and
gamble. Some of them lay with one another, men with men,
so that women are in want of them. There is misfortune and
poverty and illness everywhere." She lowered her voice,
ashamed for what she was about to say, and looked both
ways before going on. "We have even stopped addressing
our elders with respect—could you ever have imagined such
a thing?"

I shrugged. "This is sad, but some say it is the way of the
new Africa. We are becoming like the rest of the world.
This is 'modernization,'" I told her. "But what has it to do
with Akamba calling me a 'thief,' *Iya?*"

"Akamba says that, of all people in our village, only *you*
do not fear the ancestors or even the *orisha*. Akamba says
that's why strife has come to our community: Because we
no longer have the *orisha* to protect us from all that the evil
spirits want to do to us. Akamba says that is because *you*
have stolen them." She took a handful of dust from the
ground and threw it over herself to demonstrate her grief
and shame. "Akamba says you have stolen our gods."

I laughed and hugged her to me. "'Akamba says,
Akamba says . . . ,'" I mocked. "Is this the reason my

mother has been so distant to me, as if afraid of me?" I waggled a teasing finger at her. "Shame! What could be dearer to you than your own son?"

"Nothing," she replied with enormous dignity, "can be dearer to me than the ways of my people." She pulled away from me. "Not *even* my own son."

And that statement told all there is to know about religious life in Africa: We take it *seriously*. Far more seriously than people do in some other parts of the world. We do not know how to separate church and state, for example; our kings have always been our priests as well. In fact, it is one of our Oxford-educated kings who is currently the *Oba-Ooni* (or "chief of all juju priests"). According to tradition, he must perform blood ritual every day of the year but one. If they knew about his ritual obligations, his Western political and business associates would be shocked. But because they don't, they can continue to be at ease with this prime example of what they call the "new African."

But the new African exists only when Western eyes are around to observe him. Other times, the *real* African reemerges, the one who seeks protection from a threatening world through the power promised by the sympathetic magic of juju. Without that supernatural power, he believes himself and his family to be doomed. That's why juju rules in secret over his every thought and action.

So I had to admit to myself that, in a way, Akamba's charge against me was accurate. I had previously considered my renunciation of juju to be no one's business but my own. My apostasy was a sort of "victimless crime" in which I took only from myself and what I took was fear and superstition. But now, in my mother's shame, I saw that I had indeed taken something away from my people as well: the common tradition on which our social behavior is built.

I do not flatter myself that mine was the only voice raised against juju. But mine must have seemed very loud to my people, given the exalted conditions of my early life.

Besides, from all those other reformers who disparaged our
juju, we always got at least something in return—from the
missionaries who came to convert us, we got medicine and
monotheism; from the British who came to rule us, we got
government and commerce; from the scholars who came to
study us, we got literacy and science. I alone had defiled a
vital part of my people's culture without giving anything in
return. To the vast extended family that is a tribal man's
life, I must have seemed like Judas, Brutus, and Benedict
Arnold, all in one.

Still, there was a question of honor involved. I took my
mother by the hand down to the river, to the spot where all
the women gather to clean clothes and talk. In her
presence—as well as that of most of the other adult women
of the town—I confronted the slander.

"Akamba," I said, "you have called me, Isaiah of the
clan Oke, a thief."

My challenge gave her leave to speak freely and she took
advantage of it. "I have said so, Son of Better Men, and so
it is." The other women clicked their tongues in encourage-
ment.

"What do you say I have stolen?"

Her guns gleamed wetly in a false smile, her teeth having
long since been sacrificed to her fondness for *dijanga* root.
"Why, as everyone here knows," she swept her audience
with her skinny arm, "you have stolen our juju. I, Akamba,
say it. But all here know it to be true." The women clicked
their approval until they sounded like a field of locusts.

I opened my mouth to deny the charge angrily, as befits
a man. Then I took another look at the wretched, resentful
townswomen—most of them my kin—and said, "You
speak truly, Akamba."

Everything stopped for a moment with the shock of my
admission.

"But I will replace your juju with something better," I
started. "A better religion and a better life." But I'm afraid

I lacked the oratorical skill of the preachers I'd heard in the big city and I stuttered to a stop, wondering what in the world to say next. Sweat broke out on my forehead as I saw Akamba's look of derision out of the corner of my eye. "I will give you something better than juju," I repeated. "Something that does not urge you to abuse our children, to kill them for a momentary release or a chance at better luck. Something that does not spread 'slim' among us as a result of misusing blood."

But before I could really get going, Akamba cut me off very effectively by going into one of her "trances." She screamed once, sharply, which got everyone's attention. Her eyes were open so wide, I almost thought I heard the flesh around them creak with the tension. She began to shake all over and to emit low moans, like a cow left too long in the Sun.

She dramatically scanned the crowd, fascinating everyone. As she did, she gradually closed one eyelid while somehow contriving to leave the other absolutely motionless; it was like a motion picture of someone winking, only slowed down a hundredfold. Then her other eyeball rolled back into her head until her open eye looked like a white radish. I had no idea how she did it and I was as impressed by the sight as all the other onlookers. When she finally spoke again, it was through foam-covered lips and with the gravelly voice of a vulture.

"I am *Osain*," the voice rumbled. "Hear the message I bring."

There was a sharp intake of breath from the women. "*Osain! Osain!*" the whisper went round the terrified crowd. Surely, it was he, they must have thought—the one-eyed messenger of the *orisha*.

But never in all our history had *Osain* chosen to possess a women as the instrument for his message from the *orisha*. Several of the women became faint at the thought of such a miracle. Two of them even fell to the ground and began

writing in minor possessions of their own, to which
nobody paid any real attention.

As for me, my only emotion was embarrassment for this
poor old woman. I stood there watching her, as mute as all
the other witnesses. Until I heard my name.

"Isaiah Oke lies as well as steals," Akamba/*Osain* said.
"So say the *orisha*."

Those women who retained consciousness turned to stare
at me. Some snarled. Akamba/*Osain* started bouncing back
and forth in her ecstasy from one calloused foot to another.
"Isaiah Oke says he has left the *orisha*. But this is his lie:
He has *not* left the *orisha*."

"Now, see here, old woman," I said. "I ought to know
whether I—"

"I say again: Isaiah Oke has not left the *orisha*. Rather it
is the *orisha* who have left *him*," she said, getting more
worked up by the moment. "Because this Isaiah has been
found unworthy!"

The women began to close a circle around me. The foam
flew from Akamba/*Osain's* mouth as she shouted, "The juju
god *Orisha-Oko*, once incarnate in this Isaiah, has now
chosen to go . . . ," she made a broad gesture, taking in
all the four corners of the Earth, ". . . elsewhere."

For a moment, I wondered how she'd made the remark
sound so ominous. But before I could think about it, the
women around me intruded on my awareness. For the first
time, I appreciated my situation: There were perhaps fifty or
so of the village women drawing close around me, all
angered and excited by Akamba/*Osain's* ravings.

Ironically, it was Akamba herself who saved me from a
severe beating (at the least). As she neared the end of her
energy, she shouted, "He is no longer a godling, this Isaiah!
Now, he is just a man! He is just one of us!" Then, her last
reserves spent, she slumped into a tired heap like the
Wicked Witch from Oz.

The women stopped, undecided. They'd been primed to

destroy a vicious, bigger-than-life heretic. But I'd just been classified as a poor struggling mortal, just like them. Just like everybody else.

They looked uncertainly to one other for guidance until my mother settled the issue. When she saw me standing there gaping like the women, she cuffed me smartly behind the ear, as befits a mother, and ordered me to scoop up poor, deluded old Akamba and carry her home. But she walked behind me with a shy smile all the way there.

It seemed she had her son again.

SHOCKING STORIES OF TRUE CRIME

____ FROM CRADLE TO GRAVE
Joyce Egginton 0-515-10301-2/$5.50
One by one, Marybeth Tinning's nine children died—of mysterious causes. This startling New York Times bestseller takes you into the mind of a mother who committed the unspeakable crime.

____ DEATH OF A "JEWISH AMERICAN PRINCESS"
Shirley Frondorf 0-425-12124-0/$4.95
Steven Steinberg murdered his wife, Elana, stabbing her 26 times. Steven Steinberg walked away from his trial a free man. "Riveting . . . A gritty, gripping expose."—Self

____ WHEN RABBIT HOWLS The Troops for
Truddi Chase 0-515-10329-2/$4.95
The #1 New York Times bestseller. A world of 92 voices lives within her. Here a woman journeys back to the unspeakable crimes she suffered, to discover where the nightmare began.

____ DARK OBSESSION Shelley Sessions
with Peter Meyer 0-425-12296-4/$4.95
Shelley seemed to have it all, with her good looks and millionaire father. In fact, she was abused for years, the object of her father's obsession. In a dramatic courtroom trial which led to a $10 million settlement, Shelley took a stand against her father. This is her story. "Powerful . . . Vivid."—The Kirkus Reviews

For Visa, MasterCard and American Express ($10 minimum) orders call: 1-800-631-8571

FOR MAIL ORDERS: CHECK BOOK(S). FILL OUT COUPON. SEND TO:	POSTAGE AND HANDLING: $1.00 for one book, 25¢ for each additional. Do not exceed $3.50.
BERKLEY PUBLISHING GROUP 390 Murray Hill Pkwy., Dept. B East Rutherford, NJ 07073	BOOK TOTAL $ _____
	POSTAGE & HANDLING $ _____
NAME_____	APPLICABLE SALES TAX $ _____ (CA, NJ, NY, PA)
ADDRESS_____	
CITY_____	TOTAL AMOUNT DUE $ _____
STATE_____ZIP_____	PAYABLE IN US FUNDS. (No cash orders accepted.)
PLEASE ALLOW 6 WEEKS FOR DELIVERY. PRICES ARE SUBJECT TO CHANGE WITHOUT NOTICE.	319